MW01490068

CALEB LAYCOCK

A Demon's Heart

First published by Caleb Laycock 2024

Copyright © 2024 by Caleb Laycock

All rights reserved. No part of this publication may be reproduced, stored or transmitted in any form or by any means, electronic, mechanical, photocopying, recording, scanning, or otherwise without written permission from the publisher. It is illegal to copy this book, post it to a website, or distribute it by any other means without permission.

This novel is entirely a work of fiction. The names, characters and incidents portrayed in it are the work of the author's imagination. Any resemblance to actual persons, living or dead, events or localities is entirely coincidental.

First edition

ISBN (paperback): 979-8-9916960-0-5
ISBN (hardcover): 979-8-9916960-2-9

This book was professionally typeset on Reedsy.
Find out more at reedsy.com

*To my grandmother, Bonnie.*

# Contents

# Acknowledgments

Even now it feels strange to look upon this product and remember what it began as. Being an author is not something I had really ever considered. Stubbornly, I've done most of the work myself, but this never would have happened without a very few select individuals, which deserve their mention here for making it possible. First, to my good friend Richie, who sat with me and listened to all my stories back when this was just a hobby. I was just writing characters and worlds for myself, but it was your interest and your words which started to nudge me closer to thinking that it could become something more. Second, to my mentor, Dr. Lohse. We began as complete strangers, and yet you sat down with me and discussed my stories and my writing. I started without any knowledge on niche English grammar, let alone how to format a manuscript. It was your patience and generosity that started to form this work into something that resembled a novel, rather than just a homogeneous wall of text. Your work in reviewing this book from cover to cover was only part of what made it possible, your guidance and advice even to the very end solidified its creation. Third, to an honest man, Pastor George. This was a project that came about in an unwell time. The world seemed sick, and I was not in a right state of mind. Truth is not always an easy thing to accept, and your aid in that regard will not ever be forgotten. Life if a long and unforgiving road, and you helped me stand when I had almost lost the will to. There were also those of you that gave me words of encouragement in a time where I didn't have much faith or confidence in myself. Whether you just listened to me ramble about the world, or went a bit deeper, I hope you know who you are when you read this. Even if you thought it was just another conversation, the small things added up. I remember them and you, and while I won't fill these pages with a long list of names, you all deserve to be mentioned.

# Chapter One: The Wretch

A flash burst from the bowels of the cave. A sickly light, scorched into the back of his eyes. The foul magic exploded in a crackling plume; a gamble set forth. Bathed in heat, he shielded his eyes with unwavering arms. Bare skin was covered by the burgundy tongues, a lapping essence of warped human souls wailing and screeching over every inch of his torso. He held still as the spell faded, then lowered his guard.

He set his eyes upon his old foe. In the darkness, its uneven silhouette stalked along the far end of the cave. Its many bulging eyes were all fixated upon him, clouded by a carnal drive to feast and satiate an endless hunger. Both could smell it as they breathed. The charred, sharp scent of now blackened leftovers and scraps, beloved by the already present metallic tinge of blood and bitterness of rot. An orgy of carnage, wickedly stimulating his nostrils, tempted him in the same way. But the demon before him lit up another spell in its palm, showing its true foolish desire.

His grip did not loosen, no. For a moment, he grasped the bones in his hands tighter. He could see the glint of his glowing sapphire eyes in the moist sclera of his foe, and there he set his mark. Before him, his lesser kin let out a salivating growl, stirred by its prey's defiance. It raised both palms, the two mouths opening to release a fetid flow and puff of flickering soul essence. With such an opening, the balls of his feet dug into the stone. It cracked as he pushed off, his fleet feet carrying him to the side of the abomination soon enough for the yellow iris to slide in his direction. He carried the motion out as he had done ten thousand times before, his blade gliding with savage grace. The honed sword caught the bloated pink skin of the creature, sending a crescent of blood into the air.

In its defense, the demon placed a palm in front of his chest, releasing a blast of soulfire and might that thundered into the world outside. Unmoved by the rebuke, his second blade came forth. The cruel tip pierced into the gaping maw of the creature, wetting the wall behind it as it crept through the open air. He locked his gaze with the six eyes of the creature, seeing the surprise in its shrinking pupils. No pain did such a thing feel, no fear, no regret. No different from the countless others, and not far from the monster he was. Without a hint of mercy, he carried his sword up through the mortal cage, painting even the cavern roof with his artistic strike. Before the beast could flail, he performed a downward cut into the crevice, aiming for the beating mass he had nearly exposed. The sickening slush of tissue and organs splattering on the ground passed by him no different from an afternoon breeze, and for the first time in a long time, he took in the satisfaction of his kill.

Few were his father's kindred as of now, but the stirrings of human civilization seemed to bring the past back out from any crack it could crawl from. His expression was no more telling than an ingot of iron as he flicked his blades free of the corrosive fluid. With that, he returned them to the loops on his belt, standing solemnly in the dark. Quiet and emptiness returned, with just the stirring of air to whisk by unnoticed. Steamy moisture clung to his skin, surrounding the patches of viscous blood, and weeping down upon his boots. With such a lesser being, he had no runes or ritual spaces to clear, and with the space now humid and offensive to nose and eye, he turned to leave. Facing the entrance, he glared at a human face.

"I instructed you to stay outside." He whispered, noting how she recoiled-tense, grabbing onto the stone. Even for the time they had known one another, she was still not used to the indifferent tone he spoke with. Eventually, maybe, she'd see the concern hidden underneath it all.

"I ... um, well..." Lin stammered.

As he approached, he shook his head. "For one so eager to learn, you must first begin to listen," he chided as he began walking into the fading sunlight.

2

Without missing a pace, he plucked up his pack of supplies and began on his way down into the brush.

"Hey, wait!" she shouted behind him.

Still, his stride barely slowed. With a sprint, she caught up to his side. "You're not even going to clean yourself?" She held out a cloth from her own pack.

"When we get to the stream, I will wash myself," he informed her.

She retracted the rugged textiles, rubbing it in her hands. "I suppose that works ... but ... how did you know a demon was in there? We were just on our way, and you ... ran off." She could see a slight narrowing of his eyes, a very faint hint of displeasure. She immediately felt a sting along the back of her neck, and a tightness in her chest. Holding her head low, she apologized: "Oh, sorry. That's - "

"I can feel them. Like a weight in my skull." He spat the words out with a degree of spite, supposedly not directed at her.

Though that was quite a horrific thought. That meant that thing in the cave, and what attacked her ... they probably knew exactly where he was, too. Careless of her thoughts, she slipped back. The dark sky loomed overhead without even a moon in sight. Her feet carried her through the gnarled reaches of Kressel's Forest. The horrible sounds from behind, inhuman, a mass of nightmares. She could still barely fathom the thing even as it had pinned her, forcing her arms to the ground as the smell of rotten meat and filth assaulted her nostrils. The mucus that dripped from flaps of churning meat, and the tongue that had almost lashed her across the eye. Not until after she had cried out in desperation, a plea of mercy and aid instilled with virulent dread, did she notice her thigh had already been slashed by the spikes on the beast's leg. As the glint of metallic violet made a streak in the suffocated light, she was struck with shock and horror. Warm guts fell upon her, but a root brought her back from that place.

Now, though, her throbbing toe was the least of her worries. Still, she could not help but cast a glance at him. Or multiple, as they walked. Staring wasn't much in her nature, but her savior was beyond what she expected to see in her quest. His skin did not pale and thin from the purple liquid

3

that clotted and dried along his chiseled body. It was easy to see his hide with his refusal to wear a shirt, the obsidian skin with the sheen of coal an unmistakable mark that was far from what she had first seen as he stood over her. It was his eyes that had bored into her, two orbs of flickering blue energy. They had found her upon the soil with no hint of mercy, that perhaps she was to be gored with the hard-edged horns atop his head. Though his voice crafted calming words, reassured her, and his nimble fingers were responsible for how well her leg had healed up. Even as he aided her back to his camp, mostly carrying her, she expected the demonic withering to claim her, between the gash and exposure to so much demon blood.

And yet she was found by the one demon in all the land who could save her, with his strange cure. The cup he had offered her had tried to disguise its scent and appearance with herbs, but in the end, he had to admit it was a brew drawn from his own slit wrist. It was only his unwavering patience that convinced her to drink his blood. As he had explained, his own could overpower that of a lesser spawn, and in his hands, she would not suffer the full rage of the curse.

And he was right. She was still alive- owed fully to him. Which was why the question had stayed locked behind her lips for so long. Sand filled her mouth whenever she wanted to ask about it, her courage failing. She assured herself it wasn't entirely her fault. Even if she trusted him to watch over her when she slept, he was … different.

He proved this again by suddenly halting, not even completing his current stride. His head mechanically panned left, and his foot came back to stand with the other.

"Dul?" she managed to sputter before he thrust a hand in her face.

She knew to be silent, then, but her ears brought no news of what may have startled him. He still stared out, seemingly at what would just be trees and moss. But his steeled gaze did shift ever so slightly, tracking … knowing. In a slothful but steady motion, he put his arm down to his side. The other stayed ajar from his chest, the fingers chaotically moving in short bursts, like startled shrimp.

"Patrol," he remarked. "Soldiers."

She sighed, noting it to be the fourth one today. As her teacher adjusted course, she followed him along a winding ridge of gnarled roots. Placing a hand on a trunk to stabilize herself, she took it slow, despite how carefree he was about just hopping along on the toes of his boots. Still, his knowledge of the land was second to none, and the bank of the stream appeared just below.

"We'll stop here for today." He slipped his supplies down against a jutting rock.

"Hopefully they will pass by tomorrow, so you may go to town as you wanted."

He continued on to take the clear water in a cupped palm, rubbing it against the viscous stains. *You have to, Lin. It's deceptive, and he's ...* As she rubbed her elbow, the guilt overtook her.

"Dul?" she called out. He didn't turn, but she knew she had his ear. "Can I ask you something?"

He scratched away at another coagulated blob, ignoring her.

With a heavy breath, she cast her eyes low to the left. "After watching you, I just ... I don't feel like I'll be able to find my father on my own. Even then, I don't know if I could do anything if I did. I wanted to come here to follow a lead, but I hope that you would ... help me. I don't know what I mean to you, if you even care about pay, but..."

She wilted as he walked up to her, looming down from above. He snugged up even more, getting uncomfortably close. Still, she dared not take one step back. Gathering her courage, she touched him for the first time, taking up his hand. His eyes shot down without a split second between her touch and his action.

"You're the one hope I have. No one else listens. The longer I'm with you, the more I see ... the more I feel weak. Helpless before Tavora and the wilds. I know it's selfish, I know I'm already in your debt..." Giving his finger a squeeze, she earned no response. "... but there's nowhere else in Tavora I can go."

She lost her control at the end, tears beginning to well with the quiver in her voice. Yet she had no idea what pleading with such a being would bring.

"You know what dangers traveling with me can bring," he warned yet again.

She butted her forehead into his chest. "I know."

He watched her sputter for a moment, putting her even further from sensing where he stood. She wished to speak again, but the last few weeks had just proven to have taken their toll. And while he made no attempt to comfort her, he stood and listened.

"Your wishes will bring us near people who would burn you alive for seeing you near me," he said.

He was repeating himself, shrugging off the desperation in her voice.

She nodded, giving him a hum to tell him she knew that, and didn't care. Toren's followers were no help, and many pitied her for believing in legends. Yet they were the same who believed demons were all but vanquished, and their walls were safe. They wouldn't believe what stood before her existed, either.

"Dul?" Lin managed. "I don't care anymore. I want this to be over. I want him to rest. I don't want my mother to live every day knowing he's out there." For a moment, she awaited his answer, sulking in front of him.

"I've never hunted the undead before," he said.

His words battered her like a sack of rocks dropped in her stomach.

"But if it causes you so much pain, I will do what I can."

She almost shuddered as his other hand came over hers, bringing it into his view. Though larger, his near-human grasp held a fleeting tenderness to it. It quickly vanished without a trace, and his eyes opened wide again. She looked up, curious to see what had pulled him away.

"It's nothing," he said. "Focus on setting up camp. I'll be nearby."

He swiftly vanished into the trees.

Like a ghostly quill, he became nothing but a living stroke of ink being written along bark. Up and up he went, with barely a moan or crackle under his feet until he reached the canopy. From top to top, he traversed in quick bounds until he came where he could see what he wished. Panning through the fields of crops, there was little destruction. He came to the hoffen in the far end of the fenced perimeter and peered a little deeper.

Though the creatures had quite the body, capable of trampling a man as adults, or crushing them with their horns- they were still animals. The way they walked, the angle of their ears, the rate at which they breathed- they had recently been agitated. The wyrbles exhibited similar behavior. The nest-kings sat before their hens, still alert, but calming down. And that was why they were here.

Down below, he recognized the congregation that had grown just outside the town. They had come a long way from their homes, halfway across the forest, and their purpose was unclear. Lingering near civilization wasn't a common pastime for him, and perhaps that was why it bothered him more. It wasn't some sham, the leather and steel the men were clad in was well-crafted by a quality smith. And if that wasn't enough, a few of them had the star itself embossed on their uniform. He knew enough about Toren's followers to decipher that they weren't high-ranking, but it was enough that they had a leader here to show there was some official operation.

Narrowing down his view, he desired to know the secrets that eluded him. And there he saw it, at the far end of town. In a moment, he knew it to be the northernmost building, pointing into the Beastlands. A victim of a raid- but not trolls. They didn't have the power to topple a building so violently, nor did they root up sections of crops. All throughout time, man struggled against ogres. Yet the attack here looked loosely planned. They had left the far wall most intact, breaking a weak spot by the gate. He could see the path they stormed through in his mind, into the fields, and then to the home.

If he was able to get closer, maybe he'd be able to see more. But that wasn't necessity, it was curiosity. The humans were the ones that would have to deal with the ogres getting smarter, for now. He'd just finished up his last hunt, and now it appeared he was to help a young woman in her noble quest. He decided against using his magic for a closer look and summed it up to the Children of the Star reinforcing an under-manned town.

With ease, he slid back down to the forest floor, depositing himself with firmly planted boots. He reached a plateau atop the bank, and located a suitable post. Leaning up against a tree, he prepared for the night as his companion worked her bedroll out. Though even after she settled, he could feel her restlessness. Unusual, considering she had been soundly asleep many times before, knowing he didn't similarly need rest.

"Hey, Dul?" She beckoned to him.

He turned his head enough to give her an ear.

"Why do you hunt demons? You chase them all across the land, living alone..."

The question was asked for the first time in his life by another soul. Strangely, it caught him off-guard. It stirred old emotions, twisted his heart, and gnashed his throat with serrated teeth. He even found his hands trembling, disobeying his command. He brought them up, only to see the crimson stains. His breathing stopped dead, and he held himself still. Two centuries had passed, yet he could never forget. There were few alive from that time, though he could not see any one of them forgetting the war. Burying the memories once more, he found himself grounded, but without an answer one so young could understand. Still, she looked to him for one. Longing for what he himself could barely understand. He stared blankly as he wandered around in the hollow cavities abound in his mind. A place where words ceased to exist, and there were only venomous emotions. Things that permeated his muscles and ravaged his bones, the kind of scourge only he could feel.

Lin stared up at him. "I'm sorry."

Her empathetic words snagged his attention, his ears flicking at the tips. "For what?" he asked blankly, numb to the atmosphere.

She shook her head before laying down on the rough pillow. She pulled the roll up to her chin.

"It's fine. Just forget I said anything."

Cocking his head for a moment, he pondered what she had to feel sorry about. Then again, the last person to apologize to him did so when he was a child, the action quite an alien thing. Shrugging it off, he bound up, his hands grasping onto a branch as he effortlessly swung himself up into a low perch. A vantage point both to observe and to keep him out of less observant eyes that would peer through the forest. Though as he panned the shifting leaves, watching small yvera jump about above him, the question still plagued him.

8

He could not ignore it, even with the motion around him.

Once the moon was high and the little ones had calmed, retreating to their nests with whatever nuts and berries they had scavenged, there was little besides him and that mounting force. With his back against the rough bark, he once more lifted his hand up before him. As he moved his palm, he could still feel how slick they were that day. Slathered in blood … his, a demons … and his mothers. The word sent a shock through his body, a potent charm. *Mother.* The darkness around him was not so different from back then, the isolation of his room. She was the only one he had ever let see him, and she was late. Too late. The noises outside called to him, slinging him out of his trance. The pounding in his skull grew louder, harder. Until he could feel it in the back of his eyes, the mist leaking from his palms. He knew he shouldn't leave, but the sound of shattering glass drove him onward. He undid the heavy lock he had crudely constructed and pushed the handle outward.

The scent of torn meat burst into his nostrils, hounding his throbbing heart. His mouth nearly overflowed with saliva, drowning his tongue. A scream guided him right, down the hall and into the house. Dimly lit by torches, he rounded the corner. There he laid his eyes upon something more fathomless than the agony that plagued him. The door to his mother's room lay in pieces- a grotesque being looming over her. One glance to her leg and stomach shattered his weakened will, a collision between accursed instinct and wrath. Hatred won as he burst forward, carrying the monster with him. Teeth ripped into his arm, splattering the walls with his blood. Talon-like nails pierced his stomach, shredding his organs, a meager shadow to the consuming madness of the bleak void within. Dul smashed through the wall, sinking his own teeth into the neck of the demon. He tore a squirming hunk of dripping flesh away, his eyes bursting to light as they never had before. His veins pulsed brilliantly, like flickering celestial streams under his skin. He raked his nails across the lumpy chest of the beast as it thrashed at him, sloughing off wet tissue. It threw him off, but he was not about to cease. Forward he went, taking a strike across his face. With his cheek splayed open, he roared, imbedding his hands in the demon's shoulder.

He ripped free his first trophy before the nameless being threw him into a wall with a mighty kick, continuing their fight inside. Even as his memory blurred, his consciousness fading in and out, the flashes of gore did not stop. Not until he stood over the creature, his dark mist eating away at the withering husk. His broken horn buried into the socket of an eye given new freedom, nailing the head of his foe to the earth with splintered bone to accompany it.

There he stood, amidst such morbid slaughter and destruction, unphased, without an answer. Not to why he acted with such zeal, not to why his head drummed around the beast. It had not calmed, nor had his heart. This thing before him felt more familiar than any human, a connection of ominous portents.

Only animated once more when fingers had gently touched his calf, he saw his mother dying before him. That was when all left him except one purpose, and everything asked of him was his world. To retrieve bandages, to get her a drink, to get her bag and clothes, to bury their family. She even had to tell him to clean himself, yet he was more concerned with the strange wasting that was taking her. He had wiped a bloody finger over her lips by accident, bestowing her a boon then unknown to him as she fell asleep. He dared not move from her side until the warmth from the sky grew, and she once more could ask something of him. And so he followed orders, picking her up, taking her to a river, where she washed him. He carried her on by every direction she pointed to, until coming close to a city. There he gently let her down, and she cried as she was taken in by guards as he watched from the darkness.

Empty again, he made his way back home without pause, setting himself in the wreckage of his room. Rain, light, dark, cold, it mattered not. He had been there for days before another one of the demons came along, awakening that feeling again. Savage. Barely able to be tamed. But strong. Stronger than them. He alone could withstand the magic and brutal might of the invaders, and that he knew. Even as the memories faded, he remained trapped by the lingering thoughts he felt back then. That this was his life, something he could find a form of comfort in. *That was all she ever wanted for you. All she ever sacrificed was so you could make something of yourself. And you ... I won't betray your wish, mother. Not as brother did.*

Now, once more his palm came into focus, but it did not aid him in finding his footing. Instead, he looked over to Lin, stirring in her sleep. Through the war, through the reconstruction, all the decades past, he never found another like the one before him now. He had killed the few that had ever found him in defense, but she, such a young woman, had come to trust him with her life. As much of a danger as it was letting her even know of his existence, it also stcadied him. That perhaps times were changing, that all the present squabbles of man had made them forget of the time where all life on Tavora had almost been scoured clean.

He also knew it would be a fool's gambit to reveal himself. Even if ten would give him a chance, a thousand more would hunt him down to his last breath. He suddenly felt the phantom touch of her hand as she had given his a squeeze, and the drag along his calf. Closing his eyes, taking in the ache, he resigned his doubts. If nothing else, he could help another find peace.

# Chapter Two: Silver Lining

As the furs around her warmed, the veil between sleep and waking hours thinned. Slipping through the curtains, she stretched her shoulders. Pulling herself up, she looked upon the sentry who had stood throughout the night.

Slim in the shadow, he looked out into the distance, following something his ears had clamped down upon. As the wind kicked up, the row of hair between his horns fluttered, like river grass in a gentle flow. Her gut felt uneasy as she watched him, preparing to see what his anger looked like. Even if he had agreed to help her, she had still told him their travels were for her family. Not a complete lie, but he didn't know she had planned on … using him. That last part was likely the worst of it. She wasn't raised to be manipulative, but being direct with such a being was difficult.

"I would be ready soon." Dul's voice called to her as he dropped from above. "It sounds like the ogres are still nearby. Prioritize critical supplies. I would rather not be around when soldiers and farmers are scrambling about."

She nodded and began packing up her roll. Wrapping and binding it, she slung it over her shoulder, and grabbed her longsword. With that done, she took a drink of water.

"Go ahead. Meet me back here when you're done. We'll talk about your request then." Dul motioned for her to go but did not wait for a response before he shifted into the brush and vanished.

With a lightened heart, she began on her way to the rough trail leading onward. With how he spoke, it was usually a guessing game on how he felt-but he didn't seem to harbor disdain for her. There was that, at least.

As she approached the fortifications, she felt the weight of several guard's gazes fall upon her. A few hand signals were exchanged, a few grumbles and shouts followed, and one moved to the front. No weapons were drawn, but that wasn't exactly a sign of welcome.

"Halt!" A stern voice shouted at her.

The leader took another few steps forward, then narrowed his eyes. He ran some fingers through a short, gruff beard, pulling the strands along. "State your business- and make it quick. We've got a battle to fight, and no time for troublemakers." The guardsman expressed his displeasure with a flick of his gauntlet, balling his hand into a fist soon after.

"I just want to trade for some supplies." She responded surely, careful of her tone.

The man gestured over his back, spearing a direction with his thumb. "Second building on the left for general goods. The old lady at the far stead over there has some dried meats ready." The man walked back to three others, grumbling something that probably resembled orders.

Proceeding into the town, she could feel the usual buzz of urgency for any residency in the North. Except about five-fold more tense. She hadn't grown up close to the border, but her few trips to places by the Beastlands were always saturated with a melody of strife. It didn't need her father to help with that, either. But his mark was clear. He had a claim on this place, even if it was only for a short time. Others might have ignored the whispers for something on the wind, or a rustle of leaves, but she had heard it a hundred times too many. Long enough to start knowing how to follow it.

Coming to the building the guard talked about, she opened the door to find a fairly well-dressed man standing behind a counter. Crates and barrels were shoved in every conceivable corner possible, a display she only saw from those who dealt with treasure hunters.

"Ah, come in. It's good to see not everyone still fears the roads." The vendor greeted her energetically, performing a shallow bow. "Let me know if there's anything you're looking for. Although, I imagine I already know." Sweeping an arm out of view, the man procured a coil of fibrous rope. "I specialize in tools for explorers and warriors alike."

She shook her head, knowing the pitch would never end unless she took the lead. "I'm not heading to the mountains." She began, only for her breath to be interrupted by the vendor immediately erupting again.

"Ah, then for the trails, I have knives, traps, spices- "

"- I just— "

The man ignored her: "Armor as well, but let me tell you, an ostoran, a good friend of mine, has found a way to distract trolls!" The vendor hefted up a tied-up sack of cloth, which immediately exhumed a bitter odor that made her come close to gagging. "Throw it and forget it!" He began his exhibition, dramatically flailing his arms.

"I just wanted a map." She asserted.

In an instant, all joy was sucked out of the vendor. "Oh. Well, you'll have no luck with that here. I can't get any scout to part ways with one. I know where my clients like to gather, if you want to speak with them." The man spoke as he put all of his inventory away.

Lin waved her hand. "No, that's fine. I don't have much to spend on rumors. But … do you know anything about what happened three weeks ago?"

She pressed for a real answer, but got a deadly serious gaze.

"I think it's best you leave," the man muttered grimly.

With a deep breath, she turned for the door. "Maybe the next…" She grumbled before heading out into the short field. Pressing on through the creaking wood gate, she drew out an old woman from the farmhouse. She took a seat on the front porch of the building and waited patiently.

"Can I help you?" The words came out slowly, full of fatigue.

"I'd like to trade for some food." Lin informed the farmer.

The woman pointed over to her left, where a table and several racks sat stocked with hanging meats. "Bring me what you want. I'll wrap it up." The elderly woman told her.

Within a moment, Lin found herself in front of a fine display of cuts and strips. Most already salted and dried, but some more fresh than others, not quite ready. While she felt an urge to grab some of the wyrble from the top, she didn't expect it to go for what she had. Instead, she went for a hefty chunk of hoffen, and some smaller mystery strips. Coming back to the older woman, she found her with a heavy square cloth in her lap. Lin placed the meats down, and with expert handling, the goods were packed in a blink. Taking a pouch from her pack, Lin flipped it open and produced two fragments of a red gem. She studied the woman's reaction, but a long life had hardened her past being an easy tell. Reaching back in, Lin swapped them out for a small hunk of gold ore. It earned a small amount of surprise from the old woman, who nodded with widened eyes.

"Oren was always fascinated with that you all dig up from those mountains." The farmer spoke with nostalgia, sending a shiver down Lin's spine.

"He's gone?" She whispered.

The elderly woman looked solemnly to the floor. "Silvercry."

The name was almost enough to bring the woman to tears. Squatting down in front of her, Lin almost quivered. "Please, if you know anything, tell me," she begged as the old woman lifted her chin up slightly.

"Take your food, girl. I don't want to talk."

Lin took up the old woman's hand. "I'm his daughter. This the closest I've come … anything. I'll take anything you can give me."

The woman shook her off, and struggled to throw her away. Defeated, Lin took her goods and began to walk away. As she moved for the exit, a large group of radiant figures began to march past her. One carried a bronze stave, toting around a display of the almighty star above them. She shoved her way through, ignoring the grunts and sneers from those she bumped into.

"Do you have what you need?" Dul inquired as his companion marched underneath him. Pushing off from the trunk, he sailed down nimbly into an opening and darted to her side.

She nodded, but her head was hung over in sorrow.

"You grieve. What happened?" Dul asked as he slowed to her pace.

"Same thing." Lin croaked.

"The undead are an enigma. Many fear Fynor, Lin. I would not expect answers so easily."

She responded to him with a chuckle, though his expression showed he did not understand her humor.

"Do you even think we can find my father, Dul?" She inquired with a tone that weighed heavily on his mind.

"I do."

His answer was sure and short, but it seemed she wished for more with the way she peered over at him. "While I waited, I made a plan." He continued: "Do not worry yourself. I will share what I know."

Her faint smile told him he had returned some spirit, but it was tainted with something else. "I want to help, Dul. I want to be the one that lets him rest." She told him firmly.

Yet he shook his head. "If we may, I will allow it, but a hunter must be ready and able for the kill. I would not let you take up your blade against something you cannot destroy. Nor would I watch you die."

The moment of silence that followed his statement lingered around for some time, even as they pressed on through the trees. "So ... is there anything I can do to help, then?" Lin piped up from behind.

"I like to know of my prey."

It seemed the way he spoke brought some shock to his companion as she stiffened up, shaking it off by rubbing her arm. "Well, I know what my mother told me. My father was a hand-for-hire. Sometimes exploring, but he had a draw towards settling disputes. It made him as much iron as it did enemies, but he was well known for his reliability. So, when I was born, and he got an offer with a payment he couldn't pass by, he took it. He had to dive into the Beastlands and grab one relic from a cave. And he did, despite whatever stopped everyone else. He returned, went to go celebrate with his friends, but never made it. No one ever saw him again. Until the tales began to spread. We knew the sort that had hired him- they chased my mother out of town afterwards. They all wound up being found dead. Beheaded, disemboweled, cut up ... even the ones that left town. Some claimed to see lights in the dark, then ... a spirit."

Dul could hear the pain in her voice as she continued, and he stopped her before she could continue: "The undead are becoming more common now, but that's unusual. That is to say, if Silvercry is your father, I would think him to be alive … circumstances say otherwise, though. A hard working mercenary would not just leave his family, yet the dead often return mad and aimless. This is most … disturbing." Dul scratched at his cheek, reconsidering his approach.

"Dul, did you hear it when we were by the town?" Lin called to him once more, the question a potent bait he could not resist.

"No."

Lin's eyes widened shortly, but she caught up to his side. "The way you are, I don't know how you didn't. It's his mark … the only thing I can find that tells where he's been. It's like someone whispering in your ear. Noise that sounds like words, but it's not. Sometimes it's louder, and that's in places where the world seems to gray. The worse it is, the more uneasy people get. And yet no one seems to notice."

He devoured every single one of her words, tasting the fringes of an answer. "Hunting grounds." He remarked aloud.

Lin began to perk up, having some bounce in her step.

"Greater demons mark their land with blood runes. It's similar," he thought aloud.

"But you can't hear it? Or see it?" Lin pressed the question before him once again.

"No. I have never been to such a place. Though I have also never been in any towns." His gaze fixed ahead on the path, heeding what was unsaid in his own words. While the anecdote was useful, it also provided a unique challenge on its own. Or two, as he pondered it. *Perhaps three. Or four.* While theorizing would help, he needed to lay his eyes and nose on his target first.

"So, you have led us here. You know the prey's tracks. With where we have gone, you believe he is going East. But our path has been … sporadic. Unpredictable beyond that trend. Where were we going next?" He asked.

"I … well … didn't get anything this time. And the song was faint here." Lin admitted.

Dul didn't seem to so much as flinch as he heard she didn't have a direction any longer. Then, suddenly, he pointed out into the woods.

"There's a large town East of here. Carver's Triumph. If he has been heading East, for any reason, it's likely we could pick up a trail there. It is about two days by foot, if we keep a good pace." He declared.

"But ... you don't go into towns. Especially with lots of people around," Lin prodded.

"I know it well. If there is something to find, it should be quick." He explained as a critter scurried by their feet, plucking up a small rodent.

"That sounds like you want to do something dangerous." Lin said flatly.

His lack of a reaction told her he wasn't too bothered by the idea.

"If we are to find one who dwells in alleys, how are we to do so without walking the streets?"

With his next step, Dul began to bare his teeth. The surge in his chest and stomach compelled him, but discipline quickly doused the rising bloodlust.

"It is time again." He muttered quietly to himself.

"There." He pointed downwards to the town, but as he looked below, Lin only seemed confused.

"The cloth on that line will do. Meet me by the street there," he ordered, taking a small hop back. As a perfect display, his palm hooked onto the branch, and he flung his body weight forward using his core and legs.

"You're going to get past the guards and all the people in the street?"

He could hear the obvious doubt in her voice, but he could hardly blame her. "I may have taught you how to use a blade, and to survive, but I know you did not forget what I am." Biting down, he churned the mist up from within. His soul fluttered, pouring forth his power from every orifice.

Lin blinked rapidly, then rubbed her eyes. "I guess invisibility could work. It's impressive you can use so many of Alok's spells at once, though. I can't even see where you're standing."

Allowing the spell to fade briefly, his words slipped through: "Down below. We'll talk there." He kept it short, knowing the price for using such a spell for extended periods. Breaking out into a full sprint, he paid no heed to any of the humans below. With a great hop, he sailed over the outer wall, landing

18

flat on one foot. The woman working on a loom next to him lifted her head, gazing opposite of where he landed. He took two steps for momentum, then leaped the next fence. Twice more, he repeated it until he came to his goal. A heavy padded jacket was recently finished, placed upon a rack for a trip into the cold mountains. He plucked it free and slipped one arm through, finding the article to be shorter than he had hoped. Tighter as well, but luckily, the back and chest were meant for a burly brute. Even the nubs on his back seemed fairly well concealed, but that still left the final pieces.

A spool of woven rugged material sat on the ground, discarded until the worker returned. In a quick motion, he spent all there was until his hands, face, and midriff were thickly bandaged. He tied the ends off carefully, knowing the disguise could not fail. If it did, the results would be interesting. Taking slow steps forward, he approached the solid pillar fence. Bouncing on his feet, he placed a palm on the top and vaulted his mass over. He fought to pull the hood up, the fur edge catching on his horns. With a tug, he heard the fabric stretch, but it reached the apex of his rack and sat neatly above his forehead. And only then did he let the spell fade, keeping the mist at a slothful wash. He looked left and waved a padded hand in the air over the crowd. With his height, his friend had no problem locating him.

"Did anyone notice you?" Lin asked in a hushed voice.

"It's no simple spell, Lin. My time is limited, so let's be swift. Do you hear it?" He urged her by motioning with his hands, pushing them along as a small group took notice of their lull.

"I can. It's stronger here … but a way away." She responded as they began a brisk stroll further into the town.

Dul ducked his head low as two others walked by, shutting his eyes and giving a haggardly dry cough. The strangers pulled away, standing true to the one almighty rule of Tavora: the weak perish. No one, in any age he had lived through, had time to be sick. They took a sudden left, passing by a man too busy with his latest haul from the North to care for who they were. With a sudden right, they passed the ornate Chamber to Alyra erected by Carver himself. They passed behind the gathering outside, unnoticed by those preparing their veneration.

They offered their flames up to the great banner above the stone arch, the flaming hand forever reaching down from the sky to a human heart.

"... be us all ashes!" The mage violently erupted from the doors, not even a stutter between his act and bellow. "Love! Her decree that which showed us freedom! Which broke us from slavery, which taught us unity! Love!"

The energy enraptured all around them, including his companion. He nudged her back, but it seemed only he was immune to the trance.

"Passion! Inviolable! There is no world without it! Ours is this journey, as decades ago the great Bran Carver rode forth! There was no greater purpose than to serve his aspect, and to protect this land! Her fire brings her unwritten scripture to all, our history, our plight!"

He gave a stronger tug, but to no avail. When that failed, he squeezed.

"Ay- ow." Lin protested as he let go.

"I can't keep this up for long. We must move." He reminded her.

"Sorry." She muttered, her voice making it through a break as the mage took a breath.

Breaking out into a straightaway, the bustle of the town quickly faded. And as he looked around, it seemed that it wasn't just empty. There were people on their property. Inside a few homes he could hear noise, the batter or clop of various tools. Yet not a soul on the street, or in the open.

"You sure you can't hear it?" Lin checked back on him with a worried tone.

He shook his head, giving an honest answer: "It'd be difficult with this spell and coat. Truly, I hear nothing. The air, though..." He trailed off in thought, almost feeling a sense of unease himself. It was more of a sense something was wrong, and he couldn't identify it. He raised his hands to the side of his head instinctively to peel off the wrapping, but stopped himself. Sensory deprivation, something touching the stubs on his back, so many people around ... it had been a long time since he had been so uncomfortable. Or vulnerable.

Lin slowed as they entered into a densely packed portion near a low part of the wall, and his boots sank into damp soil. He glanced behind them, watching the rooftops and corners. A full sweep returned nothing, but his ears could not help him verify what his eyes told him. He took a stiff sniff in, but the earthy scent of the cloth was most of what he got back. And neither mold nor moss were a threat.

Turning back, he found Lin missing. His eyes shot down for footprints, seeing a path off closer to the wall. He burst forward, his hands only a hair away from his blades. He burst up the wooden stairs imbedded in the wall, kicking down a shower of wood dust and a cloud of termites. He hooked a right into the doorway, to see Lin standing still in the center.

She pulled a hand to her mouth, turning back to him with abject horror in her eyes. Before even the wind knew he had moved, two bone swords came to be in his palms. Taking a wide stance, Lin ran into him, not even causing him to budge. She buried herself in his chest, tears streaking down her cheeks as she whimpered.

Taken aback by the act but not breaking focus, he guided her forward with slow, steady steps. Stealth was already gone, but so was their target. The arrow imbedded in a barrel against the wall had a fresh web spanning from it to the debris on the floor. The blood that had dripped along a trail on the floor had already gone dark and lost most of its scent. And of the first he saw, the pale severed hand had set the axe free some time ago when something gnawed on the fingers. Coming to a wall of crates, he started to see the abandoned den of the beast. A body count would have been difficult, but with a kidney, three lungs, and a couple hundred bugs in a chest cavity, there were at least two.

"Lin, stay by, close. Look away if you must," he ordered as he broke away, moving in slowly. The swarm protested his approach as a threat for a meal, but he was not so feral. He lowered himself, swiping a hand through the black cloud. Such proved too thick to combat, so he let out a plume of mystic smoke from his hand. In an instant, the ground was covered with limp, crunchy blots. He ushered the magic forward, causing a foot-long scavenger to crawl out from the slack jaw of the corpse and curl up its hundred legs. With a clear view, he examined what was left behind.

Injuries were what he hoped for, but those sites were easy entryways for the skittery horde. Even then, the patterns didn't match what insects and small animals would do. There were no long cuts, but limbs were severed. A heavy chopping weapon would be capable, but a two-handed weapon would be unusual for an assassin. He brushed away the musty shirt with the back of his hand, revealing what lay under the dark splotch. A puffy, bloated chasm showed a sea of still maggots in the tissue. Though, such was enough for him to see that the attack was a piercing strike. He pulled the body to the side, raising the shirt to see the wound went all the way through.

He squinted, trying to think of what kind of weapon would be capable of such an attack. A thick, slab-like dagger might have the width and length, but not to so cleanly take off hands and parts of arms without incredible strength. To go through bone left something similar to a sword broader than his own, but to use such a tool to stab and lance would be curious. He put two fingers up to the wrap around his nose, tugging them loose. He gave a lengthy breath, smelling the onset of rot, though there was something sharp hidden behind it. Short sniffs brought him away from the bodies, towards the strange scent, as he slipped his blades back into their loops. It was metallic, but not like blood. It stung, too. The bite from the oddity only drove him closer, as he stood and walked to the wall. Almost panting, he put two fingers against a strange shadow on the wall. The outline was faint, but human shaped.

Lin stepped in behind him, covering her nose with a part of her shirt. "What..." she groaned out from his side.

She was about to hold out a hand, but he instantly snatched it, clamping down around her. "Remember what I said. If you're not sure in demon territory, don't touch it," he chided her.

Still, there were few options. Like a log burned on stone, the outline looked to have been born by a flash of something magical. Why it was darker around the fringe was just another question arisen from the abnormal sight. The remnants of something rapidly evaporated by flame left a dark, smokey outline. Though he suspected this was made neither from unusual fire, nor from something finding its end.

"What is it?"

Lin's words surfaced after a cough, and as her resistance faded, he let go. "I can't say." Dul spoke softly, casting a glance back towards the bodies. "We should go. Strangers and death don't fare well together, and we know he was here recently." He gave a gentle prod, steering Lin back around the clutter.

Upon going down the stairs, he focused in on the lingering ghost of his prey's scent. It was curious, and problematic. While unique, he would have to be close to pick up on it, though his companion could bring him closer. Together, they could narrow down his location in a city, but that left finding what city such a busy spirit would be in.

Lin took relief in the fresh air, the rise and fall of her chest controlled to calm herself. Re-tracing their steps past the congregation, he put them on an express route to leave. Lin struggled to keep his pace until he ground his feet to a halt.

In white cloth and grand blue full plate, the symbol of Toren glared at him from both pauldron and breastplate.

Taking her by the hand, Dul pulled Lin into an alley.

"Dul?" She sputtered in surprise.

Saying nothing, he squeezed them through a gap between the two houses.

"Where are we- "

Her tongue stilled as he stirred up the magic in his soul once more, obscuring the senses of all around him. With no way to fight him, he plucked Lin up in his arms and ran towards the outer wall. One foot propelled them up, the other away. Onto a roof, and then over the wall and onto the forest floor. He sprinted out into through trees and brush before setting her down and releasing the cast.

"Are you alright? What was that?" Lin asked.

"Toren is no friend of a demon, Lin. Tyxivol can hide me from them, but some Children of the Star are peculiar. There was nothing left for us there, so— "

"Damn fine leap there. I'd believe you even if you told me you didn't need that running start." A youthful voice called from the distance.

Instinctively, he went for his blades, finding the source of the intrusion. A singular young man walked towards them, unarmed and unarmored.

"But I am curious. Where are you taking that young lady, hm?" The man cracked his knuckles, reaffirming his threat with an aggressive tone.

"We're traveling together." Lin automatically responded for him, though he was the one to step between her and the intruder.

The man nodded and licked his teeth, staring right at Dul's eyes. He narrowed his own back, testing the stranger to see how much he knew.

"Hm. Alright, but then, there's a slight problem still. You just jumped the wall, wearing clothes that really don't fit you, covering your face…" The man jested dramatically with an open hand.

"Don't wander where you have no business. Leave us," Dul warned the lithe figure.

"Nah, I enjoy finding trouble. Stumbling upon it like this is a bonus." The man held up his fists and slid a foot back to take his stance.

"Naïve and foolish." Dul spoke his sentence, leading to the man laughing.

The stranger paced, planning his attack, but not for long. Recklessly, he charged with great speed. A quick jab was intercepted by Dul's bone shortsword. The stranger's raw skin ground against the edge, the man wearing a confident grin.

Dul led a stab with his other blade, but the thin core of the man bent around it with no effort. The lock broke, and a hook was thrown, which Dul ducked under. The flurry did not end, a back-handed fist strike being back stepped, a low kick being dodged. Dul slashed downwards, his opponent once more slipping past his edge. The man responded with a rising knee, which was deflected by a blade. Though the cloth pants ripped open, not a drop of blood spilled forth.

"Come on!" The stranger taunted him, throwing a singular, straight punch forward.

Dul blocked him with crossed blades, the loud thud booming out into the forest and sky above. Lashing out, Dul unleashed his unholy strength. His blades ripped forward, throwing the man back as his muscles rippled. Dul led with a horizontal strike, changing the pace of the fight.

The man was deft, slipping past his next slash. Though his foe responded with great dexterity, he was unprepared for a fight against demonic tenacity. Dul's wide arcs picked up the pace, woven in with devious lances and jabs, and the man's footwork became less steady. His violet blades pulsed as they awoke, and a slick sweep split open the stranger's thigh. A feast of mortal wine bolstered his voracity, and Dul went for the execution. With a dual flurry, Dul forced the man against a tree. In just a second, Dul guided his blade to rest against the stranger's neck.

"Dul!" Lin yelled at him from behind. "He doesn't need to die."

Though he did not dare to look away from one so slippery, he spoke: "I don't like leaving sleeping memories to wake later."

The unwavering, steeled calm of his voice and choice of words appeared to instill more fear in the man than the blade at his throat.

"If we're leaving, then why kill him?"

Her plea for his life did not sway him. "He has seen too much. And heard me speak the word." He steadied his hand, pressing the blade into the man's jugular.

"Never heard of the place, but we'll find your cult eventually," the man spat through his teeth.

"Place?" Dul murmured back.

"Look, it's all a misunderstanding. We're hunting Silvercry." Lin interjected again.

"Silvercry?" The man's eyes widened.

"Dul, put your swords away."

She spoke as if it were an order, and though he had many reasons not to, he backed off. Lin took his place, a green glow overtaking her palms. In just a few moments, the stranger's wounds closed, but Dul kept an eye sharp for any quick movements.

"A woman who knows her Breath, with looks to go with it. My thanks." He gave his compliment, but the scowl Lin gave him put him back in place.

The man patted himself down, looking at the bloody smear on his arm for a moment. Then he stared at Dul. "That's a journey few would openly boast about. And if that's your goal, I don't think you're who I thought you were." The stranger said, getting only a puff of air through Dul's nostrils in response.

"And who would that have been?" Lin squeezed for an answer.

"Abductors, at first. Seven people are missing. Your friend there made me think you all were a part of a new group from the South I've been hearing about. Puritanical types. Five of the missing people are ostorans. But if you're chasing a ghost ... why Carver's Triumph?" The man asked.

"Those people are dead. A few days ago at most, by his hand." Dul informed him.

"Here? By Illeah, what's gotten into this world? Did you find anything?"

Dul nodded. "Bodies and ... something. We have a way to track him when close, and an idea of where he might be heading."

The stranger's lips pursed. "That's more than anyone else I've heard of." He cast a glance over his shoulder, past some trees. "And I might be able to help you." He took one step, testing if he was to be pursued. Then he went and retrieved a small pack, opening it to pull out a long wooden box.

Lin seemed extremely excited, running to the man as he held out the item from a crouched position. When she closed, he pulled it back. "Not for you to have, I'm afraid. It's not easy to get a complete layout of the land drawn out. But it seems you all could use someone who can get you in and out of places without drawing attention."

The man proposed his offer but was quickly shot down as Lin crossed her arms. "And someone like you can?" The man sat the box back in his pack, standing with a chuckle. "Right, I'm Rorke." He introduced himself smugly. And while the name meant nothing to him, Lin's look was that of pure astonishment.

"You? And ... we just..." Her face became flushed as she turned away.

"I've always considered myself a man of action. Even if the ogres are on the march, this town was founded upon ogre corpses. You've got the skills, I've got resources. And I think it could be fun. Taking down a supposed legend that's been killing people for years? I like it." Rorke outstretched a hand, to which Dul stared blankly at.

"Uh ... is that a no?"

Rorke received no confirmation as Lin made her way to Dul's side. She pulled down on his shoulder, requesting his ear. "Dul, I know you don't like others, but he's a wandering hero. I know you have us in a fight, but this is what he's good at. People will talk to him. He can get us almost anywhere."

She whispered to him.

"What of me?" He countered, reminding her why he still wore the bulky disguise.

"Well…" She tried to find an answer, but it seemed she knew he would only take one answer.

Lin came down off her toes, giving him two shakes of her head. "Trust me, alright?" She looked to Rorke: "Don't make any sudden moves." She told him, taking one hand close to his face. Like a veiled sculpture, he kept perfectly still as Lin plucked at the knot around his neck. His glowing gaze weighed heavily upon her, but still she peeled away the first layer, and then the second. Tugging the wrap free, his face was revealed to the hero.

Rorke scrunched up his cheeks, his mind working away for an answer. "How'd his skin get that dark?" He asked.

The tension almost completely broke away from the two as Lin's mouth was left ajar.

"Are you … serious?"

Rorke nodded, pointing to Dul. "It's weird, but not a worry." Rorke commented.

"Rorke … he's a demon." She spoke in a low voice.

"Half-demon." Dul swiftly corrected her.

"What?" Rorke blurted out his disbelief. Even with both of them staring at him, he still had to glance between them to check again. "Half. But … you talk. And she's alive, so am I … should I be worried?" Rorke asked, as if unsure of his own words.

"I am far older than you, human. Your worry should be whether you trust Lin or not. I do not let the careless know of me and live." Dul prepared his words just as hands pulled the rope to hoist a guillotine.

Rorke scratched at the back of his head, calculating his answer. "I'll be blunt. I'm not all too sure about you. Either of you. But I know alone I can't dream of doing what you both are going for. Nor can I be idle if it's going to cost lives. I'll go with you for now, but I want answers."

"He's ignored me for a solid hour now." Rorke complained from her side.

Lin shook her head as their lead ducked under a low-lying branch. Without distracting herself, she faced forward and gave her answer: "That's normal. He doesn't talk much, anyway."

Rorke took a drink from a waterskin on his belt, screwing the cap on tight. "I can tell, but I don't like wandering blind. I know we're going southeast, but not where or why."

Sliding through the scraggly brush, she pulled free a trapped strap from her pack. "Right now, it's best to just follow him."

Rorke shot his head up, his brows cocking at an odd angle. "So you don't even know."

Lin shrugged. "He does. And Dul knows where he wants to be, which means helping me."

Rorke paused for a moment as she darted across a short clearing, careful of unburied roots. She looked back to see him shake his head before effortlessly bounding back up to them, muttering under his breath. After a moment, he came closer to her side. "How about you, then?"

She huffed, remembering his cheap compliment from earlier. "Just a girl from Toren's Wake."

Her answer was disregarded with a smirk. "Just a girl who knows a demon, hunting down a legend." Rorke remarked, his sarcasm smearing all over her ears.

"You should learn to be quiet. Might make more friends that way." While she hoped her response would land like a slap across the cheek, Rorke only laughed, wiping a finger across his chin with a sigh at the end.

"Probably right. Honestly, I just wanted to know more about you two. Lot of weird things hidden in this world, both exciting and dangerous."

As Rorke continued on, she came to a halt. Ahead of them, Dul raised his hand. A flat palm, vertical and stiff. His head canted up, homing in on something in the distance. Unlike other times, she could see the way his body had tensed. No patrol, no party of wanderers had ever earned such rapt attention.

Rorke stopped beside her, reminding her of what Dul had taught her. As her teacher slipped up into the canopy, she pressed her back to a tree, seeking cover between her and the threat in the direction the palm had faced.

"Down." She motioned for their new ally, who sluggishly slipped by another tree.

"What?" He asked bluntly.

"Something's out there." She whispered back.

Rorke was about to walk to her, but stumbled back as a dark streak fell to the floor between them, a few leaves raining down after it.

"Ogres." Dul spoke lowly, spite on the edge of his tongue.

# Chapter Three: Northern Menace

"I'd heard rumors the bastards were getting smarter; never thought they were true." Rorke remarked as he unrolled the map in his lap.

"How many did you say?" he asked as he put his finger down along the parchment.

"No less than twenty." Dul told him, standing with his arms crossed in the clearing.

Rorke groaned and shook his head. "A small raiding party. A group like that storming in could strip an entire farmstead, but there's probably more camped out in the Beastlands. Again and again, it's the same damned thing."

Lin edged in closer, peering in at the rare majesty of ink and quill. Rorke kept his finger where it was, tracing another in an arc alongside it. The moving piece came to the border of the Beastlands, and Rorke cursed. "So those reports were certainly true. Slipping in between towns at night. No telling how many have gotten through. It'd be fair to assume we'll be seeing soldiers from Kressel's Charge by the rumors, too." Rorke thought aloud.

"We did. Some up close to the Lesal Bastion," Lin added.

"I should listen to those men more often. Usually, it's a whole lot of nothing, but this isn't good." Rorke made a fist in anger, as if to prepare to beat himself for a mistake.

"You speak as if you know a lot about these creatures," Dul injected himself into the conversation.

Rorke nodded as the half-demon closed in. "I grew up on the border. Wasn't long before I started fighting back and found I was good at it. So yeah, I know ogres. Trolls, obrok, even treated a close call with a pale-eye sting." Rorke spoke as his eyes traveled just as fast as his fingers, charting paths and possibilities in lightning flashes.

Dul placed his hands on the hilts of his blades. "Perhaps then, we have what we need for this fight."

Rorke's neck jerked back, and he slowly looked up to him. His squinted eyes blinked twice, his mouth letting out a hushed and empty flow of air. "Yeah, so ... I don't want to be eaten."

His disagreement was sound, but there was no other way in Dul's mind. "That is not my goal. I would prefer not to act alone, hero," he countered.

Rorke rolled up his map and placed it back into the wooden box. "Right, no one wants a friend to be eaten." Rorke aggressively popped the lid back on. "Fighting three at the same time nearly cost me a leg last year. We'll head West, then go around by dipping South. I can get some help if we run into soldiers." He stayed firm in his stance, refusing to budge towards a fight.

"Those are Toren's children." Dul remarked.

Rorke just nodded plainly. "They're good allies."

Dul bore his eyes down on the man. "For a human. The gifted among them will know of me before they see me. I will not waste timing heading West, nor will I show myself to others. I will handle this here and now." Dul stated, laying out his words in iron. Rorke balled a fist, raising his other hand into the air.

"Do you have— "

A firm clasp around his wrist interrupted him. He looked right to see rustic red eyes, a unique scorched autumn blend that informed him of his mistake. "Please, calm yourself. There's more to his words than you're hearing."

Rorke shut his eyes, letting out a sigh through near-clenched teeth. "I'm not dying here. Neither are you. Too much ceaseless, pointless death now."

He pushed her off, walking up to the half-blood, who looked out into the path ahead. "Your companion has a lot of faith in you. Tell me then, how are three of us going to take on a band of ogres?" Rorke spat his words out with energetic gestures from his arms.

Dul remained silent, panning his head slowly leftward, away from him.

31

"That's hardly an answer," he remarked sarcastically.

The pitch-skinned demon finally granted him acknowledgment, peering over his shoulder. The strange eye of the being sent a chill down his spine, the similarities to a human undeniable. It was both his kindred and not- a phenomenon that made his stomach turn and fear swell. He held steady as the blackened lips opened: "The road nearby presents an opportunity. Safe traversal were you two to draw the attention of a few beasts. Do this, and keep Lin safe, and you shall be rid of this threat."

The half-demon's voice was sure and monotone, if only slightly unnerving with the lethal intent it carried. Crossing his arms, straightening his back, Rorke showed up on the outside what he did not feel on the inside.

"Running. You want us to run."

He simplified down the concept, adding agitation to his tone at how stupid the idea was. Still, Dul blinked and bowed his head.

"Indeed. You should know how to evade them and survive while I work."

Rorke raised an eyebrow.

"Work?"

In an incredibly swift shift of pace, Dul's head jerked up as his hands went to his blades.

"Hunt. Slay. Kill. The words end in the same place."

Dul cut each word into the thick air with the tip of his tongue, a razor which seemed to be able to draw blood on its own.

"So, you're taking on most of them by yourself?" Rorke chuffed, recalling their fight.

"You're good, but if that's all you have…"

In response to his words, Dul pulled both of his blades free. "I do not need your worry, human. We have our parts to play. Upon my word I will see Lin through, and hunt those that threaten this land. You are not needed, though the wilds may wither otherwise." Dul spoke as his fingers snaked tighter around the rugged handles, his conviction clear. He turned his attention ahead as Rorke took a deep breath.

"So that's it, then. You've decided," he responded lowly.

"Would you do any different, had you such capability? The beasts prepare to move. If they do, many others will die. Divide them, as I will. When they split three ways, they will fall."

The half-demon wielded a powerful demeaning miasma, his judgement finally made clear. But such lashings only stirred him. Rorke made a fist, rising against the challenge.

"Fine. Show me, then." Rorke retorted.

Following the dark-skinned being proved a trial on its own, as he had to bolt forward into a full sprint to keep up. The short travel ended as Dul came to a halt on a low tier of branches, pointing out silently with the tip of his blade. From the floor, Rorke bounded up and grasped ahold of a mighty branch and pulled himself up. Steadying on his boots, he found the vantage point to overlook an artificial clearing. The purple blade, like a solemn guide, unveiled a pile of refuse that unmistakably reeked of the filthy giants. Scraps of wood, broken crates, chests, and the most cherished of all: scrap metal. In the past few years, the northern menace had grown to target places with armories or barracks, taking special care to steal weapons, bolts, armor, tools … anything that had that lustrous shine.

As one of the creatures bumbled into view, Rorke's stomach turned. The pasty yellow skin of the beast was smeared with blood, angular symbols smudged by a fat finger along trunk-like biceps and forearms. Repulsive insignias of importance, along with the most horrifying sight of all. Battered plates were strapped in layers, marked by blackened splotches and craters from ogre smiths. As if it weighed nothing, the ogre raised its weapon with one hand from the muddy ground, resting the pillar of malice on a pocked pauldron. A device which still hung with flaps of skin and tissue, for cleaving apart ten men in one swing. The dark metal waved back and forth with every step, little more than a stick with several crude, stone-ground edges imbedded into a steel pole. In its spare hand, the ogre hefted a bloodied clump, opening its palm before its face. The empty face of a woman dangled over toward them, the life she once owned now frozen in an unending scream. The ogre teetered his hand back and forth, swaying the blood-matted blond hair in the air. And with a guttural humph, opened its maw and crunched down on the morbid snack. The creature froze after it swallowed, placing a hand over its mountainous stomach, which grumbled back from under the behemoth plate. Rorke felt himself tremble at the sight. Not just a youngling joining the raiding band. No adult, as tall as three men with arms wider around than a barrel of water. Never before had he laid eyes upon one of the primal leaders so closely and never had he seen one in human lands outside of his nightmares. It was a deadly innovation- dwarfing the others with another few feet, girth, muscle … and intelligence.

"Graburag!" the beast then bellowed, pointing to a smaller member of the group.

"Bahbo. Nobor don garba!"

The command was promptly followed as four of the youthful ogres thundered down the clearing, digging their feet in as they started to move more of the loot to the pile.

"Dag. Grabmok." The leader grumbled at two other sizable kinsmen, who came closer.

One carried a sack over his shoulder, one which dripped red trails down his back. A knot formed in Rorke's throat as he watched, the haunting sight not any less vehemently appalling than when he was a child. He closed his eyes as the sloughing sound of moist lumps of meat pounded in his ears, holding back the urges to vomit or scream. His mother's lessons remained strong, and his throat refused to sing its song of terror. He let himself down from the tree, walking away in a grim slump. He heard Dul drop behind him, who sprinted up to him. Rage overtook him, granting him a fury beyond sickness.

"We're stopping this," he muttered.

Rorke spun around, the care for his volume lower than it could have been: "I'm not seeing us lose this war. We're driving them back to the border. Back to the mountains." He proclaimed.

"In time we may. With your agreement, I will wait above. Retrieve Lin and take those by the edge of the camp we saw move. Do this, and I will ensure none of these creatures will feel Alyra's warmth along their skin when she rises once more."

Dul made his promise, and though it felt more like a cold bond than any word he could trust, he had no will to refuse it. He gave a nod to his companion and ran back to Lin, motioning for her to follow him. She popped out from behind her cover, sprinting to his side in a hurry. He guided her down to the left, close to the road Dul spoke of earlier. As they moved, he looked back at the young woman. Likely a few years younger than him, and from what he could see there were few signs of combat experience.

"You're from further South, ey? You ever fought an ogre?" he asked as he ducked under a low branch.

"No. And I hoped to never need to," she promptly responded.

"Well, you had that choice. A few things you need to know, your choice of weapon is fine for things troll-sized or smaller. But a longsword will do nothing to an ogre. You can't cripple them or cut deep enough for real damage. Chances are, you'll die if you get close to one. So, when they come running, keep back. Way back."

He put emphasis on the last part, the grim message well received.

"So, why am I even with you?" she asked.

"Chance also is that I don't walk away without a broken bone or two. I think he sees that. Or he's afraid they might accidentally find you. Thankfully, you have Illeah's other gift. I'll keep them at bay, but I'll be relying on you to keep me in one piece," he told her.

One boot broke out into the dirt clearing, smearing the wide tracks of wooden wheels.

With his keen eyes, he could see the destruction in the distance and smell the broken oak. On top of that, the pale-yellow hide of the ogres did little to hide them in the emerald and brown ocean of the woods. While his gut warned him of his error, the worry was obscured behind a veil of baleful emotions. Dipping down, he scooped up a dirty rock from the ground. He rolled it in his palm, feeling its weight in his hand.

"Ready?"

He did one check over his shoulder. A nod, not a confident one, but a nod nonetheless. Rearing his arm back, he hurled the projectile with great precision. One ogre recoiled as it bounced from his chest, and Rorke cupped his hands.

"AYE! Tired of eating your feces, you toad-brained lumps? Over here!"

His taunt came with admirable success as the four guards looked at each other before charging, crushing, and breaking a way through to him.

"Go, go!" he shouted to Lin, erratically pointing down the road.

Keeping a modest jog to match her, he kept going without hesitation until the stiff snapping of wood was replaced with the splatter of mud and dirt. Turning around, four gleaming faces looked down upon them. To his liking, the two that had spotted Lin quickly switched to him. Whether it was recognizing the threat, or just that he was the closer meal, he didn't care. Instead, he gathered his magic, focusing on his breath, just as the town healer had taught him. The air came in, cold, refreshing, welcoming. It expanded his lungs, filled his chest, nourished his body. It was Illeah's greatest gift to all, to breathe, to have their heart beat true. And then out, the release, the relinquishment, the return. In again, his muscles became limber, his veins dilated, every pore in his marrow answering her call. The great miracle, his body, took a stance before the charging monsters. His mind sharpened, understanding the movements of his foe. He rose two fists up as time slowed, flushing Illeah's magic through every stretch of skin.

"Rorke!"

He heard the cry of worry from behind him, as he had a hundred times before. Not many would wait until this kind of assault bore down upon them. Four wooden bludgeons raised and the show commenced as he unleashed his magic. Splashes of mud erupted, thundering booms crashing into the skies, and the birds took flight. As did he, above the destruction below, harmed by no more than a spot of dirt on his vest. All looked upon him, astounded by his escape of such a lethal entanglement. His left arm came back, and then his fist came forward. One ogre's head snapped back as he landed effortlessly behind them, his knuckles taking on the aspect's children that surrounded him. A body of mist; a hand of oak.

Before the creatures could even heft their cumbersome weapons, he struck again. A jab to the spine of one as he passed, and a flurry to the knee of another. Forcing them to spin around more and more, he slid back as a club came down from above. He closed in again in his dance, slipping around one club and passing through an attempted swipe from another. With the swiftness of wind, he swept through, vaulting off one weapon and up again. He delivered a powerful kick to the side of one's head, propelling himself back from the force of the blow. Even as he landed safely away, the tenacious beasts gathered themselves. Before him, the ogres assembled in a band. One rolled its jaw, barely bothered by the thunderous punch. Another smiled, his kick having done nothing short of amuse the man-eater. Exhaling again, he let a new batch fill his lungs.

"Gaff. Murg gobol shuug," one of the lumbering brutes remarked.

Another seemed to laugh, his round gut bouncing along the deep chortle. "Babag mobash."

It meandered to the side, eyeing him critically.

The four spread out, forcing him to take steps back to reassess his approach. There was a moment of reprieve, the two forces tugging and pulling for the other to cave. A bellow kicked off the second assault, and an ogre charged. It swung a wooden trunk, only to find it sailing over Rorke's head. His core tightened as he flung his torso up and twisted it to the side, nearly grazing a second club. He thrust himself forward, rotating his body past the next. Yet for his speed, he had not prepared for the first and last of the group to have already prepared their strikes. One downward, the other wide and diagonal- a collapse flanked by the gargantuan bodies of their kin.

He inhaled sharply in that moment, knowing he had let his rage guide him to this moment. Four on one- he would not get through this without his all. The crushing mauls closed in slowly in his mind, the end of the road for many a man. With a brief burst of air from his chest, his back reared at an impossible speed. His spine jerked and angled with his shoulders, melding him around the devastating smite from above with the aid of swift feet. In position right in front of the second strike, he unleashed what remained of his air. His lungs empty, he threw his arms in a cross as a shield before him. The filthy hunk of scraggly wood neared, and he felt the growing pressure right until the slightest touch of his skin.

The breath of the Aspect of Life had gone from him, but was not out of reach. In that fragment of a moment, the electrifying sensation of impact placed him deep within her grove. His mind became acutely aware of her gift, within himself and without. He sought that motion, submerging himself into the current. Amidst the rapids, he did not drown, but thrive.

His fist flew forth along the frothing, lapping flow. It carried him to the source, and with a shattering boom, did an ogre stumble back as Rorke dropped back to the ground. The beast dropped its weapon, its cheeks puffing as a gurgling became louder and louder. Blood ran from its fat and puffy lips, first as a line, then a curtain. The ogre grasped at its chest, fumbling about for only a moment before it collapsed onto its side. The Breathless Blow, a masterful technique, claimed more than a life then and there. He turned to the next three to see them stunned, their primal minds unable to comprehend how one so small wielded such power without flame and light. Yet it took considerable will for him to hide the stress using Illeah's blessing put upon him.

He once more held his fists up, centering his balance on his nimble feet. To press fear and shock, he elected for a frontal approach. Sprinting in, he slid past another heavy blow. He traded it for a considerable punch to the knee of one, but his attack was cut short by a furious slam. Enraged by their fallen kinsman, the three crashed upon him in a wave. He slung himself through the first two strikes but found himself too slow to pass by the next. He felt the solid impact on his left shoulder, stiff and unforgiving. He slid along the moist ground, hearing a roar from his right. Yet without a moment to recover, he couldn't move away, and blunt pain shot through his upper back. Though he had allowed the blow to ripple through him, the strength of an ogre was far more than any of Illeah's children could negate. Favoring getting away from the now crater-pocked terrain, he backpedaled.

A rather brave ogre came bounding forward ahead of the others, letting him use his acrobatics to position himself behind it. His fist flew forward, catching soft tissue. Even more savagely, he let his kick come straight up, clapping what was nestled behind a poorly treated hide. The ogre recoiled and moaned as Rorke continued on, to face the other two. A wide swing placed him back further, though the ogre had appeared to have had enough. For one of its size, it unleashed a maddened assault, carrying momentum with it as a second swing came, then a third- and a fourth. All the while, the other came from the side, wielding its club high above its head. It leaped into the air, crushing the earth below it as he was forced back by a wave of mud and might. Then he caught it from the corner of his eye. A broad hand, open-palmed, ready, and able to grasp him as he fought the slick bed under his feet. The pink-eyed beast lumbered above; the manacle of doom poised to clasp.

Until fresh blood splattered down onto the cool sludge that covered him. The beast jerked back, looking at the forgotten piece. So too did he look back to see Lin standing with her sword drawn in both hands, a slick crimson tongue along the edge. Before he could shout, a club reminded him to get distance and footing back first. Though his boots slid and worked against him, he managed to elude the next attack and find a dry patch under the canopy. To his liking, Lin had pulled back with him.

"Don't do that again," he whispered to her.

"I'm not running if it means I have to watch you die," she retorted.

He bit down, hearing that same stubbornness snap back at him. Shaking his head, he sharpened his focus.

"Stay back," he ordered as he took a breath in.

He squinted as he dissected the approach of the beasts, taking into account the one next to him. Though that was only a factor if he remained where he was. And that alone put him in favor of attacking.

He closed in on the nearest target, elegantly slipping by the first strike. He gave two punches to the side of the beast's knee, forcing it down to recover as he chambered a hook to the next. His fist sank deep into the firm layers of fat within the gut of the second after he slipped its guard, using the ogre's sturdy body as a platform to launch himself up. His aerial grace allowed him a last strike to the third, which stunned his foe long enough for him to land safely. He turned back to face the three giants, only to find one of them lumbering towards Lin. Instinctively, his feet flung him into the fray. He jumped past the one ogre, slid under the legs of the next, and prepared his knuckles for a proper blow to the back of the creature. Rather abruptly, it changed course in response, loading up a one-handed backwards strike.

39

Throwing his force into his feet, expelling all his strength, he turned his motion back into a great jump, placing him right into position.

A monumental pain crashed into his back, pulling his feet from the earth. His mouth opened into an empty gasp as his vision blurred, his back tempted between the choice to fold in two or break into a thousand pieces. The air felt hot as he felt the sensation of falling, then two hard thuds on his knees as rough soil ground against his pants. His palms weakly held him up as he flopped forward, though his elbows buckled and waved, the strength and will compelling them but a wisp. A jerk to his collar pulled him along, the change of position sapping his limbs into nothing but fleshy weights. He fought to take in a steady breath, to recover his sight or sound, but all he could manage were staggered gasps.

Still, there was an undeniable guilt beginning to curdle in his gut. He had made poor decisions before, and it was fine if he paid for it, but not another. He was spun around suddenly, causing his head to bob as he looked over at the swaying blobs of color in front of him. The beasts were taking their time closing in from what he could tell from the shifting shades of light and dark, which was fair. Ogres didn't have a penchant for long or frequent sprints. Given that, he might be able to find his voice in time to tell her to drop him. But a strange color came to view, a white-purple glint. Reflective, sharp — something of a siren's call to his eyes. It vanished, then came into view again, larger. The violet light sprang up in warm shades upon the cool canvas of the forest. And one yellow blob became stout as it lay motionless. Something of a good humor welled up from him, but so did a sense of nausea. One more bounce caused the pounding in his body to flare, and then everything faded.

Two sharp coughs pierced his senses back into the real world. From the dark, he moved to grasp his chest, only to swat his arm into something else. The dull rebuke signaled to him the slowly awakening awareness his body had, though the stimulus did nothing more than jam his brain from smoothly allowing him to transition back. His eyes shot open, the light of day no longer around to blind him. Instead, he was graced with sweet autumn hues belonging to the one tending to his wounds. With a deep breath, he let his head lay back against the tree behind him. A smile crept along his lips as he noticed not a single scratch had come upon the young lady before him.

"Thanks for holding up your end of the deal," he jested through a gruff voice, his chest likely still bearing bruised or cracked ribs from the last hit he took.

"If this is how you live, I'm not sure how you've made it this far." She muttered, preparing another swell of green energy between her palms.

Extending her hands back down to his chest, he had to grit his teeth to endure the mending of tissue and bone. After a few seconds, the tearing and searing agony faded, replaced with the usual thumping tempo. Still, her comment was a raindrop in the sea. At this point, all he could do was laugh.

"You don't get to be a hero without being daring," he said. "Sometimes I go a bit too far, but I usually scrape by." His grin apparently wasn't earning him much from what he could tell.

For someone who had seemed to have a soft side, she certainly had a cold way of holding her ground when she wanted to. Or maybe it was just him. That was usually it. When her gaze wandered back down to his chest, she pushed off to stand, leaving him to fumble with the buttons with numb hands like a writhing worm.

"Dul is out hunting down the one that ran away." She told him as she kneeled by her pack.

"Wait … he killed them? All of them?"

His eyes widened as Lin stayed remarkably calm, stunningly unaware of such a triumph. Rorke sat up, bracing his stomach.

"I know he said that … but all of them?" he continued to voice his disbelief, wishing to hear his answer from her lips.

Yet his companion remained blissfully ignorant.

"It would take a hundred trained soldiers to have wiped that camp. Maybe more."

As if his words had called out to the darkness, the spawn of the abyss dropped from above like an eldritch tear. That liquid blackness took form, opening two burning blue eyes. Dul stood tall, unwavering as his blades ran with crimson rivers over his knuckles.

"It is done," he announced bluntly.

The half-blood looked down upon him with a cruel squint.

"You, human, are quick to change your mind and words. I should not be surprised, but your decision gave the enemy a chance to retreat when I came to save you."

Rorke ignored the scorn of the half-demon, the questions and possibilities swelling up from within, unable to be held back.

"If you did all that in one night ... where have you been all this time? And this ... you hide from us? You ... there's so much more you could do." He bumbled around with his thoughts, forming little more than half-complete propositions.

Though all the obsidian skinned man did was take a seat on a stone, laying his bone swords across his thighs. His near-empty look seemed to agree with him, but gave him nothing more.

"With someone like you, there's no need for all of this. No need for fathers to die so their sons are born to fill another row of graves," he exclaimed, mustering all the strength into raising his voice that he could.

Lin looked nervously between the two, watching Dul plant his hands on his knees. The sapphire wisps vanished, and the half-demon shook his head.

"This world is not so simple."

Dul responded calmly, but with heavy weight upon each word.

"You're talking about Toren's followers? Seven or eight generations have passed, they can get over themselves! They have no power in the North. I can get you in with Alyra's church. They'll protect you, this all can end. We can fortify the North, unite it, end the squabbling between- "

"No."

The singular answer carried force with it just like the club of an ogre. It caused him to lean heavier upon the pack that propped him up, but like the tide, it was a momentary withdrawal.

"No? How ... just like that?"

Rorke felt his anger swell up again, smearing his judgement.

"You say I'm quick to turn ... you go from a savior to coward really quick," he snapped back.

Dul glared at him. Not with pure malice, but with fatigue.

"I don't think you hear yourself," Lin interjected.

"You don't even understand him, yet you speak as if you own his life." She spat back, steadily taking a position on Dul's side of the camp.

"You don't have to convince me, human."

The half-demon suddenly became animated again, slipping his blades through the loops on his belt.

"But you do not differ from the followers of the star. You alone prove that my hopes were foolish. I am still a creature to man, and I will always be. The Devastation did not change that, if it ever truly ended." Dul spoke before looking up at the rising moon in the sky, a deep gaze that left the material realm.

Before Rorke could find an answer, Lin stole his stage: "You … you lived through the Piraph Devastation? All that time ago?"

Her voice called the half-demon back down to the earth. He nodded solemnly. Just that act of confirmation caused her to wilt away, placing her hands together over her waist and bowing her head.

"What? We're still here, too. He's not the only one that fought. Our ancestors did, too."

Rorke blasted through the heavy atmosphere, clearing the fog to see Dul looking directly at him.

"You speak so proudly, without knowing consequence. Those who would seek my end do so rightly. I use the same magic that once wiped two races from this land. You would forget that to see the enemy die, no different from the Piraph when they wished to win their war. The magics of my kin … they still scar this land. The bitterness of those in Mordiv's Hold, the wastes in the West … consequence. The soil still remembers what you all do not- what happens when one thinks they can control a demon's curses. If I go and fight, what price will be paid for this victory? Will nature be stripped barren and bleed for you? Will the followers of Toren, or perhaps the tiquo take notice? The condemnation of countless lives, then and now, are they worth it for you? I have done what I have been able to for all my life, and yet … you prove them right."

Dul stood up, turning his back to Rorke as he walked off into the woods. He could show him the ogre's bodies, how the curse ate at them, how it would blacken the soil, and maybe he'd understand then what demonic magics could do. What kind of costs came with being greater than such a savage predator, that price he paid to save them. But there were more concerns than that...

His back itched, his gums tingling as his teeth ached. He had spilled too much blood too quickly. Stirring up old memories wasn't anything less than a battering ram to the gates of his disciplined mind. The words were sometimes enough- piraph, yrabor ... the races now only known by the shattered bones that farmers dug up from time to time. But the man, as arrogant as he was, had reminded him of something far worse. Someone from back then, someone who had tried to convince him of great lies. The one who had tried to pull him from self-isolation, but such was necessity. Even his mother's family- his family- had whispered behind his back. They never looked at him as a person. When others came to visit, they would lock him in closets and the basement. They knew he was dangerous. That's why he did it for them, chaining up the door to his room. Why he only let his mother see him. She alone risked everything for him, to try to comfort him. This was his fate, and he could be content with it ... alone. He didn't need the emotions of others, their words, their choices. Being drawn in by greed and hubris would only bring suffering, split the fragile human groups up more than they were. War from within was the last thing their injured race needed. As his shoulders burned, mist leaked from his skin. He bit down, mustering the strength to suppress his soul. His mark was made as the verdant life around him wilted, branches dropping leaves which rapidly browned at his feet. In a fit, he swiped at a tree, cleaving four grooves through the bark. *Mistake. Mistake.* It boomed through his very being, taunting him that he had allowed himself to walk willingly alongside such a man. The instinct pulsed for him to draw his blade, but then his sense caught the snap of a twig close by. He pivoted around, his fingers curled like the talons of a hawk.

"Dul?"

Lin's soft voice perforated his skin, ripping him open, turning him inside out. The fear she spoke with, the tone ... the same now and then. Instantly, he went limp, powerless before his caretaker. "Are you alright?"

The command was issued, and so he nodded.

"I'm sorry."

The first crack in the illusion came with a puff of dust.

"I couldn't know ... but... I'll respect your concerns. It's my fault he's here."

The second fracture formed a chasm, wide enough to force a wedge in. He pried free at that escape, bursting through into the present. With a shiver, Dul stood to full height. Turning away in shame, Lin balled a hand up.

"I should never have asked so much of you."

She stood silent after that, giving him time to find his center. While his skin still crawled with dark powers, the shock she had given him seemed to have disrupted the flow. In the last gasping breath of dusk, he struggled to control his tongue. Before her, he could not come to an answer. Not to her question, not to her apology. Just as he had done two hundred years ago at the gate, he walked away in silence. Away from the damning scourge, away from the past, away from the present, in hopes the future would help him forget.

# Chapter Four: Rot From Within

The halls were rather empty as Anuurae walked through. Not to her displeasure, exactly. The people here were fine enough to work with, but not the sort she would make any friendships with. Humans were industrious and agreeable for the most part, but she was thankful her people couldn't use magic. It just seemed to have a strange effect on people.

Opening the door on the right, she ducked in quickly, the trail of her well-worn cloak sweeping in behind her, just a hair away from getting caught as the oak slammed shut. At his desk, her contractor was scribbling away in another one of his books to the light that cascaded in over his shoulders through a broad window. His eyes came up for a peak after one more line, but then stuck back to the pages. Aggressively, he let one long stroke out and dotted something else, then calmly slipped his quill back into the pot.

During his show, she had closed across the room, and reached under her cloak. Her fingers came to the knot and quickly slipped it open, allowing her to set the lined sack on to the red-wood desk. The man raised an eyebrow, waiting for her to step back. She did, and two metal plated hands rose up, tugging the closing strap to peer inside the bag. With no more than just a momentary glance, he peeled down the woven fabric to gaze upon the trophy. The decapitated head, eyes closed, sat slack jawed towards her. Creed pulled the bag up and sat it aside, giving an affirmative nod.

"Well done. Food and board will be extended for another twenty days, and the rest will be put to the property you want. Unfortunately, I only have one bounty left," he informed her grimly, looking to the unrolled scroll pinned to the board with a knife.

"Any new leads?" she asked swiftly.

Creed shook his head, putting a hand on a close-shaved head.

"I wish I did. Reports are scarce from the East and West. The Western Wastes makes sense, we have few men out there and fewer eyes. But the East … Mordiv's Hold isn't answering us. Not that I'm surprised. They vilify us and our guide, blessed be he and his forgiveness."

Creed ducked his head with his commentary, raising a star amulet to his lips with closed eyes. He let go, returning his attention.

"Still, this is one less thief and murderer to worry about. I can divert another squad to the border. We've had about as many requests for aid from our outposts and patrols as the people. Your work has been a boon, Anuurae. The people of Kressel's Charge and beyond thank you."

With that, the Sacred Charge went to return to his logs. Yet she pressed forward. The act caught his attention, returning him to her.

"I'm not leaving if you're not giving me every detail."

Like a blade to his throat, the officer's eyes widened at the threat.

"I'm not in any position to be extorted for my reports, especially to one outside our congregation," he countered firmly.

"How many was it this week? Thirty? Fifty? More?" she pressed her attack relentlessly.

"My hands are bound where they are, Anuurae. I hold my tongue for the people. Our neighbors still grasp to their independence. I expect you to understand- we are not in a place to act recklessly. We have united a great deal of the Western Forest. Our dealings with Alyra's followers in the North go well for now … but between us and the Great Cradle we have nothing but enemies. Our contact with the Lesal Bastion in the far East has been cut for months now. Sending a messenger through their territory is suicide between malcontents and this … cult."

She could hear the hint of anger behind such a well-trained presentation, which she could understand. Any of Toren's children resented murder and cruelty.

"Then give me supplies, and I'll find him. I'm not going to stand here while my people are butchered in their homes, Creed," she rebuked his inaction, widening his eyes once more.

"Do you understand what you just said? You, going to Mordiv's Hold? If the people don't stone you, the cult will skin you alive. I can understand your frustration, I feel the same. But that … it's little more than foul suicide."

Creed still made his best attempt to hold his ground, but she could easily strike him from where he stood.

"Give me what I want and maybe I'll change my mind," she pressured him again.

"You know I can't do that. Not one page within this room can leave without my confirmation. This piece alone was handed to me by one of the Silver Command. I will not betray Toren's trust, nor my brothers and sisters."

Steadfast, Creed had both his military training and the discipline of the church to stand by. Yet she pulled her hood down, cocking her head with a bittersweet smile.

"That's why you have me, right?" She whispered, her sultry tone as slick as oil on cream. "Because if I bloody my hands, yours are clean. Right?"

Just as quickly as it came, all her allure washed away as she narrowed her eyes, biting down upon her prey with cruelty and impunity.

"If only your sense of honor could stop a blade. But no, you'd rather listen to administrators and bean counters rather than think for yourself. It's been months, Creed. I'm done waiting for you."

She delivered the twist of her knife cleanly, knowing her employer understood exactly what she meant. The well-edged features of Creed's face wilted as he sucked in on the side of his cheek, finishing with a sigh. Reaching under his desk, he pulled a loosely bound fan of papers. He tapped them on his desk, aligning them before setting them down. He gave her a discontented, flat look as he retracted his last two fingers from the stack.

"These pages never made it to my desk. To my hand. To this building. Understood?"

He spoke sternly, as if to reprimand her already. She traded with a sly smile, depositing the bounty into a satchel under her cloak.

"Never even saw them."

Anuurae spun around to leave, pulling her hood back over her head. She tucked her cloak tightly around herself with her arms and hurried back out into the streets. The chorus of the city welcomed her back as carts navigated to the market, hammers beat hard earth into submission, and boots marched on. It never stopped, not in Kressel's Charge. It was the heart of the region, a place that had great need of someone willing to engage in her line of work. Bounty hunting was a rather testing and unforgiving way to make a living, but it suited her well enough she had made it to the top as a night hunter. So too, did it suit her for getting away from the hive of humans.

Taking a right turn, she made haste to the edge of town. The terrain quickly turned to a steep rise, signaling her ascent of the old barricade. Most noise faded below as the buildings became far more disparate to the homogeny of the city. Less suffocating, with an open sky that didn't have to fight signage and roofs. She passed by some of her own kin resting on the front of their property, one flipping a dagger, another repairing a long bow as the two conversed quietly.

Two doors down, she stopped to procure a key, slipping it into the lock. The metal shifted and popped, and the door swung open. In only a moment, it was locked again, and a heavy bolt was slid into position. She slipped the latch to her cloak and put it on a hook, exhaling deeply as she threw herself on the thick padding of a hoffen rug. She lay on her back for a moment, feeling the soreness of her feet and the wear on her palms. It was quite a trip she took to scratch the second to last off her list, but that tenacity was what she had become known for.

With a bit of effort, she sluggishly worked her boots off her legs, and then went for her belt. The heavy leather decided to protest her attempts to unlatch it, further testing her patience. The smaller ones around her thighs went easier, giving her more to work with around her waist. A quick jerk let her set it aside, the ten throwing axes clattering as they were left in a pile on the floor. Then came the satchel, which she leaned up against a chest. Flipping it open, she pulled the crumpled papers out.

Creed's writing was easy enough to recognize, and thankfully easy on her weary eyes, but the first few pages told her nothing she didn't already know.

Though in the middle, a very clean sheet stuck out from the rest. No rips, no damp marks, no ink smears. Almost perfect, coming from no ordinary trader or craftsman within the city. Plucking it free, she angled it to work with the natural light from the window.

*Sacred Charge Creed,*

*We have received your summary reports on this developing faction within our territory. It has been passed personally to my hand, and I must say, bound by the guidance of the star, such perversion and glorification of violence has no place amidst our church and people. It is disheartening, disgusting, and intolerable that we have lost so many so close to home.*

*Unfortunately, our ability to act is limited. Current efforts in the North require a great deal of our forces, pushing us to reduce local defenses as a result. Our work with Alyra's most loyal is critical in once more uniting mankind, and I cannot say I am confident dispatching our men to the East. I am well aware that several of our own have "vanished" in the wilds, and though they may seem forgotten, we can simply not address this problem.*

*To take an attack from Mordiv's Hold would require us to withdraw our First, Second, and Fifth Sections from their positions at the northern border. Undoubtably, the result would at least be that we lose our relations with the North, and further, that the damnable ogres would breach deeper into our land. We must uphold our tenants and stay true to his guidance. The light of Toren led us from our bondage back to the Great Cradle of the Lesal Bastion centuries ago, and will give us the strength to endure our wounds until we may mend our bodies.*

*I will see to it that my men are kept alert, and I will see what I can do to have the Fifth Section in the North send scouts to watch the woods. The enemy may have these small victories for now, but we will not forget. Every fallen brother, every ostoran taken too early, every crime will be met with a righteous sword in hand.*

*Fourth Silver Commander Reigis*

It was difficult to finish the piece without tearing the page or spitting on the message. Creed had practically adhered to every letter. Yet the bloodstain on the paper below caught her eye. The same handwriting from the Commander stood atop it, flaunting its infallible style.

*Sacred Charge Creed,*

*I regret to say my discretion was ill-informed. Your reports, at no fault of your own, are incomplete. These papers, delivered hand to hand by dying men, are to stay in your care, and yours alone until I state any further. I will have entrusted command of my Section to my Augur, Inflector, and brother. I will personally be making amends for my mistakes by seeking the head of this man.*

*May Toren forgive me, and may the souls of the fallen be met kindly by Fynor upon their passing.*

*Fourth Silver Commander Reigis*

The shift in dire tone caused her to puff her lips out in surprise.

"What exactly were you handed, Creed?"

Her whispers faded as she looked to the true contents of the page, where several scribblings had been written at various angles. The page was filled with them, as if this was the last sheet the writer ever expected to see. Except there were three pages, each exactly as chaotic as the last. Turning it around in her fingers, she made an attempt to decipher where the beginning was. Eventually she found a pattern in the way the clumps of writing were cobbled together. There was some overlap, but understanding the theme made it easy enough to follow.

*Rev, Amlii, Pons. Dead. Someone has to know. The damn cult, it's not a rumor. Bastards showed up in their robes, they followed us, laid traps. They knew our routes. Yet they think they can wait here and find me. Tucked inside our stash, I have just a sliver of light and these supplies. I know I'm dead, and I resign myself to that fact. But I can still hear their boots above. They talk about making this one of their hideouts. And I'm not going to die without this making it to the world above!*

*Names. These bastards only talk of one. Kaerex.*

*The smell is terrible. If I wasn't able to cover my dung with dirt down here I would have thought it to be that, but I think they've moved the bodies indoors.*

*More. They're not just killing a few. They're hunting. The talked about it when they got back today. Bastards are some sort of human purists. They brag about killing our kind like it's a sport. Kaerex ... it's their leader's name. He wants to take on the tiquo, too. Psychopaths. They'll get us all killed.*

*The writing is all that's keeping me sane. I've never been one to worship an aspect. It's not like I've ever had something against Toren's followers. They keep the peace and treat everyone well enough. Alyra's people can be a bit strange or abrasive, but they mean well. And I'd be lying if Pons and I haven't been saved by our neighbor that Illeah clearly gave more than a gift with healing. I'd kill to break out of here and see that smile again. Instead it's been ... a few days more than a week I think. Can't smell much anymore. Still plenty of dried meat and berries, but I think my water is about half-way through. I need to make sure I get what I need before I make a break for it. Whoever might be watching over me ... grant my feet a clear path.*

*Three. Three stand guard nearby. They move supplies. They come inside by morning, sleep until the sun sets. Then twenty or more make their rounds inside and out. I'm going to see if I can loosen the lock here, catch a look mid-day while they sleep.*

*These people aren't right. They're covered in scars. Some self-inflicted. Their clothes are crude and stained. But there are more outside. I can see them through the window. Sneaking out isn't going to be easy ... just like I thought.*

*I saw him. His face. All of it. Kaerex.*

*Madness. He calls to Orobrex. This is it. I'll draw his face, plaster it on every city in the forest. This can't be given time! Others need to know! They hide in Mordiv's Hold, but come from the West. Whoever finds these pages, take them to Kressel's Charge!*

She quickly sat the page aside, reading but a piece on the next:

*They're like magsies to blood. I hear their leader closing in. The man holds ten weapons at once, I fear those men will not last. This is where i...*

A smear of ink and blood came across the line, but nonsensical legends were not what she needed. Tossing that page aside, she came to the last one. Even with a hole punched through it, the last sheet was exactly what she desired. Clear as day, the pride of an ostoran scout stared back at her. Exquisitely detailed, there was no mistaking the stout features looking back at her for any other. It was an oddly unique look; one she knew to be from a specific group of people. Northerners, back from when their races had met, went two ways. Those that mixed with the original ostora, and those that had refused and stayed to be enslaved or slain by the piraph.

It appeared that those that had survived to this day weren't too happy about being the losers of that deal and had found a home amidst the rat's nest of Mordiv's Hold. With a wicked smile, she looked to her axes, plucking one up into her hand. The rough and rugged hunk of metal reflected her in the polished edge, letting her admire herself. The long feathers in her hair, along her arms, black, and emerald green. Just like her eyes, the remnants of her proud heritage. The ostora were never a major power, but her kin all respected one another. Just one large family all over Tavora blended in with the humans. And it would be no greater punishment for such a crooked man to be slain by that very kin.

She felt an odd bit of pride in the thought, even coming to a somewhat ominous chuckle that caused her to pause for a moment. Normally, work was just work, but like her own lips had said. This was personal, in more than one way. In a week or so, she could indulge in quite a savory treat. Creed already had a name; a Silver Commander was on the job ... the pay would only make it sweeter. This home, food and drink for a year ... and the thrill of new lands. An ostoran could hardly ask for more, and it was enough that her mind began to let her calm for the first time in a long time. Still gripping her throwing axe, the descent to sleep was so swift she didn't even notice the approach.

She pulled herself up from the floor, yawning as a bit of grogginess sloshed around in her head and muscles. Holding herself up with one arm, she groaned, feeling the onset of the end of a journey. Still, Tavora never slept. Going upstairs, she once again ignored her bed and made her way to the dresser beside it. Sliding the top drawer open, she flung out a full outfit and crammed it into a pack to go down to the bathhouse. Even if it wouldn't last, being at least temporarily clean was a comfort she could thankfully afford. That was first on her list, then back to her house, to suit up and gather supplies. Trading her soiled clothes for food, water, and camping supplies, she said her farewells to Kressel's Charge and headed due East.

# Chapter Five: Servant of Madness

The transition over the past few days wasn't exactly what an ostoran could have ever expected. The stories from Mordiv's Hold were always a sad one, and she'd heard them many times. A group of healers established it as a camp as they followed the warpath during the Devastation. But they never really saved anyone from the withering, and instead filled fields of graves with tainted bodies. And so, the soil blackened, the trees warped, and the sky was hidden as a thick fog shrouded the world ... but she never imagined it to be so literal.

The trees had started to have darker bark and fewer leaves until some were just black obelisks jutting up into the blurry sky. Whether they were still somehow alive or just petrified husks, she didn't care to know. The cool air amplified the disturbing feeling the wood gave her, putting her on edge as she closed in at the edge of the city. Kneeling down on the edge of a mound, she focused in on the rising black walls in the distance. Watchtowers loomed overhead, with darkly armored figures occasionally slipping into view.

There was no sound that made it this far — just an ominous emptiness. Even the road bore nothing but musty footprints, as if no one ever entered or left heading West. Had the past of Tavora not been so grim, she would never have believed this was ever a place of healing. Though once more, she saw another piece of the legends. On the right, half-decayed wood fences guarded fields of crumbling tombstones. They went on and on until darkness swallowed them, the mist a guard from the past's morbidity.

That made it even more difficult to discern whether or not the unease she felt now was only from the environment, and not from the taint of the land. Ostorans weren't known for using magic, or knowing much about it in the first place. Though she knew firsthand how dangerous magic was, her bestial instincts told her when something mystical would threaten her life. If she could rely on that once inside, though- that was something she had to keep in mind … stimulus from a city, and a strange new land- her focus would travel elsewhere. And as she considered her entry, multiple guards by the gate showed her first challenge.

She looked human under her cloak from a distance. But vibrant, leaf-green eyes would surely unveil her. Her glorious colors would only be the beginning, would anyone see a feather poking out from under her sleeves. Pacing left and keeping low, she avoided the open part of the road that could reveal her as she traversed around the perimeter of the city. The walls seemed uniform, but she knew there would be multiple entrances. Slipping through the scraggly brush was nearly impossible to do so quietly, as it scratched and caught on every bit of slack in her cloak, but such a noise did not carry far enough to matter.

When she reached the other side of the city, she found her premonition to be right. The side facing the Lesal Bastion remained mostly unfortified. It still had the same oppressive walls, but no one was standing at the gate. That, and the terrain offered her an easier route to squeeze in. From here she could see some people tending to fields, raking cold dirt and pulling up pale crops from the forsaken earth. It gave her hope, watching them move about. Erratic, slow, and covered in nondescript cloth from coats and cloaks. She could blend right in.

Positioning herself where she was out of view of the guard towers, she burst onto the road, keeping her head low. She let her shoulders slump, hanging her back forward like the others. Inside her cloak, her hands pulled together the strap, tightening it closed. Unlike when she roamed Kressel's Charge, she didn't worry about the wear on the tail of her accessory. Tears and stains fit right into the sickly environment.

Proceeding to the gate, she found the entrance cracked open, left that way as if anyone who wished could come and go. Making up for a moment of hesitation, she kept her feet moving toward the city's innards. Breaching the boundary, the air hit her nostrils like a block of ice. Cold, stagnant, dead- it was difficult to keep it in. She muffled her cough, forcing herself to take a deep breath. Her body protested it like a poison, and she couldn't blame it. The air seemed to make her exhale bits of her own life.

She moved to the opposite side of the street as a group of guardsmen approached on patrol, their rigid expressions not unlike the world around them. They paid her little heed, as if she was a street rat. That would help, but with a slight lift of her head, she saw just how militant the place was. It seemed like there wasn't one person out and about that wasn't wearing leather or plate, unless they were farmers. Past the strip she was in, the bulky buildings further in all bore resemblance to barracks, and past that, billowing smoke told her that forges were busy spitting out more tools for the army that roamed around.

She ducked into an alley as a large group turned the corner ahead of her, the feathers atop the helmet of one alerting her to the officer. While grunts in such a place might be as bright as a wyrble, she knew better than to assume anyone in a position of power in this world would be the same. She kept momentum ahead, passing by the doors of what would be housing for the laborers of the place.

Two children sat on the steps of one of the houses, playing with ... bones. Some from small, predatory yvera, but the assorted collection had a rodent and a kiv skull within it. Her stomach churned, and she knew she had to find a place to stop. At the end of the alley, she pressed a hand against the wall. To her left, a small cutout allowed her a moment to hunch over and find respite. *How can anyone live here? Tainted with demonic gloom, sick, starving ... this is torture. Like the past never left it.*

She put a hand over her lips, holding back another coughing fit. If she lingered here, it wouldn't even be the people that would be the death of her. A curse from two hundred years ago seemed far more likely, or whatever illnesses undoubtably loomed about. Reaching into her satchel, she pulled a cloth free and held it over her nose and mouth. Whether or not it was a placebo didn't matter, it made her feel steadier, and her breathing followed.

Tying a clean knot, she checked the exits of the alley and made her way out once she saw it was clear.

While a tavern or barracks would be the place for her to start, she doubted the first existed, and the second was little different from walking nude into a horde of hungry magsies. Instead, she narrowed her options down to simple observation. This place was another world compared to any other, but it was a fact her foe was near. And they would never expect eyes in such a place, unless a certain follower of Toren had blown his cover already.

Continuing her stroll, she kept a watch on her sides. No one seemed to be following her, or even watching her. *Wonder if he left any clues behind. He could have been here weeks before me, or just days. They're the kind to keep records, but where would a righteous warrior rest in the den of the monster itself?*

The question was almost as daunting as the equal and opposite, where the beast lurked within this den. Taking her time, she began to piece out the possibilities from her previous jobs. Violent types usually liked to be out of sight, but these were cultists contracted by the city. The people here were unlikely to care, or even be targeted by the cult. And if the guards didn't care, it wouldn't make sense for them to even try to blend in with the masses. They would have access to supplies, aid, and if the military had control of intelligence, the two would likely work hand in hand. That pointed to them being somewhere in the core of the city, back where the swarm of soldiers had been.

What she really needed was somewhere higher up to gain a better view, but the ladder next to her that led up into the darkness of a watchtower was not too inviting, to say the least. With a quick glance behind her and to the side, she changed course for another alley. Coming to a three-way split, she found herself properly out of sight. With a running start, she jumped towards one wall, placing a muddy boot on the wooden wall. Kicking off, she rebounded with greater height to the roof behind her. Her palms planted firmly on the ridge, which she shimmied along to the right. A cusp gave her a hand up, allowing her to swing her body towards a larger lip. A window frame provided another foothold, allowing her toes to hold her up as she reached for another structural beam. By the strength of her fingers, she managed to hold on, slowly gaining ground until she could pull her chest up and roll onto the roof of the building.

She breathed heavily as he pushed herself up, admiring how smooth the feat had been for how much weight she was carrying while plagued by magic. She sat down on the edge, melding into the silhouette of a chimney, only visible to the most attentive that had discovered one of the ultimate methods of survival ... looking up. As she looked down upon the lines of soldiers, she finally began to understand Creed's worry. The followers of the great star were considered to be the largest human army, but the sort that was being belched up from the stone halls here didn't look like a militia. Every single one was hardened, toting polearms, great weapons, and hand weapons with sculpted purpose.

Furthering her suspicions, a set of wide doors opened from a low-lying building. The products of the forges came out on a cart, pulled by four men. Open top barrels displayed countless spears, with the crates under and around them no doubt filled to the brim with more weapons or armor. The cart pulled out into the street, facing towards the way she came from. Behind it a second emerged in order, and a third. The caravan marched with grim uniformity, but the echoes of pings and bangs coming from the workshop heralded that there was far more to come. Two brutes hauled the sliding the doors closed, followed by another feather-helmed officer coming up to bark orders at them. Followed without even acknowledgement, the great machine ran without a single mistake or moment of stillness.

*They know about this. And they're keeping it a secret. I guess they don't want people to panic, but ... they look like they want war. They've got the manpower, and clearly the resources. Any day now they could just march on Kressel's Charge.*

Her eyes darted to movement along another high place, a balcony on a second story. A rough-looking man in leathers strutted out, holding his head high. He locked his arms behind his back as a second man walked out behind him, wearing a crisp and unusually clean collared coat. The man in leathers gestured out to the city, while the crisp-coated one nodded. There was a pause, and the crisp-coated man walked over to the railing. He tilted his gaze down, brushing his dark, rustic hair back smoothly, only for the short strands to return immediately after. Something glinted in his eyes- a sharp spell cast from those emerald depths that pricked at her fear.

Whatever he asked when he turned around upset the man in leathers, leading to a brief altercation. If she wasn't mistaken, she heard a particular name carried to her ears by the carelessly raised voice. She honed in, hoping to drop in on what still remained.

"... I don't understand why you insist upon us waiting. The enemy is pre-occupied. You yourself know this. Yet you have our men place more supplies in our northern camps," the man in leathers exclaimed.

"And what reason have you to doubt me, commander? Have I not secured those resources through influence alone? Have I not procured aid, and led us to this very day? I know the right time to strike. Unfortunately, your tongue is too loose for me to trust you with the details. Sit by, be patient. My work will ensure success, have no doubt," the crisp-coated man calmly replied as he plucked up a glass and took a deep drink.

"It would be easier to wait if I saw real progress. Instead, we mill about in our own territory. It is time to advance! The enemy has poorly defended farmland to the northwest, which our city could desperately use. We have the strength to hold them," the man in leathers growled.

The crisp-coated man pulled out a chair, sitting down with a charming grace as he deposited his drink on the table, gentle as a downy feather.

"We may hold that ground, commander. But we still need manpower to take their cities. And if the enemy rallies the North against us, we will never win the defensive. With both Silver Commanders of Toren and the Night Witches of Alyra, our hold would be turned to ash. We must play to our strength — attack and manpower. The enemy will use their magics for attrition. We must be swift. That is why I must let out new allies prepare. Of which..." he paused, watching the door they had come from slip ajar.

"... you may enter."

The crisp-coated man interlocked his fingers, not even casting a glance to the opening door. What marched through was a feral beast that stole the form of a man, covered in many shades of dyed fur and cloth. Strips of red, brown, and gray, all haphazardly sewn and strapped together to form some sort of armor. The hooded individual hauled a body in his left hand, leaving a wide smear in his advance. From the broken spear in the chest of the corpse, the end had not come quietly or calmly.

The newcomer let go of the handful of cloth as the body thudded on the floor, and her blood ran hot. *Ten weapons at once.* Upon the man's back was an array of assorted weapons. Axes, swords, maces, bludgeons, an armory of pocked and abused tools.

"Unlike you, Kaerex has been a very fruitful worker. The only questions he asks are where he needs to be next, and what he needs to do. Take a lesson from him, commander. He achieves more than you do, and he can bring me what he knows I want. Like this unwanted pest- Fourth Commander Reigis."

The crisp-coated man held out a loose, open hand to the body.

"Silenced. Brought forth without a word."

He returned his hands to their interlocked position, giving the man in leathers a look that drained away the tough exterior as if it was only a façade.

"I am understood, am I not? Do not interfere with any of my plans."

The man in leathers swallowed hard, giving a salute.

"Understood, Rederick, sir."

That was the end of the current show as the commander hurried off, leaving just Rederick and Kaerex.

Once there was time for the departed to be a suitable distance away, Rederick finished his beverage and stood.

"As promised, for good work."

Rederick commented as he reached into his coat. He pulled forth something blue, pearly in luster, almost crystalline in nature. Immediately, Kaerex fell to one knee, his head down in submission. Rederick held out the trophy, to which two fur covered arms came up to receive. The item changed hands, and Kaerex pulled the item close to his face. The madman seemed to tremble for a moment before standing, revealing the reward to be some kind of incomplete mask.

"It appears we must make … adjustments. Come."

Rederick waved to his little murderer, who promptly followed behind him into the complex, making sure to not forget his still-bleeding toy.

She sat back, bewildered at what she was witnessing. The atmosphere began to sink in — potent and vile. All of it was crushing, unrelenting, taking a mile where given an inch. No longer was the hunt a game, a trial, or some vendetta. The scene- all of it and what it aspired to be … the death of one would not stop it.

The friend she had practically stepped upon, threatening his sanctity, seemed more like a victim now than anything else. Anuurae held a jittering hand to her face, running the side of her fingers along her lips. The nervous habit jammed her mind in just the right way to remind her of the isolated position she had, and where exactly she sat. She pulled that same hand away, making a loose fist.

*Don't let it control you. Tavora feels that weakness, and this place is thirsting to see more in the graves outside all the same. You came here for one thing, and you will have it. One death might mean little to a war, and that's why he won't be the last.*

Hearing her own voice reassured her, reinforcing a fractured morale. Anuurae pushed herself to her feet, observing the peaks of the buildings around her. There would be a need for her to stay here for some time, perhaps a few days. A Silver Commander was a valiant fighter, one of humanity's best, but that didn't mean she intended to be so upfront with her approach any longer. If her foe was inclined to prowl back, every move would need to be calculated. Who he spoke to, where he went, what his routines were.

Her gaze fell upon a flat roofed building that extended higher than her on the far end of the city, a place which jutted haphazardly above other low-lying structures. The structure seemed strangely out of place, and without many features, the purpose of it remained unclear. All the same, the vision it could provide and a possible blind spot to watchtowers would be more than desirable.

Quickly descending down into the alley once more, she began out into the rear street in hopes the long way around would avoid most of the guards. Though her second turn revealed something that made her smile. A fairly tall man, cloaked in a grimy fur cowl, hurried along another street. She changed course, following the red and gray mess. While it may not lead to a kill, she couldn't help but pass up a possible leak to a residence.

The cultist kept a swift and steady pace onward, then jutted down an alley. She dashed by a group of young boys hauling in food, earning a sneer from the rougher looking ones. Her target hung left — then out into a street. He faded into a small crowd of soldiers, causing her eyes to water. Like dust, the colors blew around, shifting, as if they did not wish to be seen. Even the sound of his boots on the wet stone faded, but still she persisted in that direction.

He took a dive into a long alley, though she could barely look dead at him any longer. The image of the man was scratchy, somehow physically abrasive to her eyes. He seemed unaware of her, but even then, she doubted this was a common illusion. She had plenty of experience with malcontents using the Aspect of Fate's tricks, but the arcane technique she was witnessing was different entirely. Whatever the spell was did not target her, instead emanating from within the caster himself.

Her target made a sharp right around a corner, which she passed by, then slowed. She whirled around, taking a few steps closer, right up to the edge of the wall. She peered around, finding ... nothing. Walls, refuse, perhaps a rat. Even the tracks that went in vanished after a few feet. Cautious of a trap or further magics, she pulled an axe free under her cloak. Silent, predatory movements guided her closer, where she knelt down to the edge of the last print.

She held a hand out, brushing the dank ground with the tips of her fingers. The domain of touch revealed no arcane imprint, no warping, no tampering by Alok's mystic ways. Though when she came to that final footprint, looking at the dirt it left behind, she could start to see why. The large boot had left a depression in the front, a substantial shift of weight. The man was large, but if he had exerted such force, he might have used Illeah's blessings to ascend above.

She began to straighten her back, looking left to see if there was anything he could have used to grant purchase, but a sudden jerk forced her back against something solid. Before she could blink, breathe, even widen her eyes, an arm had slithered under both of her own, locking her in place as a cool blade was held close to her throat. She knew better than to make a noise, even a yelp of surprise.

"Speak quickly."

A hushed voice commanded from behind.

Swallowing once, she let her wit guide her slick tongue: "Considering you've yet to use that sword, I don't think you're who I thought you were."

There was no reaction to her comment, not any ease, not any loss of aggression. *Great.* She closed her eyes.

"How do you feel about talking this one through? I feel like we both aren't from here."

Awaiting a response, she tried to avoid shifting too much, as to not provoke the man.

"An ostoran need not convince me of that. You willingly come to a place that would have you flayed. Maybe none would question your corpse for that ... but you take what little time I have left. My quarry slips away, so..."

There was a short pause, and then the edge at her vulnerable throat retreated. As soon as she was let free, she slipped two steps of space between her and the man, who had already turned his back on her.

"... I care not for you. Leave me be, less you wish to grace Fynor with your company."

The stranger warned her. Before he could take a step, she called out to him: "If you're using that disguise, I think we can help each other."

Rather than slip away, her hook had landed.

"I need no aid, huntress. Your competence is not in question, but to why you have an interest in the cult..."

The man's head suddenly jerked up. Alert, ready, he looked like a kiv who just heard a free meal break a stick nearby. He began to take steps back towards her, and that was when she caught on. A shift in the song of the city. It became angrier- the steps of soldiers faster, the shouts louder. It grew, until the sound of boots became a uniform thrum.

"The spirit has grown impatient ... blood has been spilled..." the man cocked his head sharply, then shook it. "… flee, if you can. The Sons of Blackwood will scour every rock, close this place up as a tomb."

The stranger burst past her after his warning, flying toward the wall with incredible speed. He bounced up and onto the wood, his hands squeezing the soggy fibers and crushing others to create a firm hold. The sight was admirable enough to earn a stare from her, but the clank and clatter closing in told her that the fresh gouges up were also her best bet for escape. Swiftly she bounded in the stranger's trail, using his impressions to get a head start.

While it may have not been optimal to be heading up high into the open, the way the man moved told her he had a plan he was confident in. At the top, she looked right to see several bodies on the ground. The stranger added one more, slipping out an oddly purple blade from the folds of cloth to create an elegant cut under the arm of an officer, taking the limb cleanly off. His weapons readied; the stranger bolted brazenly down another alley.

She followed close behind, watching his next lethal flourish. The attack began, and she witnessed a true master unleash the full potential of his weapons and body. Despite how tall and long the man was, he evaded every spear tip, glided past the shields. Wide strikes were let loose, claiming limb and life. In a moment, the defensive line was savaged, leaving a wreck that she could traverse without opposition.

Even more boldly, the stranger erupted out into the streets again, leaping over a group of fleeing farmers. She slipped through without a challenge, seeing the man blazing a trail to the city's West gate. Though puzzled as to why the gate was still open, she dared not slow her pace. Though even more questionable was to why the officer at the gate held up his weapon. The shortsword wasn't even unsheathed, which made everything all the more strange.

The officer battered the sheathed weapon across the back of an unsuspecting guardsman's helmet, laying him out flat. The officer then performed a decisive jab to the jaw of another of his own, putting that one on his back. With a great shove, the traitor flung the gate further open, waving the stranger in his direction. Guards moved to apprehend the traitor officer, but swift fists knocked one out, and kept another at bay.

Barked orders and growling roars beckoned a nasty fate behind her, hastening her travel towards the glint of escape. As the stranger passed the gate, out of sight and into the safety beyond, the traitor glanced to her. Far slower than his ally, the man had no obligation to stay as soldiers began to rally around him. The traitor ripped his helmet off, hurling it toward a group, which pointed spears at him. Using the distraction, he elegantly broke through the hastily assembled barrier, unleashing a violent burst.

His rampage toppled soldiers over but didn't seem to buy him much time as others came to surround him. Upon her final approach, the traitor secured one of the soldiers as a human shield, using the dastardly ploy to dissuade those daring a flanking counter maneuver. Although underhanded, the play worked, and the path outside remained clear. With no time for thanks, she blew past the city walls.

Though, as she looked upon the torn and unforgiving land, her feet began to slow. Her knowledge of the territory was poor, and any given direction could lead to wilderness, or right into an enemy town. Her heart beat harder, her mind racing, but her body came to a halt. Not once before had she been caught so unprepared, never before had the threat been so overwhelming. But like a lightning bolt, a blunt force thudded against her back.

"By Illeah, get moving!"

The traitor officer from before shouted as he bounced on his feet alongside her. His eyes darted back behind them and to her.

Such an act stirred her instinct, and though it had always favored her odds alone, this time it compelled her to follow the man. Without another word, the traitor took off to the darkened trees, flinging the stolen armor away in pieces as he picked up speed. Kicked up into motion after him, she headed for the looming woodland.

Even though the buzzing of the hive awakening behind them began to fade away, the traitor rapidly changed their path North, likely a precaution against any militant elements that would dare follow them this far alone. While she had no way of knowing exactly where the man was heading, she was far from home, without almost any answers, and now in desperate need of help if she were to ever make it out alive.

Regardless of who the two strangers were, whatever their allegiance may be, they too appeared to be against her prey. With that alone, they could hopefully come to some common ground. Vaulting some scraggly brush, the traitor officer's footsteps came to a halt. Scraping by the briar-like vegetation, she came to a clearing amidst a circle of gnarled trees. While the traitor rubbed his chest, catching his breath, the large stranger from before stared her down.

"You led her to us?"

The cold voice of the large man echoed in her bones.

"Wasn't she following you back there?"

The traitor huffed between breaths.

"Not of my will. Did I not warn you, ostoran?"

The stranger addressed her directly once more, pulling his swords from the folded cloth he wore. The unusual purple glint drew her eyes to the weapons, the uneven shape of the spine and material strangely alluring. The smears of blood, however, reminded her he was not exactly the most peaceful sort.

"You did. But between you and them, I think I stand a better chance with you."

Though it practically made her blood boil, she kept her hands from her axes. Instead, she worked at the latch to her cloak and opened it, raising her hands.

"I'm not here to fight. I just want to talk."

She took measure of the reactions to her show of civility, gauging the odd party's alignment. The traitor took a few steps forward, squinting his eyes at her.

"Unique axes you have there, ostoran. Anuurae, aren't ya? Don't think you've ever had a reputation for coming out this far."

The traitor commented, scratching at some of the gambeson he had yet to tear off. She didn't let a single hint of emotion surface as she stared the traitor down, unknowing of what her name would mean to him. The traitor ripped away at a pilfered glove, wriggling his now free fingers.

"No worries, Dul. She might be out here for someone's head, but it's not yours," the traitor told his friends.

"That doesn't give me confidence, Rorke. Especially with the way she's studying us."

A woman piped up from the back. The mention of the name Rorke almost earned a raised brow from Anuurae's frozen expression.

"Really, Lin? You usually take a liking to new people," Rorke commented, crossing his arms.

"Not when they see people as a means to an end. She's hiding something," Lin snapped back, holding a longsword in both hands towards her.

"Look, ostora are very cautious. They don't mean anything by it, and this is normal for what I've seen up North. Let me handle it."

Rorke assured his ally, but that alone didn't give her confidence. The wild born of Illeah were a quirky sort, and the one before her wasn't known for level-headed decisions.

The one they called Dul held a hand up, drawing the others in. They watched him observe the perimeter, but even as they came to complete silence, she couldn't hear anything unusual close by.

"They can't be here already, Dul. We already know how they work. We'll have time before they can form proper search parties."

Rorke's words seemed true, as the group began to calm. Then there was a clang of metal, sharp and unnatural. The pitch sheared through the world, pierced her ears, and sent a surge of fear through her very being. It did not repeat, but was followed by a low throaty exhale, one which seemed to emanate from behind her ear. Anuurae twisted around, her hands going down for her weapons. Two others shared her sympathies, though the one that didn't plucked a pack up and placed it in Lin's hands.

"Go," Dul told them.

She followed his gaze as another shrill click of metal spirited through the woods. It picked up pace as it was repeated again and again, and finally, her eyes found what her ears already had. Casually strolling up, a boxy face smiled as the head it was plastered upon teetered back and forth.

"I smell my disciple's cloth," Kaerex proclaimed quietly before pointing a chipped axe at Dul. "But you aren't him."

The psychopath whimpered, his lips now in a revolted frown.

While the two others began to back up, she placed her hand on an axe. The murderer's focus was on Dul and his stolen cloth, unaware of her ability to strike from afar. Her fingers wrapped around the rough grip, slipping it up and free.

"I would not be wrong to assume he is dead," Kaerex grumbled.

"And now we have more. More to cleanse, bathe in red and lay in black."

Kaerex advanced, his teeth bared, scarred lips peeled back. Her patience wore thin as he moved past a tree, steadily toward an opening. The impulse surged through her arms as she flung the axe into the air, a perfect spin with the head poised to catch Kaerex in his chest. And before her eyes, a limb of shimmering smoke hatched from the back of the man, plucking her attack from the air like a fly. The phantom arm grasped its new prize, perching above Kaerex like a scavenging bird.

Her mouth cracked open, a noiseless gasp fizzling out from her lungs. Kaerex snickered as he battered his weapons together in a fit. The shouts grew closer as Dul took his place between Kaerex and them.

"Now."

Dul ushered the one word, which meant the same to her as it did his friends. Rorke grabbed a pack, pushing Lin into moving away.

"Don't forget our deal,"

Rorke remarked as he began to take off, and her after him.

"In a land mantled by storm, where can one flee? Away to falsehoods and hope. Meat in a bowl, primed for us to devour. Time moves on, as it always has, turning to our favor!"

Kaerex shouted before him. Dul ignored the noise of the beast, no different than the wretches and burbles of his kin. Whether the projection took the form of words or chuffs and howls, neither had importance. Readying his bone swords, he could already hear the encroaching reinforcements, summoned by his noisy company. He exhaled, closing his eyes. He had come so close, after just four other stops. Close enough to find tracings of the spirit, close enough to find fresh victims. Evidence that had quickly pointed to Silvercry's obsession with the cult.

But in an area which felt the touch of his kin so deeply, he had to be careful of his own magics. The temptation of the feast kept his senses on edge, choking out any bastion of control slowly but surely. And that had all added up to compensating with lost time. All to stay hidden, to be rid of unnecessary death. And now, as he played with the ostoran, someone had found a victim, either new, or one he had disposed of.

The Sons of Blackwood may have not cared, but the cult did. After all, it was working its way up the ladder to the one before him, that much was clear by how the spirit hunted. It liked the game- to torture, to test minds, sadistic as it lusted for agony and torment. To crumble the mighty, to bring them low, to leave the most tenacious for last. And now, that failure led him here. Where he would break a vow and let Lin die by the hands of such a man, or to stand a chance at breaking one made nearly two centuries ago.

His gut spasmed as he held on to the strands of his consciousness, refusing to let himself slip. His eyes opened again, his vision sharp and clear. He stood in solidarity, placing a leash on the collar of what dwelled within.

His blades came together in front of him, crossed and flat against one another. Traveling from his chest down his arms, vibrant blue lines came to life, illuminating him from within as mist billowed from his palms. The swell coiled around his swords, embracing their primal origins. The very ground beneath him cried out in the presence of fresh demonic power, the soil cracking under his feet. His lips parted, an abyssal font flowing from behind his clenched teeth.

His heart thumped like a clap of thunder each time within its prison of bone, his thoughts electrified like a bolt through a midnight sky. His foe stopped for a moment, wide-eyed, but Dul knew better than to recognize it as fear. He saw the demon outstretching its arms before him as filth. Inhuman, impure, the source of all ills in the small world the creature saw. It sought not to understand, but to think of its end- death.

Kaerex sliced his right arm open with his falchion, flailing around and imbedding his stolen throwing axe into a tree as he wailed and screamed.

69

The man roared, ignorant, but not vulnerable. Dul waited until three more arms had shown, all reaching for the back of their walking armory. In that moment Dul dug in and sprung into battle, leading with a slash, following with a jab, a quick cut, and then a downward hack.

The demonic mist followed his every move, fuming as it neared another soul. Yet not one taste did it earn, the body of the feral man twirling around every strike. The man's eyes went pink as he began to muster the bulk of his magic, calling to something even more foul than the soul-eater before him.

"Orobrex!"

Shouting the name, Kaerex's body pulsed with a crimson hue.

"Damnation! Oh, master! I am yours!"

A wicked grin froze upon Kaerex's face as he twitched, his gaze abnormally wide as it stared into the sky.

Dul paced back, knowing only enough about the threat to take each move cautiously. Here, that meant waiting for the wreckage of a man to charge him in a mindless fury. Saliva began to trail from the corner of Kaerex's mouth as his body once more kicked itself back into motion, piloted by a new force.

Dul's skin tightened, commanding him to jump backwards. His foe unleashed a cruel arc with his axe, a gust thrown about from such strength as the weapon barely missed him. With not even a heartbeat between the first attack and the next, Dul's eyes shot to the ethereal host. The first arm lanced with a thin blade, carrying forward as another smashed down with a bludgeon. Kaerex's tongue hung out loosely as he hacked with his sword, immediately countering his motion and sloppily crashing his axe into a tree. The blow sent a shower of splinters and bark into the air, some unallowed to fall peacefully, batted aside as Kaerex's ethereal limbs whirled.

The man continually forced him back, leaving not a single chance for a counter. Everything was a continual act, several strikes delivered every second, with not even a breath between. Dul slid to the side, dodging a quick jab from a freshly sprouted arm. His foe made an attempt to follow him, grunting as he hefted both weapons into a barbaric horizontal strike. Both axe and sword smashed into a tree in their path, hurtling through the trunk.

The mass collapsed to the side in a great boom and crack, calling all to their position.

Dul gave one look to the man, seeing him trudge towards him, his falchion bent from the force of impact, and the handle of his axe obliterated. Still, he wielded the mangled tools with an undying grip. Such was the forsaken power of Orobrex. With both the magics of mania and wild strength, he could flatten an ogre without a single ounce of fear, but it was not without cost. Deathlust- the plague of the Mad Aspect- touched him all the same. The man could not speak as much as he could not resist the drive to butcher anything that harbored a still-beating heart.

Dul looked to the fringe of his vision, seeing the glint of metal through the bleak woods. As they grew closer, his mind hatched a plan. He waited for Kaerex to charge, then thrust himself down. Dul dove beyond his foe's strike, bounding up and over the briar. Down the incline he went, using his magic to reinforce his body. Demonic muscles propelled high up, his acrobatics placing him exactly where he wished to be. He landed in the trees above the enemy's reinforcements and turned around to see his foe charging in a relentless pursuit, drawing a replacement axe in hand.

The young ones below him thought nothing of their elite's flight, raising their weapons to the enemy above, leaving them wide open. Kaerex crashed into the line of soldiers, sending sprays of blood that spattered upon the sullen branches just below. Screams and cries of pain echoed further above into the sky as translucent arms plucked men up, ripping them apart as if they were mere cloth worn too thin. The chaos tore the force between the two of them, playing exactly to his tune.

Dul plunged down into the battle, both swords readied at his sides. He lashed out with his enchanted blade, cleaving through four men with a single swing. The mist lingered behind in the cuts, sinking into the meat, ripping away at the souls within of both the living and those lucky enough to have died from the trauma alone. He drove his other blade through the breastplate of another man, rending the armor no different than a farmer hewing straw. Mortal flesh paled before him, from fear, from the taint, sapping all color besides red from the world.

71

His vile sorcery heaved from the butchery, searching for those not yet befallen by its touch. The abyssal storm spoke back to him, its words of gluttony and authority absolute. More and more filled his soul as it returned, the raw essence a banquet to swell and fatten the corruption within. And though he moved away from the head of a halberd that sought to push him back, his dulled sense let a greatsword come down upon his disguise. It tore through the fur and fabric, though the blade was not meant for demons. It dragged along his skin, as it would if he were stone.

The shroud around him grew, disguising his sword as it slipped through the churning flume. A spurt and gasp sent a nearby foe into a panic, who he culled by removing the man's head. The sickness of the land expedited the dispersion around him, latching him onto more and more souls by the moment as he pushed forward. The billowing sickness brought with it the withering his kind were known for, swallowing up the weak and injured as it lowered itself to the ground.

The shock of such an overwhelming force had shattered the soldiers. They began to rout, the words of any commander still bold enough to stay no longer as powerful as the sight of the two monsters.

"To the gate!"

One brave soul bellowed above the discord.

"Regroup and defend!"

A captain's words cracked like a whip amidst the shuffling mass, which suffered another blow from Kaerex. Throwing a man overhead in two pieces, the berserker's eyes blinked sporadically. Kaerex wore a curtain of death over his face and arms, the smile on his face expressing great joy, reveling in the warmth of many lives. Letting the humans scramble past him, Dul held his swords up, knowing he still had to hold while his friends retreated.

Kaerex raised his battered falchion once more as he lumbered forward. The follower of Orobrex gained inhuman speed in just one shove off, slamming his bent blade downwards. Dul's bone sword caught the cut, biting through the inferior tool in a crisp chink. Dul transitioned to a pommel strike as the squirming host of ghostly hands bared their fangs, catching the man in his jaw. Kaerex's head jerked to the side with a splash of blood, yet his other hand acted without pause, swishing an axe around. Dul darted back as a bludgeon and two swords struck the ground before him.

As the dust kicked up, Dul closed with lethal purpose, using one blade to catch the axe that awaited him. His second sword melded from the darkness; a tip fated to pierce the heart of his foe.

Until a spectral hand defied him, grasping upon his weapon and holding it back with unnatural force. A staggering impact to his stomach sent Dul sliding back, a shockwave emanating from the booming contact. He let his breathing stagger as midnight blue blood mixed with sour vomit on his tongue.

Dul straightened as the aberration before him uncurled its fingers, the fist that had struck him already shifting purple and black. Spitting out an oil-like glob through the torn cloth on his face, he could feel the rush. The mist, while being of his own soul, spoke its vices to him yet again. With a forked tongue, it offered to take over, to give him the strength and fortitude he would need to crush the man before him. Such was beyond what he could steal from it, the knowledge of which quieted his own voice.

His body quivered, lapping away at the offerings it had received. Dul shook his head, attempting to ignore further temptation. It could not be silenced, especially not when it had already tasted freedom, but it could be delayed. Kaerex stooped down to the ground, his shattered hand wrapping around a broadsword. He stood with a shudder, his whole body reacting in kind, like a writhing mass of worms. Dul closed his eyes, letting his breathing steady. In the shadows of his vision, the familiar image of the only other who shared the color of his eyes passed by.

*Who are they to decide for you?*

The memory held out a hand as it strutted by, gesturing out to the illusionary creek.

*They can say what they will. They can believe what they will. That does not make it truth. The reality is that this is our power, brother. It alone cannot be good nor evil, for alone, what can it do? It acts as we command. I know you suffer more than I ... but I can help you. You deserve the same comforts that we all do. All you have to do is let me in.*

As narrow slits, his eyes once more saw the forest, and the butcher before him.

*No force for good knows only reward. No blessing ... hurts like this. Good, evil ... I need no judge to know what father made.*

He had no courage to say that before, but those words he had failed to convey for so many years could now be expressed by savagery. Kaerex slung his host forward, leading with a foolish slam. All he found was air, and his many arms fruitlessly jabbed into the corrupted soil. Dul kept to his maneuver, suppressing his soul entirely. Peeling back from the bowels of the unknown, Dul emerged with a roar.

His prey could do little more than cast a beady eye at him as the demonbone split his arm open. Kaerex's mystic array came to his defense, intercepting Dul's second sword. Three of the limbs and a wood handle snapped as the berserker scrambled away. Without a hint of mercy, Dul cast up the mystic ways of Tyxivol again. The mist that clouded around him warped, shaping his own essence, leaving the world to appear as it would have been without him.

He slid to his foe's right, preparing a swelling enchantment. His soul began to bond with the remains in his hand, and he fixated his eyes upon the end. Aiming a lance for Kaerex's skull, he could almost see the splash of brain and fluid. Arms folded in as a shield around his foe just before impact, a blanket defense of sheer desperation. The bone sword punctured the shield, sliding to a crawl. Dul drove the savage thorn in deeper and deeper, growling as he jerked one sword free, slashing with his next.

Kaerex met him equally with a mace, driving the battering ram into his ribs from under his magic bulwark. Dul staggered back, watching Kaerex do the same. Around the cut on his arm blood burst forth in waves, the shriveling skin around the laceration just the beginning of sickness he would not forget. More of Kaerex's life wept from his chest, a shallow wound from the last attack. Even then, the cultist remained animated, ever-seeking senseless death.

Dul's grip tightened as he prepared for the next trade, but his eyes fell upon the tattered sleeves of his ruined coat. Patches of his skin shown through rips and tears, caused by the swelling of his own muscles. It was already and tight fit- but if it fell apart near such a place, in front of such a man ... he would be known for more than his unusual eyes. The rising pain in his back and head signaled to him that a choice had to be made.

The shuffle of men in the distance preparing for a second attempt to slay him forced his decision. Raising his swords, he knew it was best to leave the hunt where it was for now. He slashed his blades in a downward motion, unleashing a cascade of mist, a rising plume that devoured even the light as it clawed its way towards the sun. Dul turned around, and flew off into the woods, his last gift one he hoped would claim the monster, a sacrifice he would make even if it delayed his hunt.

Though as he began to flee from the death and chaos, he felt the consequences of his actions fester. His flesh moved on its own, re-arranging itself. Not just his splintered ribs becoming a single piece as they were meant to, but his frame itself adjusting. His back burned as he ran, just another weight upon him that the past was beginning to surface yet again. In his shame, he erred his path left, driving himself beyond the fallback camp where he knew his friends awaited him.

He ran until he found the lowest, darkest place around, surrounded by decrepit moss and wicked briars. In his cradle, he stood for just a moment before erupting in anger, tearing at the sullied cloth around him with tooth and nail. He threw the shreds away before collapsing onto his knees, burying his fingers in the back of his head. The pounding in his bones grew, harder and harder until his skull felt like it was outside the skin.

He frantically ran his hands through the soil, biting down as two bones jutted out from his shoulders. Blood spattered along the ground as he panted, spires of skin growing like vines from the gaping wounds. His vision shifted from blurry to abnormally sharp as he reached for a discarded sword, placing the flat of it parallel to his back. More memories surged alongside the horrors of the present, tunneling him down a path with one way out.

He began to cut in to the new flesh, passing through with little effort until it came to the bone. He forced the edge in, jerking the blade back and forth. He bit down as progress was slowly made, up until a point where he felt the appendage begin to bend. He forced the blade forward, snapping the bone and sending a hunk of himself flopping onto the dirt at his side. The mass of flesh spurted and wriggled, still trying to rebuild itself after being severed from its body. Swallowing hard, he took hold of his second sword, positioning them over his back, ready to shear off the second growth. He widened the implements, unaware of his company.

"Dul?"

His name cast cold shackles along his limbs.

"What … what are you doing?"

Lin's voice was filled with an uncomfortable dread, fear she herself likely did not understand. Just as he, who barely knew himself now any more than she. The world itself had not seen him as he truly was since the Devastation, and now, in all his glory, he was returning. His nose scrunched as he tightened his grip. He jammed the blades together, his bone putting up just enough resistance to catch his weapons. With one play of moving them back and forth, the next mass dropped to the ground.

He discarded concern as he proceeded to jam the tips of his swords into both bleeding patches on his back, the muscle and tendon clinging to the treated bone. That which was peeled back sucked in air, slurping and gurgling. An acute squish announced his dive, his mutilation a slippery and disorderly symphony. He dug out the bit of cartilage that was buried within, cutting out more, gouging, slicing. Even after what remained of his wings was purged, he continued, as not one uttered a command to stop. More and more blue ink splattered near his feet, scraps of black skin and dark tissue splashing down on the occasion like a macabre rainstorm.

Even his face was alight with the accursed maelstrom, itching as his jaw and nose stirred under the surface. Like a pox, the plague's scorching touch grew until he could hardly bear it. In a throe of great agony, he thrashed his blades, sundering a tender cut of muscle from his back. Dul lost his grip on his swords, staggering to the side before collapsing. His fingers latched over his face, clamping down upon his skull.

*You knew this would happen. You starved yourself, and now you can only want more.*

Heaving unsteadily, every breath in seemed to be one closer to his chest bursting open. His nails dug in until his blood began to trickle down his cheeks, and even then, after all of his struggle, a hazy motion drew his eyes up. Once more he was given a single moment of clarity, to see Lin's face close to his. Vulnerable, hurt, fragile … so close, so trusting. His lungs emptied, refusing to be refilled. His fingers trembled as his body weakened, and he was drained of all humanity.

His limbs felt as if they were going to burst out, doing as they willed. The voice boomed for him to open his jaw, and that it did- strands of saliva stretching from roof to floor. Falling deeper out of himself, the instinct was insurmountable. He was just a part of it, a conscious to the raw and insatiable gluttony. The words she said fell afoul of his ears; all the acute devices would tolerate being the beat of her heart. The thump rolled in his ears like thunder, her scent filling his nostrils, the taste of this human flesh a mystery his mouth could hardly await.

His tongue slithered forth, flicking and dancing as the mist began to return from its ebb. It appeared no amount of disgust with himself could give him power to take control, the mutilation only a delay to the vile bond. He quivered, beginning to rock and tip, shutting his eyes in hopes she would run, to escape him before nightmarish memories would be made. And then, a catastrophic bolt cast through him. His whole body jumped back, averting itself from the intrusion.

He sat on his rear, heaving staggered breaths as his mind and soul clashed. In a blink there was a lapse, enough of a space to wedge through a single command. His right hand flew up into his mouth, where he clamped down hard enough to hear the snap of his bones. In that pose he sat as Rorke and Anuurae came before him, setting their eyes down upon him. A throwing axe was ready for him, and Rorke made his way between him and Lin. The hero turned his head away from him, trying to whisper his cruelties like all others before him had.

"Move, can't you see what he's done? He needs help!"

Lin rebuked, pushing Rorke to the side and making her way towards him. In her approach, he found an unusual calm, no rush of mist as she took his side. As she crouched down, he let his hand drop from his lips.

"Stay your hands. Healing magics do not work on me."

He muttered softly, warm blue blood running through his teeth. Lin stopped, the others taking in the sheer amount of his blood on the ground.

"You never mentioned anything like this, Dul," Rorke commented with a condescending tone.

"It astounds me how much your kind can forget in just a day. Still here to try and convince me, yet here's your proof you were wrong," Dul snapped back.

"You mean those risks you won't shut up about? That ... fog? Those men had fear in their eyes as they fell down and choked for air. And you ... I never imagined I'd see something so sinister. I don't understand all of what I saw ... but you almost ripped Lin apart there. If anything, I'm forgetting all this and running to Kressel's Charge."

Dul's expression dropped from pained to grim the moment the threat was uttered. "Do as you will, human. If righteousness against me is worth the thousands that will follow me to the grave, then go. Find how far I will let you run into the forest." Dul began to raise his hands, flexing his fingers slowly and steadily.

Before another word could be said between the two, a dry cough called him to the right. "So, I hate to skip introductions and break up the fine discussion you two were having, but aren't we a bit close to the city for this?" Anuurae asked.

Dul shook his head. "I doubt they will follow so soon now. The land is blighted between here and there now, and they must tend to those the withering has not yet claimed."

The ostoran nodded in return.

"Good to hear. But now I have a lot of questions for both of you."

Dul cast his gaze left to Lin, then back to the ostoran as he stood.

"Your assumption I will answer by word is ... intriguing."

With an expert maneuver Dul propelled himself up, throwing one sword into the air with his boot, catching it, and swiping the fouled weapon through the air. To his surprise, the ostoran remained relatively unmoved, her change of stance and grip showing lessened aggression as it slackened her limbs.

"I know when I'm outmatched, and after that show down there, I'd rather stay on your good side. And since you're not on any of my lists, I'll hold my tongue about your ... condition. Consider this nothing more than an offer of aid."

Dul pointed the tip of his sword towards her as she spoke. "I need none. He alone has proven that."

Dul hacked the attempt to create a bridge between them down with impunity. Still, the ostoran did not relent. She snickered, throwing her hands about.

"Him? Of course that was a mistake. There's a good reason he's not had a group or team take him in. People would rather mine deepstone than take him on. I'm not offering my advice. You're a fighter, capable hunter, and you know more than I do. I'll be extra hands, eyes, and ears. Together, we can get what we both want, and then part ways."

She proposed her offer with a keen emphasis on certain parts of words, force and grace applied where it was needed to feel convincing. It was no lie- it had no need to obscure truth- the statement was forged with all the intent of someone with proper conviction. The letters upon the paper were clearly laid out before him, and though he could sense her curiosity, her presentation and the way she carried herself was beyond even the ostoran hunters he had observed ambushing the beasts of the North.

And though Lin remained silent, he felt an odd affinity to agree with Anuurae. As much as he disliked the allure of that option, he had indeed been able to escape much easier with Rorke's distraction. She seemed to know that he had less aversion to help than the one offering it themselves, placing herself right into that position. And though it was astonishingly foolish to offer aid to someone that looked and acted like him, the ostoran seemed wise enough to gauge the possibilities before her. Rorke crossed his arms as Dul continued to think, scoffing as he shook his head.

"You're wasting your time, he's only going to sulk before laying into you. Besides, you saw exactly what I did."

Anuurae slipped an axe out from under her cloak, bobbing it as she spoke:

"Restraint? Yeah, I did. He ran wide of us, and we saw something we shouldn't have when we followed her. There's a lot of things in Tavora that'll kill you, Rorke. You give them space when needed, and both of you should have been smarter if you knew the danger."

Rorke's eyes widened.

"Danger? This isn't like the stories our parents tell us. They haven't seen this- all of this- " Rorke thrust a hand towards the jagged canopy above. "- it's a nightmare. It's real. Just like him … a demon," He stated with plain hostility, lowering his arm slowly, extending one finger, a harsh judgement placed upon the darkly figure before him.

The ostoran didn't seem to even flinch at the theatrics.

"You're right, he's not like the stories my mom told me. And I'm sure he appreciates you constantly pointing it out."

Rorke leaned his head forward with an open mouth, almost aghast.

"Sure. You can say that because you see him calm at her side now. But don't act like you wouldn't kill that if you saw it alone outside your window."

The huntress shrugged.

"I think I'd rather hide. But fortunately, I've had the pleasure of speaking to him, and the displeasure of meeting you."

Tucking her arms back under her cloak, the ostoran dismissed Rorke with a swift side-step and turn.

"Back to business. So, what do you say?"

Anuurae stood at attention before him as he glanced between the two, the show that was just performed quite the spectacle. Between the options of killing both of them and adding another, the proof of his new ally's worth was displayed by how quickly she had silenced Rorke. The man stood to the side, squinting at her furiously, without any clever retort. Rorke was more useful to the common folk alive than dead, and if she could maintain that command, it was perhaps possible to keep him that way.

Slipping his blade back into the loop, he placed one hand in the other, rubbing the patches where new flesh had already grown in.

"We will have much to discuss. With the guard alerted, it would not be wise to stay here. There were plans to move Kaerex West, but today may have changed this. We must watch from the shadows, and strike only if necessary. Our prey follows one another closely now, and this volatility makes the task no easier."

He addressed her question indirectly, but the ostoran took the skipped formalities in stride.

"You've got a plan," she deduced.

"I still need time to think. Silvercry is a restless worker, but he has shown caution. We were close to his trail in the last town, but here ... he acts strangely. But tell me, ostoran, from what you have seen, is your quarrel with this man all you truly desire?"

He plied at her motivation, matching her cunning and testing her with a harsh gaze. She took a moment to shy away, making an unusual movement with her lips. Then she returned: "He's a start. Taking down someone like him should slow down the enemy, if nothing else. If that's what I can do, and I can avenge my people, I can accept pulling back to fight another day. It sounds like people have been asking a lot of you- I don't know what kind of pay you take, but that's not why I'm here. I help you, I still get what I want. After that, your business is your business. We've all got our ways of surviving this world."

She answered with tempered stoicism, cleverly remaining distant, but not from fear of the beast. The intuition she had was astonishing, hitting every note so sweetly to his ears. Knowing he no longer had to maintain his front, he let the grimace on his face return. The great apparition of torment still flew about his body, banging its chains and wailing. Dul tried to open his lips, but a flash of pain caused him to lose balance. Lin caught him under the arm and pressed into his chest, barely sustaining his weight. Dul blinked, focusing on regaining his center. With Lin's aid, he found some grounding, but her touch reminded him of something far more serious than his wounds.

"Watch the blood, Lin," he muttered.

"I know. I'm being careful," she assured him.

Dul nodded, testing his legs' ability. Slowly, he parted to stand on his own.

"I can accept your terms, ostoran. I must take time to settle. It will be good to discuss our strategies when we make camp," he spoke softly as he walked forward, finding some trouble in bending down to pluck up his supply pack.

"You're still bleeding."

Lin reminded him, her concern for him something that twisted his gut.

"I will be fine. Moving should calm me," he affirmed.

Still, she held her ground, even after he had told her that a monster such as himself could not be healed.

"Lin, right?" Anuurae piped up again from behind him.

"Yes." Lin responded curiously.

"Anuurae. It's an honor to know one of Illeah's graceful that's still brave enough to leave home. I know you're trying to help, but your friend there is thinking with us in mind. He wants you safe before he is. Let him lead for now, it'll be better for both of you."

The ostoran weaved her words swiftly, ending with a muted snicker.

"Just remember to be hard on him afterward for disregarding you. Got to make him a better leader."

The delivery earned a lighthearted chuckle from Lin, and there was a pat of cloth that encouraged her to get moving. With his pack in hand and two of his party ready, he began to march into the woods. After a few paces, he turned around, seeing Rorke beaming back at him with crossed arms.

The man failed to hide the softness in his eyes, which darted away the moment they made contact with Dul's. He seemed he was torn between his own views and principles, whether or not to oppose that which he perceived to threaten his people. It came from a good place, but unerring in how it viewed things that were unknown and dangerous. Dul was indeed a part of the shapes in mist the man vehemently vilified now, but he could not ignore his earlier words. Rorke surely recognized that his hands could not knock the walls of Mordiv's Hold down. Without aid, that meant he was powerless to stop the bloodshed that was coming.

That too, the man hated. He was a defender, never to be helpless like those he let cower behind him. Now the beasts had emerged from the veil, with one devouring the others. Unexpected, not understood, he was a phenomenon Rorke had clearly never once imagined. Even then, the man looked back to him one final time. He exhaled deeply through his nose, shaking his head solemnly. His ego rightly bruised by Anuurae, he may have become humbled enough to cow his head to reality. Rorke began after them, his pace slowed, and tongue silenced. As they went down the path, Dul could still feel the accursed power running through him. Oddly, the shock of Illeah's magic seemed to have stifled it. For now, that power staying in its den was all he could hope for.

# Chapter Six: Before The Maw

There was a muted creak behind him as a branch moaned under the weight of another that sought to ascend to the heights of the canopy. Dul did not turn. He already knew who it was, considering the late hour. Lin needed her rest, and Rorke was overspent from his infiltration, whether or not he would let it show. He allowed his new ally to take a seat on the branch opposite him on the trunk. Anuurae stared out into the fog with him.

"Sorry about earlier. Stressful times like that can be volatile. I'm not sure how I came across to you, but I want you to know I will stand by my words." She spoke softly over the slothful breeze.

"I understand. I may have been your only way out, or just seemed like it. My hostilities … born from necessity. You, though, have shown a rare level of control and reason. So, I will delay our business no longer."

While the rush had faded, it still took effort to speak clearly. His eyes unfocused, Dul let himself relieve some tension as he relaxed his shoulders, placing his hands upon his lap. He assured himself that, in this moment, he would not be overtaken.

"Those soldiers you saw have united under the name The Sons of Blackwood. They have been pulled together by a man I know only by name-Rederick. The man has a mind like few others, one I wish we did not have to suffer in this time. He has not only united and focused his people, but even the one you seek."

Anuurae was silent, recording every word.

"Whatever tricks or techniques he used, I am uncertain. My time there was limited, my prey being Silvercry- yet with them entangled so closely now I managed to see the ideals of the Cult of Orobrex and the Sons align. And with a leader so wise and cunning, he has seeded his men as far as the Western Wastes." Dul explained calmly.

"That sounds like they're not just preparing for war … they've already won. If they've infiltrated our cities, cut us off from Lesal … they just need to slit our throats," Anuurae responded grimly.

Dul paused, curling his hands into loose fists. Lying just wasn't in his nature, no matter if he forced it or not.

"I cannot say for sure. Your kind are resilient. Be certain, however, that war is coming. One death will not stop that. Which is why I must ask for your aid. My current promise to Lin binds me, and I wish to be free of it by the time I am needed."

As Dul unraveled part of his plan, the ostoran's legs stopped swaying.

"Do not think me deaf, nor blind. I will not forsake your plight, either. With the spirit's demise, so too will Kaerex fall." Dul promised.

He could hear a sigh fighting to surface above the whispering wind.

"I suppose I have to let go, don't I?"

Anuurae let out a chuckle that could hardly obscure the nerves that provoked it.

"Dreams are dreams … and even there I wouldn't have the strength to kill a nightmare like that," she murmured.

Dul nodded, placing his hands loosely together.

"I know it is difficult to trust a stranger like this. Especially one such as myself. That is why I will tell you, while Silvercry deserves his end, Kaerex's death would not just be for you. An oath I took long ago would demand it, and I do not break a vow."

He solidified his words in his heart, the actions sealed to fate. Such was the power that he spoke with that silence befell the two in the shimmering moonlight cast down into their deathly environment. While he expected her to leave, the ostoran stirred, shifting every so often for a few minutes.

"I don't know where you came from, or why … but thank you," Anuurae whispered to him.

He let his head hang low, the words he had perhaps heard the least all his life filling him with strange emotions. What he assumed was meant to feel nice curdled as his demon blood surged in, summoned by such stimulus. Upon finding a lack of food, it quickly joined anger, which only festered as he began to cage it. The two sides barked at one another until all was just a howling, snarling cauldron in his chest, forcing him to shut his eyes.

Deep breaths brought stability, but no balm to settle such a burning. As he once more opened his eyes, he needed something to keep his mind focused that would aid him in keeping anchored. While he could not leave his post, the one next to him appeared just as restless.

"Would you like to know?" Dul asked.

There was a short pause from the other side of the trunk.

"You trust me that much?" Anuurae inquired.

"I would not dare tell such a story to one as innocent as Lin, nor as unpredictable as Rorke. I have a need to keep steady, and this stillness is as much my enemy as silence."

Though she was once more silent, Anuurae did not leave as he pulled his legs up and crossed them. Looking up to the smeared blot of moonlight above, Dul let himself recall the darkest times, the stories of his mother, the things he let shape his very identity.

"Two centuries ago … I remember those days well. Such was a time of great expansion and revelry. Before that, however, there was very little to talk about. The past was lost because it was stolen from man. What I know is most of what any great archivist of Alok would tell you. Humanity began in Lesal, the eastern ring of mountains that shielded them from the rest of Tavora. A calm place, away from ogres, away from the piraph.

"At some point early on, the yrabor, the race that inhabited what is now Kressel's forest, found humanity amidst the trees. They were a peaceful people from what mother said … simple. They lived in villages, led by shamans, gifted tribesmen that protected their people with crude fire magics. Their peaceful nature allowed man to work side-by-side with them, and the yrabor introduced improved tools and helped humans advance their language. That was about all the time man was given before other greater powers took notice.

"The piraph, the mighty underground empire, saw the use in a new, poorly developed race with a malleable mind and dexterous hands. They sent armies forth to raid and steal humans, forces that the yrabor could do nothing about. Ever watchful, the giants in the South, the tiquo, emerged to do the same. Given time, not one man or woman was left in Lesal. The stories here diverge greatly, kept by mouth for many generations … but few truly know all of what happened over the centuries.

"Much of what you see of this world is stolen from others, down to the words we speak. Though none know the language of our lost allies, we still use it. Hoffen … not a human word. But of all the stories to come of our early times, three things remain constant.

"That one woman stole the flame of the piraph to join with her lover, one taken from her. She burned away the metal bars that held her, incinerated those that stood before her, and made an inferno of the lands she trod. She did indeed take her man from their captors, but the proud piraph did not let their insult go unpunished. They sent a force beyond counting from one of their cities, to which the cornered lovers responded by sealing their own fate.

"The woman engulfed them in her warmth … turning all to ash in a great explosion that left few standing. Both the human slaves and soldiers in the army that remained returned home, speaking of her name in fear and reverence: Alyra. No effort made by the piraph elite could silence her tale, and there they discovered an inviolable fact. Those who love, will blossom love in others. Those who are passionate, will arouse passion in others. The tortured, oppressed, and now inspired people took to their tools, stolen arcana, and fury.

"They broke free and smashed the weakened piraph army. This great rebellion spread, unquenchable, until almost every man, woman, and child had escaped their chains. When they came to the surface, those who had smuggled books recognized their icon above. Toren too, burned brightly in the sky, and his followers rallied everyone to follow his glow. It guided them back to Lesal, where knowledge of masonry, metallurgy, mining, carpentry, the labor once forced upon them, became a boon. Man built the Lesal Bastion, blocking the one pass through the mountains with a massive wall.

"The yrabor, now rallied by such a force returning after such a long time, harassed the piraph going through the forest. It was not long after that your people arrived from the North, just a few thousand strong. But neither man nor yrabor refused the ostora, and they formed a great alliance. In the West, weakened by the uprising, and now facing an armed and fervent force, the piraph grew desperate. And that was the world I was born into. About this time, my human mother and father were one of the old frontiersmen, like those on the northern border."

Dul took a pause, recalling how wide his mother's eyes had been when he had first asked of his origins. Such an expression had baked into his very soul, and never again had he asked. But with her kind heart, she had not left him without some answer in the end.

"I know little of how I came to be. I know the misery my kind can bring. I've lived it. For a human it is often too much, and this … this demon that did this … likely one of the first to have escaped. She said it only left her alive … it let her flee, carrying me and my brother in her womb. To this day, I still do not know why. Some greater demons, they understand souls as a resource. But … that one did something to her. To us. And many months later, we were born within a family home in the outer rim of Lesal.

"The first child, my brother, was of fair skin and known for his vibrant eyes. Then there was I … with skin of coal, bumps upon my skull, and flaps of skin along my back. Mother … she was not like the others. She loved me all the same as my brother, but he was beloved to all."

Dul cracked a shallow smile.

"He hated it. He hated how people treated me, enraged that the one who shared his blood was treated as some abomination. He was all I could ask for, given my condition. Sometimes he would take me out into the woods when the others weren't looking, and teach me about the fish and plants. He'd try and make me fight for myself, but … I could never lay my hands on them.

"Brother knew I had power … he saw how poorly I could control it.

Sometimes the mist, it would pour from my skin uncontrollably. It was a great shame to me, but not to one as patient as my brother. For years, he never gave up on trying to help one as damned as I. But I don't think I could have ever seen the next few months in my darkest nightmares. I sometimes see things when I sleep … things I cannot explain. I struggle to distinguish some of the next days from those dreams.

"One day, brother grew enraged with our family. He denounced them, cursed them, pointing a wicked finger at them and shouting a vow that he would find the answer to their sickness. I watched him leave through the crack of a door, and that was the last I ever saw of my brother. Such was a shock to everyone- but brother had a deep contempt in him I think only I saw. No matter how many women of any age swooned for him, no matter the power offered, brother never smiled. I cannot imagine where he went … nor that he would be alive this day.

"And that was not the end … two days passed. I was awoken by the noise of snapping wood in the midst of the night. I crept to my door, and listened from behind the lock. There were heavy thumps, and another snap. I was drawn to undo the lock I had made, and to that…"

Dul found his words had stopped, his throat tightened, and his lips peeled back to show his teeth bared down. His muscles tensed, a shadowy fury swelling in his gut. Just like that day, the pain in his limbs was such his skin felt as if it were boiling, his head weathering a bone-splitting cataclysm.

"… I found a slaughter. For some time, I had felt ill, something pounding in my head. Now, there was little to the world besides instinct. A scream drew me down to the darkness, blood and saliva pooled at my feet. I found one of my kin standing above my mother, and that was the end. I had never killed before, but that night, I found what my hands were capable of. It was … I don't want to say what drove me. We ripped away at each other, tearing, biting, flaying … until I drove my broken horn into its eye.

"It was no lesser being, yet I was alive, and so was my mother. My own cursed blood saved her life, and so I took her to the Bastion itself. What you see before you now was born from this… and that was not my last fight. More found me in the wreckage of my family's home. After that was where

89

I made my vow. My mother raised me with only one wish, that I could be content with a good life. And so, I find satisfaction in using my curse to hunt my kin, and fulfillment in giving the enemies of man and ostorans something to fear before they sleep.

"And I did indeed find satisfaction many times. The Piraph Devastation lasted forty-eight years, and saw two races be banished to fading memories. I fought on the front, away from the eyes of others. And yet, here I am. A half-demon, one of the last of that blood still alive. Knowing this, I think you should understand why you can trust me with Kaerex's life."

Dul finished regaling the events that had led him here, but flashes of the war still came to his mind. Horrid sights which would never leave him. Caves filled with wailing pits of blood, strewn about with pulsing symbols and assemblies of animal parts. Humans and ostora, still alive, thrown upon altars without hands or feet, legs, or arms. Eyeless, broken husks of women and children in crude cages, left for further use. Mutilation and macabre perversion on scales incomprehensible to even his mind. Such horrors could hardly be retold, no words able to match the taint of demonkind.

To this day, the only ones that might understand what he saw would be the tiquo. Though he avoided their part of the war, he had seen them on the front. The long-lived race would no doubt have many alive to this day, veterans ... even in the mind of a thick-skinned beast, he doubted they could so easily choose to forget.

"With that much time ... you could fill this night with the past and not cover anything more than a fragment of your life."

Anuurae's comment drew him back to the woods.

"I suppose that's true," Dul hollowly responded.

"So why did your brother leave, anyway?"

Her question caught him off-guard, causing him to perk his back up.

"That ... it's difficult to say. Brother never told me he was going to leave. I don't think he wanted me to know. From his yelling, I can only guess at what he meant. He had a sharp mind not clouded by our curse, and he understood how to use our magic, so I only hope he found what he was looking for."

Dul spoke softly, the distant possibilities of what could have been creeping in.

"You don't think he's alive?"

Anuurae inquired.

He felt there was a certain level of ignorance to the question, but somehow the twisted fate his family shared earned a grin from his unusual mind.

"I doubt he fell so quickly in his journey. The problem is mistakes like us don't have a way to know how much time we have. Is two centuries most of my life, or am I still a child? Is this body to thank for my seemingly timeless nature? I would think so … and I would think my brother would be lost to the ages, even if we had common blood."

The weight of his words appeared to sink in, his company finally assembling all the pieces. What he had not spoken of was not a complex tale. Long decades of hunting, watching over the blood-soaked lands that never ceased its struggles.

"Damn."

Was all she managed to mutter under her breath.

Dul looked out into the mist as the strange shape of a small bird, just a dark shadow, darted away from a blur. The show continued as the larger bird of prey reassessed in front of them, then vanished, no less a figment than the thoughts in his mind.

"Is it strange that the more you say, the smaller I feel? It's like when explorers come back from the caves and far North. All the insects and dangers … a new land, right beneath our feet, and just over the mountains. And here … with you, and them … I never thought I'd see a half-demon in my days, to say the least. The stories we're told as kids … they could never prepare us for this."

Marvel and dread were laced in his companion's words.

"Many don't even question where their ancestors came from. What the past held. The present is enough, the struggle of survival all they know. Is it a surprise you don't comprehend fully what I am? What is known of the history of man and ostora can fit onto but a few pages. I am no less what has been lost than the life I lived."

He paused, deciding to carefully complete his thought.

"The same can be seen with those in Mordiv's Hold. Those graves around the city- Thousand Stones- named so because every follower of Illeah was said to have laid a thousand markers before their job was done. Once unified by a cause, suffering together, the founders were brave and altruistic. And behold, those most tormented by loss could not have their scars fade so easy. The purpose has warped, still to help their fellow man ... to save it from the inhuman. Such a fate ... there is a sorrowful wish in my heart for them to cease."

Dul finished, rubbing his knuckles, pondering the loss of life that would come with yet another war to cut down on the struggling race. Perhaps a sign that they were, as a whole, unfit to survive such a place. Unable to conquer, unable to finish anything without aid from their poorly understood allies from the South. Beyond the giant stone gate, a land none had seen ... Tiquatzek.

It was always a fear of his that one day the tiquo would break their distant vigil and decide other races were just a threat. While their strength was unknown, their display during the Devastation would likely mean a weakened and divided humanity would be crushed like eggshell underfoot.

"So ... have you ever stopped? Made a home?"

Anuurae passed him another question.

"Stopped? No. Home? Tavora," he responded distantly.

"Do you ever plan to stop?"

She continued down the same road with her questions, which unfortunately led no-where.

"I am not one to foretell futures, but to plan for it ... no."

He spoke calmly, but Anuurae seemed to take more meaning from his words than he intended as the gloomy air became heavier. She sat near motionless in silence. He could practically feel her contemplation.

"For everything you've done ... survival isn't the most impressive. After so long, you've labored to keep your sanity, and you value the lives of people you could cast aside. You don't have to do any of this, yet you still have the honor to."

She suddenly broke both the eerie night and his composure. Taken aback,

92

he had no response.

"You asked for my help earlier, and now that I know this ... I know it wasn't easy. It'd be all too easy to just see us as liabilities, either getting in the way, or as a loose tongue. But that you chose to confide in me, I'll return that trust. I'll lend my blade fully to you while our cause aligns and do what I must after."

The sudden barrage of compliments caused his distorted mind to pass over some of her words, but it was soon after he knew what he should address.

"You do not fear me for the same reasons they do. You don't see me as one, nor something to control. You can know my story because I know you will keep it well. Better for you to see me for what I am, than a great mystery you will hunt until death."

Dul said as he scratched at his back, the unnaturally warm skin greeting his fingertips. Smooth and moist skin slid along, and as he pulled his hand to be centered in his sight, he once more was met with another few patches of shed skin. Flicking the tissue that regeneration had rejected down to the ground, he tasted the truth in his words.

"The night is still young, and it appears you would hear all I have to say. I would tell you the tale of your people, or demons, if I knew them. But it is likely you know just as much about both as I," Dul said. "But if it is the past you wish to understand, I can tell you all I know of the Devastation. If you have the stomach for it, that is."

Once he had finished, he gave her time to walk away. Truly, he had never spoken of those days to another soul. He could already guess how others would react, and he would never force such knowledge upon anyone. But Anuurae stayed opposite him in the canopy, and Dul nodded.

"As I thought. Very well, let me continue my story. If we were to go back to the time I made my first kill, there was little for me. I had nothing besides my family. My brother had left, my mother ... I gave her safety and life, at the sacrifice of my own desires. Then and there I had just my clothes and some trinkets I had left at home. I gathered those remains and returned to my room.

"The fight had left little behind, just graves and a few wrecked walls among piles of rubble. Somehow, that wasn't what bothered me. I don't think I really perceived much- I had no true purpose or guiding star like the humans. But demons … I learned quickly that they hunt by sensing souls and their potency. As do I have this sense, near one of the same. I felt the Devastation begin. Endless days of my head pounding, my veins so tight they felt as if they could crush my bones, it all amplified.

"From there, I could feel my kin approach. Those that came were not the strongest of their ilk, and were splayed out as a warning to whoever discovered our home by sunrise. However, the more I tore apart, the more my mist claimed, the more I changed. It is a chaotic power, but strangely serene. It overwhelms and breaks everything about you, as if your soul is trying to wrest control of your body and mind. And when it did, I did not suffer pain. I did not have anxiety about life and the future. There was only the present, lorded over by sensation. The slightest scent can be narrowed down and trailed across the land, sound can fade until it is only the prey that is heard, and eyes can see forms mingle in the darkest caves.

"By that, demons you can say are creatures of impulse. Thankfully, some of my mind remained, and rather than hunt man, my vilification of my kin put my body prowling towards them. Westward I went, unafraid of the smoke and red lights creeping upwards into the trees. The soil, just moist enough to cling to my palms and soles of my feet, heralded their coming. It became crisp- crackling ever so softly under my weight as frost broke. Unusually cool winds brought me more than I could have asked for.

"In these strange lands I had never trod before, I found stained and broken bones, strewn remains all about the woods. Of course, as I was, I could only see the macabre nature of what was before me some time later. Being the embodiment of bloodlust, I came upon the scent I had followed. An yrabor village, whose tents lie collapsed and trampled, and residents no different from the animal remains I had passed. Splintered, scattered skeletons whose forms were disfigured by gouges and gnaw marks lay everywhere. Symbols had been carved into the soil, flashing amidst the fires that lit the world in unnatural colors. Effigies had been made of skulls and spines, still stained pink in some places.

"The scavengers, the lowly demon kin, began to emerge from the bushes. They were what I imagine you all picture demons to be. One of blistered, red skin that looked to be a legless man's torso had crawled from a collapsed tent. Another, pink skinned, flesh warped like tangled roots, staggered around a tree, covered in hardened pale plates of natural armor. It's true they come in many forms, especially the weakest. But what many do not speak of is their resemblance to man's form. Despite the many limbs, mouths, heads that some have, there is no doubt they are a twisted jest of the human form.

"Before them, I stood, the demonic viscera that clung to me cracking open to the air as I moved. My unwashed scent drove them mad, and they growled, chittered, and chortled. At their sight, my very being twisted with hatred until I howled back. I barreled into their lines, and under the moon, ripped them apart. No matter how many times I was bitten, cut, burned by their sorcery, I did not so much as blink. I was made whole by their death, invigorated by devouring their essence.

"As before, I have told you what this does to sense. Honed beyond physical means, with a near undying body at its disposal, it makes me a near perfect killer. And that was what I needed, as that night I found a greater demon. One gray hulk lumbered from the wreckage once many of his pack had fallen. Far taller than I, covered in teeth and horns, it was a spiral of jagged shapes. The whole body of the thing was wide, full of recesses and bloated buboes, topped by no head, only a swollen mound whose many mouths ran like rivers.

"The fumes it spewed at me rotted and melted away the withering plants at my feet, but this was only the start of what I found it to do. How such a monstrosity, lacking even a head, was such a gifted magic user, I will never know. As I tore at its leg, grappling and climbing onto it, the demon unleashed blasts of soulfire from its body. Not from any palm or staff, but conjured with arcane might from its skin. Such a force threw me off and to the ground, where it flung a handful of mongrels at me. It used them as sacrifices, charging their souls to explode.

"Even blinded by that, I still flung myself at the creature, hungering for its bright essence. It caught me, slammed me into the ground, but made a mistake. Assuming me weak, it attempted to rip my soul from my body. Such a spell is incredibly dangerous. Unlike any other, demonic magic requires essence to cast, every spell eating away at the caster themself.

"Were you not an ostora, I would tell you no more, but I know you would ask me this later. This mist you see, it is of Tyxivol, the art of manipulating soul essence. It is our corruption, and what causes the withering. What you have seen happen to me and my flesh is Alshivex, the magic of our twisted bodies. It allows us to change shape, grow limbs, and defy sense. Nyr is how all this came to be, as our kin rip open the fabric of the world itself. Anything besides a demon suffers through the use of these arcane spells, and even to us, there is a significant risk.

"My father's curse was quite mighty and proved too much for my opponent. The spell backfired and split the demon asunder. As it recoiled, I leaped onto its chest. I placed my hands onto opposing lips, and pried away until muscle tore, and the sound of joints popping signaled me to execute the foe. I folded my wings in, plunging inside. I followed the uneven bumps and thumps through sludge and tissue, and with my hands, I pulled both hearts of the demon to my teeth.

"It was not long after I was striding free among the woods again, my mist eager for yet another kill. Such was the craze that I raked my fingers along the corpses of the slain, just to watch fluid and blood seep forth. Some shred of conscience kept me there, wandering, prodding aimlessly among the dead like some lost child. And that night, maybe I was. No ordinary child, but one nonetheless. Nineteen years since my birth, many a year lost to isolation. And yet … I had no need for sleep. I was to seek nourishment from death, heeding nothing and no one else."

Dul took a moment to grasp his hands tighter, taking strength from revisiting what he had overcome. Unlike previous memories, it bound him tightly in pride, and the refusal to allow what he felt to dominate and regress him into such a thing.

"If I were to say that start was just a calm, a hint at things to come, it would not be a lie. By morning time, I had fought a few more off. To my benefit, it gave me time to battle myself as well, to once more realize myself, and my wishes. I think of that day as a warning, a tipping point … it showed my what the gluttony within me can do.

"I had never seen an yrabor while I was young, but what had come to litter the ground was no less disturbing. Marrow, drained and hollow. Long bones from arms and legs, scratched from tongues, scraping every bit left. They devoured all, only leaving their blight behind. And that taint, though I did not feel it at first, came to make even me feel the pull after I was fully cognizant again. The beginnings … if even I felt it, I do not believe my perspective can unveil how sick someone like yourself would have felt, even sitting in your home in Lesal."

He took a break from his long speech, letting his companion take in his words.

"Didn't they come from the piraph lands all the way to the West? How did they make it to Lesal without anyone knowing? That's everything from the coast to the Gate of The Star."

Anuurae asked a question that he knew came from an innocent place.

"They did come from the caves in the West. And they did spread to Lesal in the East. You are correct," he responded promptly.

"How?"

She once more pressed, her enthusiasm strangely admirable.

"It only took them two days if you believe the tiquo. Their ancients, as they called them, played a large part in the war's front. They claimed from their findings that once the first demon gate opened, it was not even a day until the piraph had been devoured. By the end of the second day, all that remained of the yrabor were two mortally wounded shamans who made it to Lesal.

"I do believe it is possible, as while the piraph were warmongers and had large, capable armies, they were attacked from within. As for the yrabor, they had no walls, no fortifications. Demons need no rest when feeding, so that would be no different from a wildfire in dry brush. Much is owed to those two survivors, though. Their warning before they passed was what was considered by many to be what saved humanity, but I would credit the guard at the wall for their haste and vigilance. That, and the timely release of the slaves from the tiquo had greatly bolstered humanity's defense. Demons could have avoided the Bastion's outer wall by going through the mountains, as they did to me. But the worst never came to pass, I suppose."

Dul did not know if it was his tone that had finally left his companion truly tense, but she seemed to retract into a ball.

"Two days?"

She repeated in a hollow echo.

"It was all they needed to bathe Tavora in blood."

# Chapter Seven: Bleak Dawn

Letting go of the branch, Dul dropped onto the soil. Even as the group packed their supplies, he still felt an urge to hide himself as his stretching moved the maimed stumps on his back.

"Anyone moving about?"

Rorke's question abruptly batted the thought aside.

"Not nearby. With the casualties they took, our foe appears to be choosing to take the defensive now," Dul delivered his report of the night.

Rorke chuckled, rummaged through some of his loose trinkets in his pack, and then stood.

"That works for me. There's more than a few of the modrot I'd rather not see again, let alone creeping up on me in my sleep."

Rorke grumbled something after he finished, rubbing a new mark along his face. While the wound was tended to promptly by Lin, they had to be careful about showing such power when they were deep in the Hold. As such, the faint itch of a mending cut likely reminded his companion of the rather sadistic nature of a select few Sons of Blackwood. Rorke tossed his hand aside with a huff and wrinkled pout. While his inexperience with blending in had led him to some bumps, his contribution to gathering information was fantastic.

"While that works for you, your prey being spooked like that generally means they'll be harder to work around."

Anuurae piped up before Dul could, stealing his next point, if not his exact words.

"What you say is true. When Silvercry attacks is not a matter we can control, and to distinguish our involvement from his won't be on a soldier's mind. With what we know now ... Rorke, your map?" Dul said.

He gestured towards the sealed tube with his hand, crouching down in the center of their camp. A moment later, Rorke tossed the treasure over, where Dul fluidly popped it out and spread it across his thighs. He stared down upon it for a moment, then squinted. In his silence, the others appeared in his periphery, but it was Rorke that shook his head.

"That's not going to do you much good. After that sprint, it's as good as useless until we get our bearings," he commented.

Dul stood up, carefully sticking the drawing back inside the protective sheath. He handed it back, looking left and right, compiling everything he understood about his prey.

"Three towns lie to the West in the path of Kressel's Charge. Our foe is injured, but alive. He may be zealous, but it is unlikely he will seek any conflict until he recovers. If he wishes to go unnoticed, I see one way he could travel. The followers of Orobrex have frequently been moving supplies. Much of it right into Toren's cities and towns. They work at night, but that will not be our problem."

Rorke and Lin slung their packs and readied themselves.

But Anuurae, as usual, tore into every word.

"You're saying that like you know it for sure. And like you can tell where he is."

Placing his hands upon the pommels of his stowed swords, Dul nodded appreciatively.

"The mist. A skilled demon may augment their essence, store it, shape it. My soul still feasts upon him, if only drop by drop. I ... do not like to call upon such gifts. Or leave any afflicted by my touch. But to find one man in all of Tavora is no simple task."

Dul paused, raising one palm to face him. With some concentration, Tavora became muted, and his soul became sharp. There was a tug onward, a clairvoyant gift to reunite the piece of himself he had seeded in another.

"He remains somewhere in the city for now. Our best choice is to stay ahead of our foe. Kaerex must go West for their plans to succeed, so in the West we shall wait. There we will find our moment, and if all goes well, act before Silvercry."

He declared his plan clearly, taking his own pack and putting the straps over his shoulders. No longer did it sit flush against his back, something that he knew would bother him on the road. Such was something he would have to endure, at least until he was once more on his own. He headed forward, past the group. Both women followed him.

Rorke stayed where he was, before voicing another gripe: "And what makes you think that way is West?"

Dul turned and pointed outward with his left hand.

"There is where I sense Kaerex. If Mordiv's Hold is that way, and we ran some way North of the city out of the westward side, and we cannot see the mountains of Lesal, is this any way but West?"

His words seemed to sting as Rorke scrunched up his nose, then looked around. He crossed his arms, as if the concept of relative positioning was difficult to process.

Anuurae shot into the conversation, bluntly smashing it apart.

"I get that you're used to doing your own thing, but someone clearly has more experience and knows the land better. It's one thing to check with people, Rorke. But if you really can't feel safe around him now, don't make it our problem. There's work to do, and I really don't think we have time to take care of children."

With that, Rorke gave Anuurae an intense glare, but her insult got his feet moving. With everyone ready, Dul plotted a path through the dark woods. Compared to the rest of the land, Dul found it easy to traverse. It was far more open, with fewer shrubs and trees. Leaves were moist, soaked into the soft ground. Unfortunately, the magical taint of the land was to blame for what obscured his vision now. Only a glint of sunlight made it through the thick blanket of fog, an enemy of the kinds which he had come to hate. Not only did it block his eyes from peering into the distance, but the cool wind tingled his skin as it blew by.

Moisture would build up, and at times that meant droplets fleeing down limb and face. If there was any more rot over the scent of stale, near lifeless earth, his nose would have likely also have been useless. Thankfully, all of this applied to his foes. Knowing this, he kept them at a steady pace, choosing areas where nasty vines and other sorts of growths did not hang or sprout up. Not only could they snag and cut with how sharp they were, but it was best to ensure a potential enemy had no more advantages than them. In such a place, sound would be the fatal tell. Even arcane senses would be muddled for the unskilled, if Toren's kind were to have somehow made it so far East.

Coming to a fallen tree which spanned upwards, towering like a great wall, he looked left, right, and then up.

"We go over,"

Dul remarked quietly before jumping up onto a broken branch. Far wider around than any man, it did not squeak under his weight.

The other three came to the base of the wooden bulwark, sizing up the gargantuan obstacle. To no surprise to him, Anuurae was the first to grab onto a knuckle sized lump and scale the bark, even skipping by him and going on. Such began the race as Rorke launched up after her, advancing with admirably nimble swings from both his arms and legs. It was only a few seconds before he was pushing into the fog, displaying that when it came to athletics, he was still at the top.

But at the bottom, one remained. Without a word, Dul laid flat on his stomach and extended an arm. Lin only managed to reach his fingertips, requiring him to stretch a little further. With a small jump, her arm came high enough for him to grasp it. Though she winced as he pulled her up, the weight proved little challenge. With his other hand, he pushed himself up and sat her next to him. She rubbed her arm when he let go but judging from the selection of options for the next twenty or so feet, he would not have a spare hand or place to rest.

The idea that came to mind was not what he would have preferred, but Lin was agreeable, which gave him hope that there would be little arguing. He reached for the clip of his pack and swung it off, and walked up to her. She said nothing as he fastened it to her own, though the extra weight did her no favors. Next, he turned his back to her and kneeled down.

"Hold as tightly as you need," Dul said.

"Thank you." Lin muttered shyly, barely hiding the embarrassment in her voice.

Her arms wrapped around his neck, and he stood. He sensed her begin to shift rapidly, about to fall, but her legs shot around his waist. While it would make moving his own legs around a bit of a challenge, it seemed Lin had found a way to keep herself mounted. Digging his fingers into the bark, he advanced fist by fist, choosing the quickest way up over any other.

Upon reaching a point where the incline became shallow enough to stand, he trudged on. And once there was a decline, he panned around to see if there was an easy way through. Usually, just jumping would work, but he had seen humans fall from heights that were but half what lay before him, and the results weren't pretty. But with no real ledges, branches, or even another tree within distance to leap to, it was hand over hand all the way down, just as it was going up.

Once his boots touched the mud again, he crouched to let Lin down and retrieve his pack. Anuurae and Rorke split off as he approached them, letting him pass and take point again.

A strange scent caught his nose. A sharp one, one that put his body to a full stop. The others saw the change in his composure, grinding to a halt.

"Down. Stay down, wait for me to return," Dul spoke in a hushed tone, hanging his pack on a branch as he let his mist envelop him.

He commanded it more fiercely, conjuring a cast more powerful than he had done in decades. The call, once more, unsettled the storm within, but he could chance nothing. In the air, he had caught a sample of fresh blood, from many bodies as well. The second strain of scents was partly familiar. He could swear he had caught trails of it before, and perhaps long ago there was a particular musk he had come across that was similar. It was enough to cause his entire body to tighten up, and that threat he did not like.

As a shade to the world, he prowled closer and closer, the alluring scent filling his nostrils. It was ravenous, the combination of mystery, remembrance, and discovery. A hunt that melded many times to one, and felt like it spanned so many centuries. Slipping past a curtain of briar, Dul placed his eyes on a wrecked camp. One not assaulted by the hands of man or paws of a beast.

The first corpse lay in a shallow grave, created by being pummeled and utterly obliterated by something that concaved steel no different from clay. The arms of the body still reached up into the air like friss reeds, as if the man had died so quickly his body was unaware that he had been struck down. Controlling his urges, Dul emerged slowly, creeping past a limb that had become separated from its owner.

A heavy footstep snapped his ear to his left, around a well-scarred trunk. His boots slipped over a discarded and bloody sword, where he found splatters of more and more blood. A torso with its hands grasping onto warm, leaking organs lay before him. The tissues were bruised, the separation less of a slice, and more of a crushing type. Another heavy thump resonated through his bones, making him bite down. A few more steps around a pile of crates showed that the place was being set up as a staging ground of sorts, with raw materials and construction tools lying about.

And with a few of the corpses bearing mixed cloth and fur, the Cult was directly involved. A sharp moan and creak drew Dul's attention ahead, where he carefully maneuvered wide of the sound. Past a pile of unopened crates, he set eyes on a giant shadow in a large tent. It stood as tall as a young ogre, with a small box in its hand. It cast the object aside and turned around, ducking to emerge from the tent flap.

Dul dared not to move, his chest even coming to be as still as the dead at his feet. Slick, inky armor sat atop brown fiber wrappings, obscuring part of what was underneath. Some details were still out for display, far different from any usual traveler in the forest. Humans and ostora did not have webbed feet of darkened green hide, nor beastly black claw-like nails.

Nor could man ever dream of shaping the most rare and enigmatic metal that the creature wore, a treasure many had died for over the centuries that this being had lived. They would never make it past the tail behind the beast, nor what the warrior hefted to his shoulder. Placed to rest, the great two-handed mace still dripped crimson from its masterfully crafted head.

The helmet covering his face did nothing to hide his identity, no matter how much it concealed. The design was molded to mimic much of what was underneath, a face that had a name.

*Shajhu.*

The tiquo legend marched back into the camp, taking his helmet off and mounting it on his waist. A forked tongue slipped out into the air, a red-pink flash. In and out, it poked around the woods. The near-inexpressive yellow eyes of the tiquo showed milky for a moment as a membrane flipped over. Shajhu turned in his direction, looking around where he was hidden. Such was almost as disturbing, if not more unnerving, than being seen.

For it was not the fact his kind were able to smell and track demons that allowed him to discern something was off. He could not know that there was a demon nearby, as the arts of Tyxivol smeared his essence to nothing but a blur. As a creature bound more by soul than flesh, it took little more to render his kin undetectable. But the perils of such a strong cast resulted in a mild anomaly. A place which didn't seem quite right, one where the flow of magic and wind seemed off.

And that was just it— nothing but a hint that something may or may not have been slightly off- that had aroused such scrutiny in the tiquo. Under that watch, Dul dared not to risk retreating. Only when Shajhu looked away and reached for his helmet did he bolt off, unable to outrun the larger problem. Even in a land that carried with it an age-old scent of his kin, what distance would ensure their safety?

Flying from the brush, he gritted his teeth and let his mystic cloak wane. His boots skidding across the dirt, he threw a hand towards his new path.

"We move now," he commanded.

Honing an ear in to the world behind him, he awaited it. The slightest crunch, the most meager clank of armor, and he would have to vanish.

"Quiet, but quick. Words later," he said as they mobilized.

With their heads down, he kept the misty shroud steady, taking any measure to obscure the essence he emitted. And though they kept pace for some time, lips shut tighter than the doors of an ancient vault, the sight haunted him. The name crackled in his ears like the raging fires of the Devastation. His preoccupation must have slowed him, as a tap on the shoulder sent his hand down to his blade, and his body twirling around.

Lin staggered back, wilting away from his overbearing aura. Even Rorke and Anuurae were bothered. Their eyes widened with primal fear. Forcing himself to calm, Dul nodded, accepting of his mistake. To them, he was now a near unstoppable force. A thing unimaginably strong, but truly, there were many things in this world he had to bow his head to as well.

"My apologies," he whispered lowly.

He turned, unwilling to fully pause, but knowing their voices would not carry far enough any longer.

"What'd you see?"

Rorke's words came softly, his weariness surpassing any bravado he had left.

"Someone I wish I wouldn't have. Someone I have always avoided for so very long," Dul said, vaulting a log.

Dread and curiosity silenced the three, their minds likely trying to imagine what one person he spoke of. That alone told him they were unfamiliar with him.

"Do you all recognize the name Shajhu?" he asked them.

"Mother told me a few things. She knew someone who followed Alok, and he spoke of trying to piece together a tale. One about a tiquo … he survived being captured alive in the Devastation, right?" Lin said.

While her words came about slowly, he had to raise a brow at Lin's knowledge. Even the others looked at her, to which she seemed to fade away with such attention.

"Survived demons? Wait, they capture people?"

Rorke did a quick double take on himself, his mind jammed by multiple concepts at once. Anuurae, however, did not seem surprised in the slightest.

Turning to the front once more, Dul nodded.

"That he did. I did not witness everything, but I watched his walk back to Kressel's Charge. He is beyond his kind in tenacity and might … I dare not challenge him. And it is best for all of us if he never knows we were ever here. His kind are of a unique mind, and his persistence to find judgement that satisfies him would only be questioned by the ignorant."

Once the silence of the wood returned, the fog grew heavier. Dul understood why. It was as he had felt in the beginning. The land itself was stirring. Tavora seemed to have a way of smelling the blood coming, and the land of death always awaited its next offerings. The more the younglings saw, the more they realized they weren't the only moving parts of the world. It was also difficult to blame them for wanting to remain ignorant … knowing the truths of such a place was enough to drive many to the edge, if not over it.

Knowing that, hearing the words inside his own head, he looked to fix the problem. It was a fact he wasn't the best at comforting others, yet there remained the option of diversion.

"Lin, what kind of man was your father?"

Dul's words struck firmly against the icy atmosphere, the shock of such a question plastered plainly on her face.

"Um … I … can't say much. He died when I was only two years old. It's easy to say anyone that goes for the path of a bounty hunter is a stubborn and tough one, but mother said he was soft. Bright and forgiving. He cared less about the price or problem, just wanting a peaceful place for everyone to live in. He considered his job a duty to others, and that's what set him aside. He was that way with no aspect's touch."

Lin rubbed her hands together, as if losing her ability to continue.

"Interesting. I've been thinking … watching my prey. I don't understand all of it, but I believe your father may have come back as an unfelled." Dul said.

Rorke immediately shot his head up, waving a hand.

"Woah-ho! I get the legends and all, but that's a serious thing. Besides, that doesn't make sense. Unfelled always have a strong affinity to an aspect. She just said her dad didn't even use magic."

Rorke raised his voice, and for an apt reason this time. While undead were indeed an increasingly common sight, unfelled were something no man wished to ever hear of, let alone be hunting.

"He is no forsaken, Rorke. I have come close to him. There is some tangible form to his body, not just arcane imagery," Dul countered.

"So, he's a befallen," Rorke said back.

Dul shook his head.

"He has too much sense for one. He does not mimic any old life. He thinks. Plans. Moves beyond and learns."

Lin bit on her lower lip, and pulled nervously on her shirt.

"I've considered as much. But ... what are you thinking, Dul?"

He took pause for a moment, noticing a moldy arrow imbedded in a tree, very close to his stomach height. Noting the sign, he slowed his pace.

"I cannot say I understand it all. But the one piece that does not fit is the last task you told me of. The relic in the cave. That is the one unknown that bothers me, perhaps the seed of all this mystery," Dul said.

Before Dul could take another breath, a spout of mixed words jumbled together from Rorke and Anuurae. The two glared at each other, engaging in fierce mental challenge, before one backed down.

"Considering I wasn't around but too long after, I knew some people who knew the story. Quite a few were after that piece. The problem was the caves of the Beastlands aren't really meant for people. And that old bit of treasure seemed to attract the worst of it. No one knew why, but it was this pale thing, looked like salt if you asked them, was sitting on an oddly flat rock. No one got close enough to see exactly what it was, because all the bugs and creeps around it all saw them as food. Since it was likely magical, the reward for it was ... well, I never thought twice about taking the job."

Rorke's eyebrows twisted for a moment as he finished.

"Oh," he grumbled.

"I don't know what sort of relic such a thing could be, especially if few eyes have seen it. But to bury the dead with anything found below, anything magical ... I would not doubt the possibility it is to blame."

As Dul finished speaking, he took a quick pan around for any more signs of hunters. It made sense to see the arrow, a missed shot left long ago if they were on the fringes of a township. His feet came to what was barely a shuffle, searching for any rope dangling down from branches. Traps- snares, particularly, could put a damper on their pace. Turning leftward, he instead took notice that his teeth had clenched down. His jaw, strangely, refused to move.

The ridge above his eyes itched, and he put a hand to his brow. Turning around, his gaze fixated on a tree. Just above, magic splintered and danced. The imagery before him was a lie. The illusion then burst downward, his body surging in kind. His arm jerked up, his core tensing just before the impact. Blood burst onto his face as his palm was impaled, and hot lines combusted along his stomach. His rage leaped from a simmer to a boil as he heard Anuurae yelp, and his unholy taint blighted his ally. Though he had caught one barbed lance, the many that had lashed him had done a fine job of dispersing his flesh.

He rolled his hand into a fist, his fingers uncaring of the new hole in his palm. Before him emerged another one of his kin. All it took was that one look into its eyes for him to tell it was no lesser demon. The white, slime-coated spheres blinked at him with intent behind them. It was thinking, gauging him as their essence began to mix.

It saw him for what he was, just as he did it. Wisely, it detached the spiked appendage willingly, pouncing backwards to cover, writhing spears along its back sampling him in a joyous dance. Dul looked to the barbed cone imbedded in his hand, the venomous liquid that spurted from hollowed openings now dripping down his arm. Without an ounce of hesitation, he gripped onto the splinter, and ripped it free.

Behind him, the three scrambled, and though his curse quickly came to claim his mind, he ordered his lips to part, and his tongue to march.

"Nearby. Stay." Dul commanded.

Ripping the latch to his pack, he dropped his supplies and drew a sword in each hand. His kin clacked its teeth as it paced on all fours, the rounded glands and boneless limbs on its back exhuming poison gas and venomous flows alike. Most despicable wasn't that it wielded toxins, but that some of the five eyes looked right through him. It knew he was going to be a challenge to face head on, so it was now considering the one afflicted with his withering.

The dulled sound of panic behind him seared through his clouded sense for a moment, and though the thoughts were jumbled, he deciphered the threat. Unless he remained in control, Anuurae's life would be taken by his hand. His foe disrupted his gathering rage by hurling a spine at him, which anchored him in reality as he threw it aside with the flat of his sword. Even the sweep of his arm tempted the scourge within, the time between the last call and now far from sufficient to rebuild a proper defense.

Yet there was no choice. A fight without the consent of one was just a slaughter. In a blinding charge, he engaged, slashing down low. Hopping like a toad, the demon plastered itself on a tree beside him. Rapidly, it came back in, rearing several impaling limbs. In just a blink, he slashed through one with his sword, moving to spear his foe with his other. But such was only a jest by his enemy, as the world exploded into a dark orange hue. Dul continued his strike, but at no point did he find contact through the fuming gas. The poison stung his eyes, but it did not fool his instinct.

Jumping free of the distraction, he placed himself among the low, hearty branches. In a split hair of a second, he latched onto the scuttling movement below. Fangs bared, Dul descended with a merciless wrath. While his party offered both fists and longsword in defense of Anuurae, the demon caught onto him. It sprung to safety as his swords dug into the dirt. Ripping his blades free and flipping his grip, he gave not a breath before bursting back into range. He slashed wide, feeling his skin alight as if he was standing amidst the battlefield once more.

His mist trailed behind him, phantom images of his quick assault. The venom that was in his arm, ravaging muscle and vessel excited him, adding fuel to speed the dynamo. Unfortunately, they were two of a kind. Taking advantage of his next low lance, his foe went up, vaulting over him. There were three faint impacts on his back, followed by the sound of ripping flesh. As the faint sense of agony spread through his torso, the calling became louder.

Not whispers as before, no promises. Demands. No longer having the patience to lie, to lull him into submission, the collar had been removed. It sought for no master, to breach equilibrium, to become all that it could be. For less than everything was never enough. Forced to a standstill to deny the totality of his power, barbed edges whipped his back. Flaying his skin, throwing it upon bush and dirt, his flesh itself pulsed.

*Life. Promised.*

The words scorched like a brand on his face. Though his stare ahead was blank, lost between the two sides of his own war, a cry made it to his ears. It was agonized, helpless. Upon the ground she lay on her back, the blood upon her that of a demon. And as he looked up, the cool rain dripping down upon him, his purpose became the only absolute.

Sensations fell apart as the stinging scent of his kin scorched his nose. Burning, a wild blaze conjuring up images from times long past. It gagged the bickering sides, and blinded him to a much smaller world. There was he and it- *demon.*

With an overhead slice timed with a turn of foot, Dul's sudden maneuver brought the fall of four limbs. The demon recoiled, looking to distance itself as it lowered down on its contorted front arms. Dul came forth like a bolt in a dark sky, the forks reflecting pale purple as he brought them down. Passing through the joint and into the earth, he claimed a critical piece of his foe with that deft hack.

His head tracked his prey perfectly as it rolled away, struggling with the loss of an arm. Bending at the knee and leaning into advance, Dul poised his blades like tusks before the enemy. Like an arrow he flew, impaling the lowly being and hefting him into the air. Tearing his swords through the bowels of the demon, he freed his weapons and returned with fury. Severing the legs and spine with two inward arcs, the chunks fell.

Flipping his swords with his fingers, it was the end. High and then low, both tips unwaveringly burrowed through the skull of the demon. Standing above the twitching mass, the enemy still fought to free itself with the one arm it still had. With an inhale and jerk, Dul split the head asunder, obliterating what was left in a squishy gush. His wings fluttered down gently at his sides, lowered down with a knee.

Touching down to the earth, the soul flowed openly to him. Even so, he sniffed- searching for another beyond this pile of flesh. Nothing more did he yearn for but another to slaughter, to break and make him feel his hatred. But without a trail to follow, the rage spurned and sputtered, dying down with the beating in his chest. Without aim and overloaded, his strained consciousness faded.

He looked at his sword, and the oddly deep red blood that adorned it. It had already clotted, a process that was not unusual to be rapid for his type of prey. Still, that meant at least some time had passed. But how much, he wasn't sure. There were gaps again, and this land did not like to unveil the sun above. Details had started to trickle back, bit by bit. He remembered where they were heading, and some sort of fight. He felt the urge to look at his other hand, and he squinted at it.

It made him feel … jittery. Turning the palm and blade away from himself, he found a small tab of skin hanging off. A flash of a gaping wound landed like a hammer strike, and he immediately found himself staring dead ahead as everything pulled back together. Anuurae was on the ground, hurt … but now, gone. The faint tug of his blood now led in two directions, one closer than the other.

Making his way down a slight slope to a flat patch of dirt, he found his party. Rorke took notice of him, giving him some brief glances out of the corners of his eyes as he worked at a small animal with a knife. Lin sat with Anuurae propped on her thighs, intently keeping a vigilant watch. With the slight flow from the ostoran, he knew she still drew breath, but he had taken a lot out of her.

He kept his approach slow, but he placed himself next to the two. He dropped his swords, taking note of the usual symptoms of the withering.

"Could you help her?" he asked quietly.

"I cleaned the blood off. But, Illeah…"

Lin's voice trembled, the empathy that came with her healing touch now brutalizing her. Though the two sides of Illeah took the threat and idea of death differently, he could see their pain clearly. Rorke sliced with a bit too much vigor in his fury, cutting into a bone. Lin sat her hand on Anuurae's cheek, nodding slowly to herself as old tear streaks shimmered.

He understood from what he had seen over the decades. Man was uneasy around death, and though seeing someone drop dead was one animal, holding another in your arms as they slowly faded away was another entirely. Those of a good heart always wanted to stop it, whatever it was, out of an inclination to act. Another example of responsibility he could only somewhat emulate. And here, there was nothing either of them could do but watch. A special kind of torture for those of the Aspect of Life.

"She will survive. As you know, my blood is not a pleasant drink … but it will not kill someone unless I let it. We're close enough to where we need to be, so let us set camp here and wait. With some rest … she will be fine."

Dul paused, inspecting Lin's hands.

"You did good work. Keeping steady in times like this, being able to consider both risk and action, both take time. And you're getting there." Dul complimented her, relieved that she did not add yet another affliction to his list of problems. From the pile of cloths tossed aside, she had also remembered that he kept special spare towels in his pack for cleaning his blood. Yet she squinted at him, not yet assured all of them were safe.

"And you … the venom?" She murmured.

Dul shook his head.

"Weak. Gone now … not a worry," he assured her.

Behind them, there was a solid thunk. Turning around, Rorke's knife was imbedded in a log he had pulled up for a seat. He stood with hide gripped in a bloody hand, a twisted and scared look on his face.

"No worries? This … I can deal with ogres. Men. Maybe even obrok. But you, and that? Nothing in this world is like you. Squirming while impaled through the head … you say you're a half-blood … but what are you, really? You and them … you kind of look like us. But you're just…"

The words of the hero bounced off him, his heart unbothered by any malice that made its way into his companion.

"Wrong. That would be the word, wouldn't it? You're missing a piece of history, like the rest of humanity. Our name came from the mouth of one of the surviving yrabor. The bare man, skin of pine straw- hayamen. The wrong men- daeyamen. So quickly forgotten, for how fitting it is." Dul said solemnly as he retrieved his swords.

It was a shame that what was common knowledge upon their arrival had failed to be carried down. It was likely that if that one translated piece had made it, humans and ostora would see the foul spawn as more than some strange animal.

"I ... don't think that makes me feel any better. None of this does."

Rorke shook his head after he spoke, mulling about with whatever else was going on inside his head.

"I would say there should still be some comfort taken in this path you three have pushed me along. It has let me see how I must act to aid the flow of this war. It will be a busy time to be alive, but take it all as a lesson. This is the way of the world. All moves ever onwards, bringing change and the dangers of it. You get to experience both the pleasure and torment of it all, with such limited time. No matter how dark the night, Rorke, do not reject any sunrise, and what it may reveal to you," Dul said.

Confronted with such a challenge, Rorke let his shoulders slump as he looked at the meat. He let out a puff and sigh.

"I'm going to have to start a fire if we want some food."

Rorke spoke lowly, a deal of his energy taken from him.

"I must wash myself and my swords. Prepare, and when I return, I will keep watch." Dul responded.

Rorke then took a rigged spit out, lined with enough cuts for a few days. "How did you hunt so quickly and have time for that?" Dul asked.

Rorke smiled sheepishly.

"Don't worry. I re-armed their traps. With luck, I don't think anyone will notice."

# Chapter Eight: A Grand Madness

He scratched at his skin, dragging alongside scabs. It burned, itching more, his anger nearly causing him to draw more blood. That he could not allow. The wounds had been hidden from the master, but the magics did not stop, and that was problematic. It was not Toren, no. He had been burned by the glowing armor and swords before. The same for the flames of Alyra. Nothing … nothing had ever caused his body to ache so.

In a fit, Kaerex smashed an axe into the table, breaking it in two. The candle rolled along the floor, burning the corners of a few letters. Pain … torment like this had to be repaid. Blood had to be spilled, more than before. As he panted, he remembered Rederick's orders.

*You are critical to the success of this attack. Your followers will only listen to you, so I must rely upon you for something very important. The city of Kressel's Charge will be no easy target. Long ago it served as the front of the Devastation, and it is a mighty bulwark few could challenge. Soon, we will have you moved in, and an informant will give you the tools and knowledge you need to bring us victory. Prepare yourself, Kaerex, and rally your followers. You will lead them to the bowels of the enemy and rip them apart from within.*

A faint cackle escaped his throat, his fists now clenched and shaking with excitement. So long had he waited, even longer had his predecessors waited. Their suffrage, the attempted extermination, every single death to preserve humanity against any foe. Now that a man with both the proper passion and ruthlessness was in charge, the end was in reach. No more pettiness between man. No more feathered liars, no more vile demons, and with everyone in arms … not even the tailed ones would lord over them. Man would be one and whole, safe … safe. No more slaves, no more slavers.

Taking up the candle and sitting back down, Kaerex plucked up another paper from the floor. Freshly drawn, it laid out the tunnels dug below Kressel's Charge. The one and only, it had many scribbles and many errors. However, with the second page, it was still useful. Many supplies had been hidden, and many loyal followers of Orobrex were already strewn about. But the enemy would still not fall so easily.

The followers of the star were rigid, hardened by their virtues. While decades of laxity had softened them, none in Tavora were so foolish as to give up the fight. They had steel and faith- substance and morale, the very reasons to resist. All the same, they had lost the feral edge of instinct, and let themselves be blinded. Orobrex gave them the strength to break iron with their bare hands, and to disregard the looming threat of mortality. With the ease that one plucked a fruit, one mace would rend their precious armor to nothing but a dented burial casket.

But no matter how much of an advantage they had, the problem Rederick had pointed out still stood. Even if they came from below, the street structure and form of the city provided no opportunity to take all targets at once. Barracks were positioned to have a response to an attack from any side of the city. Important structures were near inaccessible from the tunnel system and paired with elite holds for their best soldiers and commanders. Street paths were mostly wide, but few in number. Every minor detail was crafted to be in favor of the defender. And Toren's children were surely the kind to respond with heavy shields and bold spells to buy time.

*That is why this role cannot fail. Even if I die, if we all die, we do it for our cause. Whatever they send at us, we will prevail in the end!*

Touching trembling fingers to the broken mask upon his face, he smiled widely. Such power had been given to him … for a reason.

*I will die. And it shall be glorious! I will cast aside this war, for this is my battle!*

Taking up a few of his letters in a bunch, he read through the names and options quickly. Finding the building numbered for their leaders, he returned to the surface map. In the western portion of the city, there was a marker in the outline of a large building.

*Evalom Star-skin. Aeralei, Hand of Toren. Brightwalker Alvor. We will accept nothing less. I will take your light, throw you into darkness, and show your people the weakness of complacency.*

Casting aside what he did not need with the sweep of an arm, he rolled the drawings up and sat them in a pack. In attempting to walk away, he stumbled and went to catch the wall with his arm. Upon contact, it jerked back in pain. His shoulder impacted the floor hard, the phantom magic surging through his bones and flesh once more. Gritting his teeth, red spirals twisted around his skin. Fresh blood dampened the bandages, but he planted a palm and pushed himself up.

Climbing up the rungs of the ladder, he pushed the trapdoor to his room open and stepped up and out. Following the stairs up, he came to the hall, where many of his cloth had gathered. Seeing a peculiar scar from across the grand room, he made his way to the table and sat down.

"How are your wounds?"

Stern as ever, his second in command dealt him a very fine mercy.

"They do not seal right. This hex ... does not fade," Kaerex responded bitterly.

"Rederick would certainly have a healer for you. I would see no shame in such a time in asking something of him."

Rahkev's words sent a surge of anger through his entire body.

"Master cannot know I failed. He cannot know they have ... that man. We have suffered too many to Silvercry, but we are strong! No loss or warrior will stop us!" Kaerex's shouting already stirred grins and a few cheers from his men.

Such voracity is what he hinged everything on. No creature from the North or this brutal land had ever subjugated them. A fierce land had only made fiercer men. Still, the one at his side remained still as he took a drink of water. Such temperament was mildly unnerving to the others at the table, who sat down in silence. Even Kaerex had to admit it, were Rahkev blessed with a more potent affinity to Orobrex, he may have had a chance at taking his place.

Calmly, the mug was set down, the water barely rippling within. A hand peeked from Rahkev's robe for a moment, showing the layered mass of scars underneath.

"I understand. But you must, too. We are all willing to do what must be done. But we must not give ourselves to Fynor in vain. I have fought the star children many times, under your order. They do not go quickly. We are a device to remedy this, Kaerex. You must know we stand no chance against all sides of this war. Do not squander your gift in an attempt to appease another. We do not need his kindness when we lie broken. What we wish is greater than such trivialities."

Rahkev's scolding hit like boiling water, making his stomach churn. Again, the wisest among them spoke with wicked reason. Rahkev's foresight called to darker skies, a cruel pressure, an anxiety to work against making foolish mistakes.

"Where does our path lead us, Kaerex?" Rahkev's harsh words coaxed him forward.

"We will not waste time burning their foundations. We will bring them a vengeance unseen! Our brothers and sisters will work with the Sons and rip open a way forward. I will lead my chosen and go for three heads. Evalom, Aeralei, Alvor. Those who survive will raid their storehouses, set fires to their homes, and savage those that come. Be they a kind to plea or fight, this will be no time for parley!" Kaerex shouted.

He quaked with enthusiasm, but a hand grasped his bicep. The excruciating sensation tested his patience, but Rahkev bore not an ounce of fear nor doubt upon his face as he stared into his drink. Unlike the others, he did not use his one good eye to lead him astray. His ears had heard enough to find doubt, and his hand would only discover the truth. Rahkev's advance was firm, prying and squeezing. He observed every tense and withdrawal from force, and only loosened when he found disappointment.

"Mighty are you, Kaerex. But this shall not do. Long ago, I witnessed Alvor. Aside him is a warrior even stronger, despite his youth. Only you and I are capable of such a triumph, but not like this."

Rahkev let him go, but a pounding phantom of his fingers stayed behind.

"Go see Rederick."

With that declaration, Rahkev took another drink and closed his eyes.

The followers around them were roused, expecting some form of violence to spring up from the actions of their superior, but Kaerex did nothing until he stood. While an act like that would normally have brought him to raise some sort of weapon, the younglings did not see the crushing defeat he had just suffered. To attack such a man was to hurt all of them- to chance their fate. Rahkev needed no eyes open to know he would not be struck, nor would it matter. In such a pose, he could draw and parry before one of them could blink.

With his head cowed, Kaerex pulled his hood up and made his way to the door. He flung open the heavy wood with ease, slamming it shut before jumping down to the road.

"As it must be," he grumbled through his teeth, picking up a fair pace towards an alleyway.

The maiden song of war played about him as officers shouted and metal clanked, drills and exercises for the unbloodied now ceaseless, day or night. Once the incline began to turn sharp, Kaerex took a right into an unsuspecting corner beyond some old buildings. Against the wall, he saw the dark metal door at the top of a short stack of stone stairs. Even as his tongue dried and his throat seemed to swell shut, he banged his knuckles against the metal sheet. Within a moment, the sound of a heavy lock moving welcomed him inside. He lifted the heavy handle and pushed, walking inside of the sealed tower. As instructed many times before, he shoved the door closed, only to watch the lock move itself back into place.

"Kaerex ... you are not well," his master said.

Both calm and knowing, Rederick was scarcely one that needed to ask or receive.

"Come closer. Let me have a look at you," Rederick commanded.

The order came clearly, but Rederick did not cease his writing. He dipped a quill once more, his strokes artful and focused. With slow and steady steps, Kaerex made his way closer to the brazier's light. Rederick's nose twitched, and his eyes squinted as he held his quill, ceasing movement in a deathly omen.

"I had my suspicions after that day you had met someone powerful. Perhaps another Silver Commander, this one with skill- but you found something far more interesting."

Rederick stood without a sound and began towards him. Kaerex stopped as Rederick studied him. Rederick outstretched a hand, pulling up his fur sleeve. Underneath, he found a white wrapping his expression showed no fondness for. His finger a razor, the bandages drifted to the floor. Bowing his head further, Kaerex hid his shame. Rederick gently brought his arm up, running a finger close to the cut.

In an instant, his flesh became ice as a powerful spell imbued his body. Kaerex choked out a feeble breath as a solid knot traveled through his throat and chest, the sensation little different from a fist being shoved down his gullet. He managed to hold his legs in place until tears welled in his eyes, but even he could not withstand the violent spell. Trembling, he dropped to the floor. He heaved heavy breaths as Rederick stepped back, tapping a finger to his lips.

"Hmph," Rederick remarked before nodding.

"Tell me, Kaerex. What do you know of demons?"

Kaerex tried to muster enough breath to answer, knowing the man before him was not one to entertain silence.

Still, Rederick went back to his desk and took a seat.

"It is known by many of Alok's followers, and even by the greatest of Toren's followers, that there are three kinds. The lesser ilk- weak, exceedingly common. Near mindless, poor magics, but still dangerous. Then stronger demons, which have been shown to be able to plan and reason to some degree. Users of their arcane arts, and far more difficult to deal with. And greater kin- monstrosities beyond imagination. Many, even I, thought them to be entirely gone. The hunts following the Devastation knew the threat they posed, being able to organize those below them, and displaying ambition for their own gains.

"You appear to have met one, Kaerex. Most concerning, this is. I have stifled the taint within you and mended your wounds. No matter my talents,

I doubt your arm will ever fully recover. But this must not happen again. I have gifted you now with the ability to sense demons. You will know it when one nears, and I need not tell you what to do next. But do oblige me- what enemy has themselves such a being in their control?"

Rederick glared at him from his desk, peering into his soul as moonlight crept through a forest canopy.

"I ... I know not. I saw no light or flame. From their clothing, I would say they came from the North, Lord." Kaerex said.

He gave his best as he kept low on hand and knee, awaiting his master's response.

"I would expect as much. I do not believe Toren's children could ever swallow their pride to wield their sworn enemy as a weapon. Alyra's followers, on the other hand, they would treat such a creature as a penitent, would it join them in battle for the right reasons. This ... is not desirable. While they have shown this to us, only your own would stand a chance against it. They must know this."

Rederick looked up and pulled a rolled paper from a shelf. Shuffling around a few items on his desk, he sat back down.

"I must attend to informing our commanders about this. Cinderstone holds many unknowns, and not even I have set foot inside the city. If they hold such things within, the upcoming battle will be far more important."

Rederick tilted his head, rubbing his fingers along the surface of his desk. He tapped them on the hard-wooden surface before he looked back to his loyal servant.

"Go now. Work must be done, and now there is nothing to hold you back," Rederick dismissed him.

Pushing himself up, Kaerex placed a hand on his chest.

"Yes, master."

With care, Kaerex approached the exit and, with great care to make as little noise as possible, shut it behind him. Itching at his shirt, he had to take a few deep breaths. Understanding the workings of strange magics was hardly something he could fathom, but if it was a test ... he had passed. The heaviness and unease were gone now ... but something had been put in its place.

Though what it was mattered little. Rederick knew, just like he did, that this next battle had more worth than what was fathomable by most. And that the enemy had a demon- the most vile, the Great Enemy, the old devourers! Such was not simply unacceptable, but disgusting, putrid, black of heart, and dull of mind! The very fact any could ally with consumers of their own flesh and blood ... they would feel his wrath.

*Not just mine ... but the damned one himself. If I am to become nothing but a memory, I will unleash the blessing given to me, and drag your city into oblivion with me.*

Pulling his hood down, he walked forward, feeling the chill in the air. He looked to the fading light above and shook his head. Both sides had voiced their reason, but in both, he saw his own in the dying day. With the touch of the great Rederick, his life was no longer fading from his grasp. That was because he had shown worth, and was valued, if only he was alive. Rahkev saw their path pragmatically, knowing they could live, but it was not to be so. In the end, maybe a few would live for some short time. But he would not be one of them.

Throwing open the door to his cult's hall, he raised a fist to his brothers and sisters.

No longer could he contain himself: "My friends, men and women of Orobrex! Raise your hands for me! Gather the stores, sack them dry! All grains and meats will we give to the people! Know this, where we head at the end of the next day will serve us our final meal! There we will give all we are, so that our bones may lay forth the path to a new day!"

Waving his arm about, many took from their chairs to rally to him. Finally thrusting his finger to the rear of the hall, he gave his next order: "Go! What may be given, shall! To the streets!"

Scrambling about, the disorderly group began to break down the home they had been given in but a blink of an eye. Barrels were dragged before him, others carried cloths with wrapped goods between, and some had grabbed blankets and sprigs of medicinal plants.

"Come! Quickly now!"

Kaerex barked at his cult, throwing his hand out towards the alley. Leading the line of his followers to the street, he headed towards the East with his head high. While many of the Sons of Blackwood looked upon him and his band with disdain, their small minds could not conceive of the forces at work. Though they listened, it was for far more primal reasons. And for that, he could forgive their ignorance in the face of greatness.

As he went, the rot within the hold became distinct. None would be blind to it, nor unable to pass by without hearing a sound of suffering. Turning into one of the larger streets, the pavement became nothing more than rounded, crumbling stones imbedded in mud. Buildings of ten different shades of wood, repaired by cloth, slumped into the old earth they were placed upon. Children ran from him as spindly mothers corralled them away, fear found in the eyes of men whose bodies had been broken to raise such a place.

Only one remained outside upon their arrival, whose right arm was tied and bound. Under his ragged hair, his worn and tired face did not show he had a thought of cowering. As many more of his faithful arrived, Kaerex shot a hand into the air. Unfolding his fist, they all dropped their hoods. Without a sound, he turned and approached a follower, who held out their bounty. He took the makeshift sack and approached the man.

His boots brought new mud upon the creaking old steps to the home until he came before the veteran. Though his form was lame now, he could see the one before him was once a force to behold. But the signs of stitching across his cheek, along with the many jagged marks that could not hide beyond the stretched folds and tears of his shirt … Tavora had already condemned him.

Kaerex raised the bundle as the old soldier peeked down at it, shaking his head.

"You'll not get use from me. Take your offer elsewhere," the man pushed off the railing, as if he had been dismissed.

Slapping the food into the man's chest, Kaerex caused him to stumble.

"Orobrex expects nothing for his gifts. Alok takes what he wants. Alok gives what he wants. Orobrex shows us the reality of this. Such is the grand struggle of all," Kaerex said.

As he spoke, the thin man took up the bundle in his good hand.

"This ... is more than any of us should have," the man whispered.

Kaerex smiled widely, giving up a low chuckle. He knew the situation the city was in- long had this land failed to provide. The growing city could hardly ever feed everyone, and now most of what was harvested went to the soldiers or farmers themselves. Even elsewhere, those that offered no worth would struggle. Here ... they were just another nameless marker to be thrown in Thousand Stones.

"It seems wrong, does it not? Why would any give to another for nothing? Struggle more for another in vain. Lose to lose ... take what Orobrex has given you."

He left the man with his bread, returning to his comrades.

"Not just me. All of you! This is our ascent, to the finest of days! Act as if you are worthy!" he bellowed.

Though it was not a decree of violence, he saw very few had come out of their homes. It hurt, that they saw them as a greater threat than starvation. But it was as Rahkev said, the man's words a harsh truth for them. Orobrex was not an easy aspect to understand, and those born with his touch had to overcome much. While with his own kind, there was no alienation, to the people that wished only to live, they were hardly any more than savages.

Still, that did not mean he would be stopped. Taking up a large waterskin from a crate, he carried it to a locked door and deposited it by the steps and went back to grab another. Alongside a follower, he carried a sack of grain to the next house. With repetition, braver souls came from further down the street. Taking pause over his transportation, he watched his followers intently as they off-handed their supplies. Even the ones with a strip of black fur along their hoods behaved well under his command, despite Orobrex having exacted his fair toll.

Through the crowd, he saw a woman limping to them. She barely made any progress with her walking stick. Such a thing was a poor substitute for what was missing below her right knee. Pushing through his own, Kaerex shoved those aside who had become infatuated with their gifts. He could see it. A knot went down her throat with a stiff swallow at his approach.

There was resignation, her acceptance of helplessness, but to that he gave no second thought. Such a thing would not even be appraised by his own.

Forcing his broad frame under her arm, there was no struggle as he usurped her walking aid.

"Come," he told her, taking a slow step forward.

She made an effort to move with him, and with patience and a slight adjustment, he led her towards the center.

"Thank you," she whispered quietly to him.

He shook his head.

"Save your thanks. I will hear none of it from one who has been cast down as you have. Tell me, who cares for you?" Kaerex asked.

"My father and brother. They work the fields, but ... they need this more than I do."

His boots ground the gravel into the dust once those words were spoken in his presence.

"Need ... more? No."

He refuted such a terrible concept, his very loins rumbling with the call of his patron. It took him a moment before he was able to take another step.

"You are his daughter. Human. You bear the gift of Illeah, her breath, life. No greater than another. You need no less and no more than they do. Than I do."

He decreed his truth, the firm ruling of the world, and the great Orobrex.

"Tell me, the cold comes. Are these rags all you have to wear?" He rapidly shifted the conversation.

With a little shock and a cowed head, the young woman nodded. Gently, he moved to let her down on top of a crate. His fingers reached to the straps of his coat, pulling them open with little effort. He yanked the heavy fur sleeves, pulling the layered piece off and setting it in her lap. From the rear of the supplies, he pulled more thick furs, setting them next to her. Packing dry goods and other lasting offerings into the wood sides, he dragged the small crate around to her. With wide eyes, she beheld his gift with reverence, but he could see the curiosity within her.

He knew how long this could last, and how much it would cost a family to trade for. And yet, he desired nothing more than to give it away.

"Brother!" Kaerex shouted without looking.

Immediately, the follower that was walking by came to his side. He pointed to the handle on the crate, and the man nodded.

"Is there anything else you need?"

Kaerex stood ready.

"Um ... no ... but..."

Before she could finish, he offered her a hand and spoke: "This is my will. Our beliefs. When we arrive before Fynor, and leave fair Illeah, these things will be but a memory."

Taking her up once more, he marched to where he first saw her.

"Then ... this is because of the war," she muttered.

He could hear the despair in such miserable tones.

"Do not dwell on it. Orobrex has gifted us so that we may suffer and die for you all to live. We will rid this land of hubris and taint, so that not one may place man beneath them again. When we are finally gone, there shall be no demons. No longer will your stomach growl, or nights be filled with sorrow," Kaerex said.

Even with the confidence he was sure he held, and his appearance, she still seemed to shake at the thought. Before he could ask which home was hers, he saw the circular marks of the walking stick in the soft ground, and where they led. Adjusting his path, he had little else to say. He pushed open the door and led her to a crude chair in the corner of the room. His follower stowed the crate in the wall and left them, but before he could turn around, he felt a tug on his bruised finger. His head came down to the lame woman, seeing her wrapping an arm around his coat.

"You say you do this for your aspect, but, Orobrex ... how is it you do more than Toren? What could possibly compel you?"

The questions came to him, lighting every torch in the hall, dropping fuel in the hearth. Through his grim scowl came a smile, and he took a knee before her.

"A brave question. A keen one. I can answer with one word, but that in itself means ten thousand," Kaerex said.

He readied his exposition, giving her pause, waiting to see if she wished him to continue. By her brow, there was no doubt. Crossing his legs on the ground, he wiped his fingers across his chest.

"Madness. Can any say what it means? Madness ... long ago, my ancestors saw the coming enslavement. They sought any answer, for freedom was worth any cost. Their cries awoke an aspect, one who had long slept. When Orobrex stirred, he saw us bleed and die, copulate, and bleed and die. He witnessed a world in which every idea brought forth growth, and in the same the very means to undo it.

"He heard us, but could not understand what he witnessed. He was unchanging, undying, unable to feel pain. All that we were, he was not. So, he conceived an idea that we should know peace, as he saw it. Orobrex yearned to create unity."

Kaerex held up his left hand and pointed one finger, and then his right, making a circle. Placing the two together, melding his fingers together in a mass, and then crafting two angles to make a box.

"From the unlike, to create like. He could not create order without disorder, and was lost to his own cause as he was enveloped in our world. Orobrex began to see only his goal, viewing his followers, and every other being as the buboes of this sickness. His power became twisted, just like his view, turning man into something worse than a beast.

"It gave us what we wished for at a great cost, one we had to endure. Whether one of us killed or perished, both brought Orobrex closer to his goal. But that was not our end. Our fate did not come so soon."

Breaking apart the box, Kaerex moved his hands up and out.

"For we had purpose. He had given us that back. We suffer, as that is who we are. We fight, even though we create division and war. We take to give, as that is what we do. Endlessly chaos to order and back. To battle every breath was our creed, to make our own peace. To follow Orobrex is to reject him, and in doing so, become closer to him."

Kaerex moved his arms in arches and then slammed his palms together.

"I need no reason besides the act itself. It is my desire. I will cater to the weak because I am no more than you. No more permanent. No less finite. I am what I am, a fool, that will help another because I feel the need. So be it if it hurts, I am meant to feel it."

Pushing himself up, he could see the effect his story had on her. Doom and hope, the great duality and contradiction of life had been temporarily revealed. In her shock, he stood, giving a sharp nod.

"Only nothing is nothing. We are all something, as we are what we make ourselves out of the flesh and blood Illeah molds us from. On this path, I will do what must be done. Bloody my hands in the gore of the ignorant or innocent. I will be the fever that shakes man, so that a place like this will never need to be again."

Still silent before him, she moved her lips, lost jumbles of thoughts a dancing spirit along her tongue.

As he turned, she called to him: "Hey! Um … you … you don't plan on coming back…"

With a glance, he saw her bundling some cloth nervously in her hands. Though she overcame her timid and weak nature, looking him dead in the eyes.

"… I'd like your name."

Kaerex's eyes widened for a moment. He saw a spark in her weary gaze, a certain emboldened force he would normally appreciate. And while it stoked his grin, it also invoked a mired sadness in his chest. Taking up an axe in hand, he placed it across his chest, lowering his head as a formality of his kin. Closing his eyes, he delivered her yet another answer: "Kaerex. Among the honored of the Aspect of Madness, I lead."

# Chapter Nine: Tavoran

Lin watched as Rorke moved his fingers around in the small tin. The gritty mix was clumped and packed, just to be smashed back down again. Rorke then pulled it apart, using an oddly particular method as he sorted out what just looked like the same bits of wet earth. But as he took one sample, raising it to his face, he continued the same pattern he had started when he sat down. The resemblance to tree bark along his skin was almost uncanny.

As Rorke continued his painting, she looked over at Anuurae. With an unrolled cloth, the ostoran had put a full range of tools on display, which she now used to pass along her dagger. The green tint of malarite was beautiful, which meant she had dedicated a few valuables not just for the blade, but for all the delicate, small tools she used to keep it. Moving a small stone along the edge, the night hunter had an unnerving focus on ensuring the mirror polish was flawless.

But as she looked to the box in her lap, the feeling she had earlier became prevalent again. While she passed the time sewing up her clothes, the two before her had gone through a plethora of their supplies and skills. Half of which she had never seen anyone do in Toren's Wake. It reminded her of the many tales she had heard of as a girl.

While she grew up with the old walls protecting her, these two had come from the frontier of human civilization. Places where farmsteads were wiped out overnight, and groups of people lived on the fringes with animals. A place where men made riches from breaking open the earth and pulling stone from deep below or risked even more and ventured beyond into the farthest reaches.

"You got that look on your face again," Rorke commented as he rubbed under his eyes.

"I'm just thinking," Lin responded gently.

Rorke snickered.

"Guess you do that a lot."

Rubbing her sewing box soon came to finger tapping, which she caught onto and forced herself to stop.

"Well … you both give me a lot I end up thinking about. Just … it's not only Dul. Has this made you think at all, that even as humans, we've become so divided in such a short time? We hardly had anything before … and now … what's the word?" Lin beseeched her mind but found nothing.

Fumbling around for it, there was an idea she knew she wanted to convey, but the easy way to say it just wouldn't match up.

"I guess I really don't know. A century is a long time, yet, with the distance between us all, we've become so … dissonant, and the time just … makes me feel weird. Can you imagine what Lesal is like now?" Lin asked.

She couldn't tell if she had dragged it on, but as Anuurae slipped her dagger back into her sheath, she nodded.

"Scary, when you think about it, really. Reminds me I've not traveled enough, and that maybe I shouldn't get that house."

The night huntress' agreement felt nice, but her approach could not have been any further from the same sentiment.

"But you're not scared of things like the ogres? Obrok? Just the people?" Lin inquired.

Anuurae shrugged as Rorke stiffly inhaled.

"Ogres, maybe. But everyone, and I mean everyone that comes up North expects to see an obrok. It's kind of funny to tell them the things are about as rare as finding sunshard," Rorke said.

Looking back to Anuurae, Lin found the ostoran leaning back on her pack and looking up to the youthful night sky. "I think the town I grew up in had one incident. 'Course, all we really saw was the dried bloodstain."

Without even stopping his camouflage work, Rorke continued the thought:

"You get a lot of bad images in your head when you only listen to people that like to focus on the destruction. Really, the fighting just recently started to widely spread with the ogres, and they're the biggest threat up there. But they've never gone after one of the bigger towns or cities. Mostly that's because of Alyra's followers."

"They're more common folk than a military at some points, but that's what makes them strong. People look out for each other up there. Ostoran or not, family is crucial to your life. Friends are, too. Trust me … I wasted all that. If it wasn't for my gifts, I would have never made it."

Despite the severity of what he said, Rorke almost seemed to crack a smile.

"So … what is it really like up there, then?" Lin asked.

"Cold," Anuurae immediately shot back without hesitation.

Rorke looked blankly at the ostoran for such a response, but it didn't seem he was going to disagree.

"I'm not exactly the best to ask, I guess. I was pretty useless to my parents when I was a kid. Spent my days exploring instead of working. That alone was probably a sign of my affinity from birth. Sure you noticed yours as well."

Rorke implied a bit with his words, but she knew what he meant because they both were born to Illeah, just the opposite ends.

"I guess. They say we're never drawn to conflict unless it's to protect others, and I just let myself get pushed around. Same for my mother. It's why we had to move towns. We never stood up against those thugs," Lin said.

Anuurae yawned, crossing her legs as she took an even more relaxed pose.

"And see, you'd never get that up North. Issues like that are rare, and when they do happen, you get some manners beaten into you. Or it's worse … and you draw the eyes of a Flametongue from one of Alyra's Chambers. But hey, your type of peace in the South gave me some fair work."

Anuurae spoke about her job casually, if not with some joy.

"Guess it makes sense, though," Rorke rapidly took back her attention. "This whole thing's for your mother. Pretty selfless act, which fits you perfectly."

131

The hero's comment seemed genuine, but it brought her no pride. If anything, it was almost bitter.

"But how'd you end up here, then? I know Anuurae said you're not well liked, and…"

Lin stopped herself, watching Rorke's face for the usual springy attitude. Instead, he was still oddly calm. In fact, he nodded as he sat down his mixing tin.

"You're not wrong. It was a wild ride, and like I said … I'd have been doomed without my gifts from Illeah. I started to go further, some days. Wandering off into the mountains. And now, that's a proper death sentence. Not only do you have the ogres, but at that point you get trolls, stonegores, stranger things from the caves … anything. And it gets worse the further North you go.

"But those same places are where the treasures are. And all was forgiven when I started filling my pockets with some shiny rocks. Dad said some of it was unarite, or something. Very valuable, very tough, and Alyra's smiths love the stuff. Alyra's faithful also like rubies, and I managed to get some. Trolls, though … they apparently can like shiny stuff, too. You'd think they'd be dumb as hoffen, but … some manage to pick up and use weapons.

"And lay traps, as I found out. One almost cornered me one day. I could cross gaps and scale sheer faces pretty well, but the damn thing got me in a narrow pass. I got around it, but not without getting smacked a time or two by its wood club. I ended up with the town healer afterwards, and that's where I suppose you can say my legend started."

Rorke finished his tale, lending her mind to a certain strain of thoughts. Lin curled her lip and raised her brow.

"What's with that look?" he wondered aloud.

"You just … found out you could use Illeah's magic. And went off? Just like that?" Lin asked bluntly.

Rorke leaned forward onto his elbows, shaking his head with confidence.

"Wasn't like I never considered fighting every now and then. But that day showed me I was capable. Training showed me I was efficient. And if it was hiding again when the ogres came by, or taking it to them … I was going to walk away or die knowing what it was like to truly feel alive. Wasn't like I never got a good beating. Skin of Stone and Bones of Water both let me stay standing, and that's what I found mattered. People do better when they don't feel alone. When one person stands up and takes that risk, others follow that."

Rorke chuckled, rubbing his dirty hands together.

"I suppose that's the story of Alyra, isn't it?"

He seemed to leave the rhetoric for himself in the open air. Yet ... there was one thing that bothered her about his sentiment. Something missing.

"You don't sound like you did any of this out of hatred, though. As fired up as you get when you fight," Lin pointed out.

Rorke squinted, interlocking his hands: "Hatred ... wrong word for it. I get angry when I think about it. I don't know if I should or shouldn't. I want people to live a good life. Be healthy and strong. That's why I don't hate the Sons of Blackwood. I get what they're doing ... they've been struggling for a long time. Doesn't mean I think they're doing the right thing. There's a way you go about things, and others don't have to like it, I guess."

Lin felt her eyes widen as she stared at Rorke.

"You know, there's more going on up there than I think I gave you credit for, Rorke," Anuurae shot back into the conversation.

"Maybe if you weren't so aggressive at first, you'd have learned a bit more," Rorke swiftly countered.

Though as he spoke, Rorke's eyes wandered to the fourth of their group. Lin found her vision meandering over to him as well. Fast asleep, Dul was still leaning against a tree in the very same pose he had started in. His breathing, slow, steady- controlled, made everything feel like a lie. Like he was just closing his eyes, waiting for one of them to give him his cue. In fact, the only thing that seemed to be out of the ordinary was his facial expression. It looked more pained than well rested.

"Maybe ... I can't blame you. This is all just ... a bit much, isn't it? Feels normal to talk about home, then you remember where we are ... that he's here," Rorke commented.

The hero's words lingered like an early morning fog, narrowing down the world to feel so small, yet even that little slice of reality was almost enough to be overwhelming. It didn't seem to like the nostalgia that came from her lower gut, or the longing to return to the safety of home. It didn't seem to matter how fast the days blew by, the months she had been gone stacked up high all the same.

Rorke pushed himself up and gave a glance out into the distance.

"Well … this is it. First step towards the end. I'll go keep watch over the town."

Finishing his declaration, he took one long look at Dul. As he turned, she was barely able to make out the mutter under the hero's breath as he departed: *Illeah, preserve me. Ophora, sleep soundly.*

Even against the ogres, Rorke had not shown such a fear of death. All that was asked of him was to watch the people. Again, that was her father's presence showing through. His song was faint, but still present. Even if only one other here could sense it, it still had the same sinister influence. In the town itself, it was likely Rorke would feel no better. Not only was there the magical miasma, but the knowledge of what lay just out of sight.

"You know, it's clear that the road's not been too kind to you. I take it he's taught you a bit, but this isn't something you're made for. You ever considered just moving North? Alyra's followers treat healers better than their own sometimes," Anuurae presented a new topic.

"I don't think I could leave my mother," Lin responded.

"You wouldn't have to. It'd be a bit of a journey, but you shouldn't have to hire on more than a scout or two. If you're worried about finding a place to stay, you'd only have to show your talents. Any den of adventurers would trade your help for a bed."

Anuurae almost made it sound too easy, but she had learned early on that any place that needed a mending hand had a good reason. The North was always busy, and now with the prospect of war, there'd be no shortage of injured men to treat. It'd be a consistent and reliable way to make income, just with the threat of the war getting a bit too close … which might not mean much if she was whisked away to the rear to do her work.

Though that was not something she could decide alone. Or even now. It would be better to think about such a drastic shift when she would be calm and level-headed. Lin rubbed her hands together, realizing that in all of this, they had left someone out.

"What about yourself, Anuurae? We go on and on about ourselves, but you've barely mentioned a thing. What brought you here?"

Lin found her words opening the verdant eyes of the ostoran, which seemed to show genuine surprise.

"You ... actually want to know?"

Anuurae spoke as if completely baffled, speaking as if this was the first time someone else had taken interest in her. The night huntress sat up, pulling her well-worn cloak tight with her arms.

"I ... guess I can tell you. I don't think I can match you or Rorke. I was born to a couple of scouts, not really even in a town. They drifted, like many other ostorans. I was raised on the border of the wilds up North without any siblings. I had nothing but to learn the tricks of the trade, and that was most of my life."

Anuurae looked down, shuffling her boots underneath her cloak.

"Sometimes it got rough. Bad hunts, farms getting raided, not a scrap from scavenging. Not enough food to fill you up, nothing to trade. When the one shot you have is the difference between sleeping soundly or hunger pains ... you learn to not miss."

Anuurae stopped there, her cheeks going pink as she wore an odd expression. She shuffled her arms underneath her cover, a strange show that almost looked like she really needed to find a spot to pee.

"Are ... you alright?" Lin asked, leaning over to reach and check for a fever.

Anuurae suddenly jerked back, shaking her head.

"I'm good ... just... yeah."

Anuurae straightened herself out, shifting her lips around, carefully preparing her tongue.

"I don't know if I want to say it," Anuurae finally admitted. Lin exhaled deeply, finding the situation almost comical.

"Is it that embarrassing?" she asked.

Anuurae leaned forward, taking a moment of pause: "I took my first life when a man named Morgan thought he had enough manpower to start a gang. He came North to target less defended areas and started roughing up farmers and miners. It was us or them ... and the pay for taking them down was better than anything my family had ever seen," Anuurae said, tone heavy with a viscous gloom.

Lin shrugged as the supposed secret was unveiled.

"I don't think there's anything wrong with that. Bandits are rare, but they threatened your life."

Though, as Lin finished speaking, Anuurae wore an almost guilty smile. The culmination of behavior gave her an odd feeling, one that tried telling her to be afraid.

"Yeah..." Anuurae whispered from the back of her throat. "... until the rumors start that you can pierce a man's heart without waking his friend within arm's reach, or take a runner's leg out from fifty paces ... then people start fearing the little girl."

Anuurae's grim humor seemed to subside but was replaced with a much darker shadow of something she hid away.

Lin squinted as she stared at the night huntress. "Anuurae ... do you like ... killing?"

Tucking her head down into the collar of her cloak, Anuurae obscured part of her face as she looked away. Between them, a moment of stillness broke out, until Anuurae tucked herself further down into the cloth and pulled up her hood.

"Not just ... it isn't just that. I can't ... it's a lot to say at once, even if I don't think you'll hit me," Anuurae muttered shyly.

Though her limbs and neck had already warmed beyond their usual bounds, Lin held herself as steady as she could.

"That sounds like ... a heavy confession," she admitted to her friend.

Anuurae nodded slowly. "You saved my life, so it's only right that I'm honest with you. I ... not even my family took my decision to become a huntress easily. Everyone thinks they know why, but no one lets me talk..." Anuurae trailed off, scuffling with a troubled mind.

"Well ... you give off a certain aura when you act like this. I didn't think you had a side like this ... but I'll give you a chance," Lin responded as genuinely as she could muster, trying hard not to let any bit of panic trickle in.

Anuurae looked her directly in the eyes, giving a subtle shake of her head. "It's not like I just kill to kill. You can see that, right? Most people think it's an obsession among all night hunters, that we enjoy this thrill that comes with the pursuit."

Lin could feel the involuntary narrowing of her eyes, and see the result of it as Anuurae began to manage to somehow retreat further into her cloak.

"I don't want to scare you. Or hurt you. I promise. Not a lot of people have treated me like you all have in the past few days," Anuurae said before taking a brief pause, looking into the darkness under the fabric mantle. "I know it was a rough start, and I know how I was. It feels like we're a bit of a mess, but I like that."

Lin sighed, resigning herself once more to the complexity of the situation. There was so much right and wrong mashed up into one mess that it being incomplete would offer nothing but more questions if it were to be studied. Therefore, the answer would have to be sourced from belief.

With a half-hearted chuckle, Lin assembled what she hoped came off as a simple smile: "I believe you."

Anuurae seemed to sprout from the recesses of her cloak, showing off a bit more of her face.

"As strange as it is, you make something good of it. After all, you came here for Kaerex. And you're kind enough that Dul took a liking to you. And if he likes you, I don't think you can be that bad," Lin said.

She found her words bringing out some kind of shimmer in Anuurae's eyes until a sudden jostle at their side caused her to yelp. As if he had heard his name, Dul's muscles had tensed up. His arms flexed fully; he looked ready to rip someone apart as he flared his nostrils. His lips parted, and he emitted a low, guttural noise. And then in an instant, all the steam for his fit was lost, and the half-blood returned to his sleep-like state again.

"Do you think he's dreaming?" Anuurae inquisitively prodded.

"He's normally the one keeping watch, so it's not like I know if this is typical. If I had to guess, it's more of a nightmare than a dream," Lin gently whispered.

"I'd like to say everybody has nightmares … but part of me wants to know what can make something like him feel … that."

Anuurae seemed to take the words right from the back of her mind. Plucking up her worn shirt, Lin rubbed her fingers around the tears.

"I'm not going to dwell on it. As you were saying?" Lin found a fair response coming from her ounce of encouragement, drawing out the childish glint in Anuurae's eye once more.

She quickly ducked back down again, drowning out that twinkle as she took a moment of silence.

"Do you ever wonder why we fear death?"

Anuurae's words came from her lips like a surprise hook to the face. Lin found her mind locked at a standstill by the question. Death was something she sometimes thought about, especially at the beginning of this journey, but not in that kind of way. It sounded closer to the question the scholars of Alok would propose to test someone. Perhaps the same could be said of this, but what would the test be?

As her mind wandered, her friend's words sliced in: "It's universal. Trolls. Ogres. Hoffen. Wyrble. All walks of life, even simple insects don't want to die. You pluck the wings from a blightswarmer, and you can see it panic when you set it down. It wants to run. But it can't. You move far faster, and it should know this, but it still fights to live, no matter how futile it is.

"Such a simple creature that we disregard with the swat of a hand, but it still shares that desire with us. It's a self-centered thing, too. Do you know how many have tried to bargain with me when the knife's been to their throat? Willing to betray friends, family?"

Anuurae began to pull her arm from behind her cloak, an act which instantly brought a surging sensation in her body to run. Watching the huntress' hand with a dreadful concentration, Lin saw the dagger come free. Anuurae flexed her fingers, then deftly flipped her grip. With her other hand, she brushed fingers across the edge, deeply absorbed in her own mind, yet not a single drop of blood came from either pass. Just an aid for recollection, or some nervous habit- it wasn't clear. Just as it was brought forth, Anuurae returned the dagger deep within the confines of her shadowy haven.

"The only thing lost in death is life. We cling to that thing … life."

Anuurae paused, her eyes coming to slits as she placed her palms together, rubbing them back and forth.

"How many people do you know that could define that word? We use it so often. But what is life? Is it this thing that links us all? Is it a gift from flesh that we spawn from our mothers? Some claim it a mystery, something beyond us. But how can it be out of the reach of words, when we have a word for it? This thing … intangible … we want it. We don't want to lose it to Fynor.

"Yet his embrace isn't painful … many pass peacefully in bed, a smile on their face. If it is not a fear of pain, are we just greedy? Is it that we want life, or don't want death? I don't think those are the same. But I found when you get close to someone, and they begin counting the drops of blood they have left … you see things you wouldn't otherwise. To witness that little ember in the eyes of a criminal fade … it's not an answer."

Anuurae's grip became firm as she locked her fingers together.

"It's the only way I've ever come closer to one. The hunt lets you witness life and death. How we think when threatened. How we change when pushed just that far. With so many years, I've only found that we're slaves to that instinct. A drive to survive at any cost. And from that I find myself questioning what exactly we are."

Anuurae abruptly let all emotion melt from every speck of her face, a mudslide of ominous portents. Her leafy eyes snapped straight to a corner peak, right at her.

"So, Lin, born of Illeah, Child of Life … where do you stand?"

Just that one sentence toppled the weight of the world, throwing everything upside down. *Would the wrong answer kill me?* She couldn't shake that thought from her mind as Anuurae waited for her. But just as her hands had fumbled with her blade as she first began to train, nothing had prepared her for this moment. Her mouth became ajar as her throat became dry and her limbs cold.

Then Anuurae smiled warmly, a swift sweep of her arm once more concealing all but her face in her cloak.

"It's fine if you don't know, Lin.   Nobody seems to.   Life, death, consciousness- buried deep in Alok's choreography.   When you think about this, treat it like a hole in the woods. You'll never know who or what dug it, and the more you look inside, the more you'll feel like you're falling in. And once you're over that edge, you never know how long until you reach the bottom."

# Chapter Ten: Where They Once Stood

*Dul pulled his blades from their loops. Firm, rough, championed from the remains of the mightiest fallen. Bones ripped from one lithe and intelligent, which kept his strength and arcane skill. Tempered further in the wicked violet blood tapped from a nigh-ethereal demon, they had a latent consciousness of their own. As rain ran along the freshly honed edges, frost was left behind in slithering streaks. The cursed, cold air whispered to him, hushed hellish bargains that coiled around his heart.*

*He struck them down and held the swords to his sides, approaching the looming mass ahead. The pelting rainfall struck both him and the earth, and he could almost feel the sting of every drop. Truly, Ophora had no mercy for any single soul this season.*

*Tucking his wings in, he ducked down and observed the corpse at his feet. Trampled, the rear of the breastplate had been pierced by something the size of his own head. And within the caverns of what was once a living, breathing man, was nothing but mud and fragments of vertebrae. Despite that, the lingering essence of his kin married with it the knowledge that this was fresh.*

*A crack of lightning conjoined with a powerful gust kicked a chill to his bones and lit up the outline of walls in the distance. Still standing, neither the rage of Tavora's Aspect of Fortune, nor the otherworldly onslaught had toppled the packed stone bricks.*

*Barrier-towns, he had heard the name from the lips of soldiers. The greatest hope of creating a blockade against the darkness. Taking his feet forward, he walked through the remnants of turned earth, and the wrecked outlines of where fortifications may have been erected. Torn cloth and broken weapons lie on the ground, carrying with it a solemn and grim message.*

*This was all he had come to know- they were a storm that came without thunder and darkness. Thousands suddenly appeared as a flood, as if they had been beneath your very feet. As he stepped over the impaled body of a demon, scorched lines of earth beheld the first defense. He stepped over the markings, feeling the agony of Toren's light wash through him.*

*His inhuman eyes looked upon the incline up into the town, and to the countless lost souls strewn before him. Taking care not to disrespect those who lived with honor, every step he took was placed upon stone if it could be found. Nearing the top, it became impossible to avoid the bodies. As the rainwater flowed down his face, he stared upon the mounds of demon corpses.*

*Like a bank of sand carved by the tides, the wretched force surrounded two statuesque forms, which stood in the dark, neither having given up their fight, even in death. Dul walked up to the soldier and his great foe, observing their eternal struggle. Even now did the great servant of Toren grasp his spear, the thrust sealed everlasting within the chest of his opponent.*

*With both arm and tentacle buried deep in his gut, his legs had not given out, despite the numerous wicked gashes in his pants showing there was little left to hold him up. And yet it had not been enough. His head lax and slack backwards, a spine went clean through to the back of his helm. Such a show of bravery in the face of damnation- one of many great men he had seen in such a manner.*

*Yet he knew better than to try to bury this human with honor. He had learned that his wicked hands should not dare to even approach the true Children of the Star, for his tainted blood boiled and wailed as his skin peeled away ... even from the enchantments of the dead.*

*With sullen footfalls, he came to the gated entrance of the town, seeing the malformed shapes of demons parade around in the streets. The moonlight revealed much more than just that, against his wishes. Reflected upon the drenched walkways were the beginnings of their totems. Strangely ordered stacks of gnawed and splintered bone, artistically endorsed with runes.*

*Maddened in their slaughter grounds, none did so much as to acknowledge his presence. Surmounting the air of dread, hatred and rage surged to his throat. His own curse came to a head, and he unleashed it in a harrowing roar. He peeled his lips back, baring his teeth at them. Some began to look and gather, so he gave them more. Snarling, howling, he issued his challenge.*

*Glowing dots appeared from the recesses of destruction, and like hail amid the rainfall, the horde dropped from shattered windows and ledges. The streets flooded and swelled, the gazes of countless warped beings upon him. Biting down, he let the mist take hold once more. His breathing turned to panting as his muscles swelled with unholy power. Desire wrenched away fear, and he began to move forward. In a berserk charge, he plummeted into the wall of teeth, horns, and nails.*

*A series of dull, sharp pains ran through his body as he slashed with his swords. Unwavering, his limbs carried through a sea of flesh as more and more clung to him. Breaking free to the other side, several demons came with him. Jaws clamped onto his arms, fingers tangled onto his legs, he glared at them with a vehement spite. They dropped from him like rotten, sagging fruits, some seizing as he ripped their essence away.*

*Diving from above, another demon sank fangs into his neck. Blood and venom burst into his throat as his wings knocked back others, and with a gargled cry, he drove a sword through the heart of the leech. Before he could return his focus to the surging mass, a burst of unholy flame knocked him aside. His boots slid against the slick stone underfoot, but his eyes fixated upon the skittering form in the ruined home.*

*Many arms carried it out and away, no doubt to strike again come the opportunity. Another demon leaped to him, yet his instinct had awoken. His arm threw out a quick slash before he could think. Entrails splashed against him as black fumes erupted from his pores. His swords reacted in kind, accepting his power if it meant another chance to feast. His fingers tightened down, welcoming the weapons as family.*

*With a dart forward, his arms carved and reaped. Without fear of the whirlwind, a demon with an enlarged arm charged him. Putting every ounce of force it could into the blow, its swollen feet slid as its mangled fist dragged it forward. He hacked into it with his shortswords, but quickly learned why fragments of wood and metal jutted from such a puss-filled and horrible weapon. The edges of his swords stopped within the putrid sack until it connected with him, flinging him back. His wings caught the wind behind him, slowing his slide.*

*Bursting from the dark, crimson bolts were conjured and thrown toward him. The barrage exploded around him, such bright light no different from Ophora's lightning cast within his skull. Simultaneously, a burning force wrapped around his wings, yanking him back. Blinking rapidly, Dul fought against the bindings, frothing at the mouth, venom and saliva overflowing.*

*Runts and minions sprinted towards him, though that became less of a worry as a shadow was cast over him. The presence of the greater kin grew within his soul and mind. It was his captor, and as he looked above, his executioner. He dug in his boots and fought against its grasp, but failed as he was dragged closer. Engulfed by the shadow of a great limb larger than his whole body, he knew there was no way out without sacrifice.*

*With all his strength, he threw himself aside as the blade-arm came plummeting down. It cut through him effortlessly, smashing into the street and sending him tumbling away. He pushed himself up with his right arm, sputtering out a gushing torrent from his left side. And yet an arm and wing were not his life- and barely worth a thought for what would be replaced.*

*His mind slipped further away, the warmth of the slick flowing wound fading into obscurity. As tissue and vessel writhed, he yearned only for more. He slung the tip of his blade toward the encroaching foes, who screeched and flopped into a charge. He tore into them with a swing of his sword, smashing some lowly scum beneath his foot. Yet they were not what he really wanted. His gaze fixed upon the cleaver that was raised back up to the side of the goliath greater demon.*

*Covered in a strange series of hardened colonies, fingers and branches of a skeletal material adorned the master of this army. The head of the greater spawn canted towards him, the two glowing eyes matching his own with their golden spite. What could be called a frown was gifted to him as the many tentacles swayed in the place of a mandible. It appeared to even try to shake its head, but what little neck was recessed between such distended shoulder and back muscles could hardly move.*

*Dul watched as soul bindings dropped from the palm of the smaller arm's hand, which reared back to strike. Like whips, the attack struck him as an order. Flying towards his foe, he slashed through an intercepting minion before dodging a great sweep from the blade-arm. A deft stroke from his brush christened a new palette, and he took a dip from the vulnerable elbow of the demon commander.*

*It quickly folded its arm to crush him, but Dul bounced up and tossed his blade into the air, his hand wrapping upon the strange protrusions of outer armor. His body trembled as his muscle spiraled and crept over bone, and skin crawled overtop. His regrown arm awoke as nerves fired up, and caught his sword. His other palm ripped open against the crude surface of the demon's armored skin, executing a perfect swinging launch into the air.*

*He dipped into his own paint, slicking his blade's edge wet in a tantalizing mixture of two souls. The concoction lit up in tainted tongues of flame as he plummeted, dashing the face of his foe with a masterful mark. Upon the ground, he dodged the demon's counterattack with a roll. The gargantuan blade was lanced forward, still an accurate attack, despite his foe's skull being split wide down the middle.*

*But such a powerful attack required commitment. The demon's blade-arm crashed into a building as Dul closed in, slashing at the groin of his foe. Despite the organ being as warped as it was, it earned a moan as Dul ran towards his discarded flesh. With the stomp of a boot, he sent his second sword into the air, out of the grasp of a withering corpse. He spun on his toes, keeping balance with the flap of his wings. Flames exploded around him once more, and the minions returned to the battle.*

*But as the soulfire flickered around him, he closed his eyes. His nostrils took in the smell of his foe's blood, his soul seeing the path forward. The stones cracked underfoot when he pushed off, a streak of black lightning as Ophora witnessed him. His first strike landed with the heart of cataclysm itself, sending shards of ingrown plates and calcified branches around him.*

*Mercilessly, he opened his eyes to see the gap in the organic armor. With a swift slash, foul liquid poured out from below its knee. The great demon listed as it was forced to use its greatest weapon to prop itself up, and Dul wasted no time in ascending upwards. He drove both of his blades into the soft tissue above the waist of the debilitated foe. His arms came to his sides as blood showered him, and he dropped to the ground once more.*

*The excess contact of blood kicked up a blistering storm physically and spiritually, a taunt from his foe that he was no easy prey. He turned to see the host finally being assisted by his army, as they climbed upon him and formed a bulwark between them. The smallest among them crawled into the open wounds, vanishing beneath like a beetle under the leathery skin of a corpse. Though such pockets soon flattened as their commander worked with the sacrificial power bestowed upon him.*

*His foe devoured his underlings in an instant, his lantern-like eyes flickering with amusement. A lump traveled up the greater demon's gut, vanishing somewhere near his chest. A moment later, two lame arms sprouted from the depths of its throat, pulling the two halves of his split head together. Skin, bone, and burned brain alike sealed without consequence, reminding him they were two of a kind. Potent enough was their wretched mark that they were beings of soul far more than flesh.*

*Glowing whips once more dangled from the hand of the commander as it held out the bladed limb as a decree, and the lull was quashed with murderous force. Sniffles and growls brought forth the tide as the casters gathered in the furthest dark corners. Dul charged as lights began to flicker and flash in the back lines, and a new wave crashed upon him. Rapid cuts brought him through the first onslaught, and as the arcane ways of Tyxivol were unleashed, his wings wrapped around him.*

*The magics battered his wings; the flames eating holes in their webbing. Through these, he saw the lash of the demon's magic whips. With a dart left, only a chunk of his right wing was cut away. Leaping up through a broken window, he used the vantage point to shoot himself from a balcony at the casters hiding among their master's armor. Below, many demons jumped and stretched, popping up like grease on a cooking pan.*

*Engulfing himself in his mist, he became a black comet, soaring with one purpose. Bypassing the blade-arm, his illusion had worked. With a thud and hiss, his mist exploded outwards as his boots ground against the hardened flesh. Inside the crack beneath his legs, a nest of purple eyes glared back. He thrust his sword into the center, feeling the meager resistance of frail bones.*

*He jerked and threw the lanced corpse aside, his tongue writhing in his mouth as he felt a pulse within the craggy bulk below. The greater demon began to shake and run, a feeble attempt to stop him. Even more hopeless was the raising of the magic lashes, as he had already set his vision upon the future- the end of a life.*

*Ducking under the glowing lashes, he stabbed both blades into the shoulder of his kin. Yet another blast of soulfire sent him tumbling from the titan and back down to the stone road. The greater spawn wasted no time in thrusting its injured arm forward, though Dul flung himself away with foot and wing. Dul led into a retaliating strike underneath the commander's arm, severing a muscle with a deep cut. And as he did, the armor plates beside the wound crackled and vibrated.*

*He barely had the time to throw his arms in front of his eyes as it exploded as blood and shard, the fragments ripping him apart. Thrown back first down upon the street, joint and tendon jammed or shredded by shrapnel, each movement was rough and spouted more blood. Raising his battered limbs to lift himself, the battle did not wait for him.*

*He staggered back as the massive blade cut into his chest; the gust kicked up from the strike swept aside the rain and blood. Debris was spit from gash and gouge as he distanced himself, leaving a trail on his retreat. The horde came for him in his greatest moment of vulnerability; the shard jutting out from his right knee still inhibiting quick movement.*

*Though this was not the first time he had been brought so low. This war had brought forth a part of him he knew would never sleep again after it was over. And now, it outstretched a hand to him. He flung his arms out, splashing blood on the ruined walls around him. And with it, he allowed it in ... and felt a deep unsettling. At first, it slothfully acknowledged its chains had been cast off, and then it saw the wondrous carnage before it.*

*His pierced lungs took in a steady breath, no longer concerned about the trivialities of death's boundaries. It was indeed a grievous glory, a reason to revel, a tribute to the weakness that hid such might. Long claws raked away at his skin, flensing bone to air. Spines sank into his stomach and legs, all but hastening his departure.*

*In the back of his mind, there was fear that survivors may be tucked away, a child or two hidden by cunning parents. Dropping his swords, he stepped across the threshold. His vision faded, his bones re-arranged, and blood flooded from his wounds, until it seemed the last drop had come. Yet he was a vessel, and what he was to become had no concern to share with flesh.*

*His boots squeaked as stress tears appeared all over, and his belt popped. His*

147

*pants turned to strips and fell away, leaving him bare. Lurching forward onto his hands, his foes dropped around him as his mist enshrouded his form. A great pestilence manifest, a conjuration of what baleful evils he was made from.*

*His eyesight became filled with little more than darkness, a blindness that mattered little from the growth of his other senses. Every soul was a beacon, a siren's song, felt and heard, pulling him towards it. As his new body settled, the greater demon's whips swung with futility, foolish attempts to assail the unfathomable.*

*Shoving up on his now inhuman palms, his snout locked onto the whip. So greatly infused with magic, his teeth caught on and crushed down. The spell dissipated, absorbed into his cloudy aura. Nothing but raw instinct compelled him forward, seeking the source of essence before him. The greater kin's form was outlined in his mind, and lethal clairvoyance spoke of every move he needed to make.*

*There was not even time for the bladed arm to be raised before Dul closed the gap, forcing the limb up with only one hand. His other arm thrust forward; he tore free a hearty chunk of meat with little effort. A frantic defense of exploding armor peppered his ever-shifting body, with all the success of a sword swipe through a cloud of gas. In exchange, Dul swiped again, reaping another harvest of fat and juicy meat.*

*Then his fingers wrapped around ribs, cracking them as he ripped open the great spawn. He let fly one more handful, only to then come back to the living feast with two wanting hands. He flung open the great treasure within, taking no time in snatching it for himself. He held it for just a moment, feeling the last beat of his foe's heart. Gulping it down, the great hulk fell to its side.*

*Still, he kneeled down over it, tearing free another morsel. His broad hand shoveled it into his mouth, his flattened nose pressing into the dripping mass. The liquid flowed into his nostrils, dripping into his throat. Nothing but bliss was found within the subjugated soul, bliss that pushed him onward for more.*

*His fingers ran along broad bones, pulling tendons out from joints. Cartilage could be plucked free from soft points, and his teeth could crush it with ease. Organs offered the most, but such vascular treats did not last. None of it did, as he found his anger driving him to snap the freshly stripped carcass open for marrow. Not until complete exhaustion was he freed from the trance, pulling himself back from what he hoped was not the point of no return.*

*Curling his elongated digits into fists, he cast quick glances around. It appeared the same as always. With the fall of the overlord did the mongrels flee. No longer being controlled, without a reason to be devoured. The word quickly brought a roiling sickness through him. Placing a hand over his swollen abdomen, he hoped for an urge to vomit. Yet no such thing came.*

*The form he had taken would never relinquish what it had taken in. Before he could rub his hand across his skin, he pulled back, feeling the sticky coat coagulating. All he could do was close his eyes, and try to steady himself. He shut himself away in the torrents of Ophora, repeating the words to himself.*

*In. Out. In. Out. Steady.*

*But among it, he could still hear the curse speak to him. His stomach was not yet full, it flaunted. Around his head, in his hands and feet, the lingering power was ready to seize him once more. With his greatest effort, he attempted to push against it, but to do so would be an act not unlike shoving a mountain. There was not a budge, not a sliver of hope, just hopelessness. It was the will of his own veins and soul, to become this ... and more.*

*Opening his eyes, light twinkled as it pierced cloud and mist alike. The rainfall slowed, and he walked forward through the streets. Glass crunched under tread as he took note of just how barren it all was. Rain had washed away the stains, the earth drinking as he did. What was left was just a shell, and this ... this was all they had. To create fortresses against things like what he was, to resist and bite.*

*Pushing open a cracked door, he ducked down to look inside. A pair of weapons, discarded from the dented armor aside from it, lie on the floor. Little else could he see through his miasma, as there was nothing but death to be found. There was a faint hope within him that there would be some left, a valiant group for the next to rally behind, but even a faint life would not be hidden from him. The door creaked as he retreated and shut it.*

*Going up the incline to the main wall, he found the final front of the battle. It was there he began to shrink and revert, the full sight of the battle something he could never find words for. While Ophora had domain over disaster and weather, this alone brought doubt to him that it was not Alyra's anguish that was drowning the land. A gigantic chunk of the wall had been torn out, and around the stone brick plateau were familiar deep gouges.*

*Bodies cast around in halves, scorched lines of Toren's magic on the ground. Some had set up shield walls, just to be trampled and overwhelmed. Others had made an effort to help the wounded, only to be taken down themselves, their hands still entrapped together. A few in the center had given up, died in the embrace of another, until their arms went slack and cold. It was draining to look upon until a dim light sparked to life again.*

*It flashed into sight atop a mound of charred demon bodies, as if to draw his eyes to it. The greatsword, encrusted by charred flesh, seemed to bark at his presence with its enchantment. The wielder was just nearby, further up the throne of corpses. Dul shuddered to look upon him, his final defiance a message that had even parted the horde.*

*As the man had collapsed from his many wounds, he had held out an amulet of Toren over the edge of the wall. The silver effigy of the star still dangled, sparkling in tandem with the sword it once sat beside. Just that, by its chain, unleashed a burst of magic that forced him to step back. Its blazing radiance caused the nearby impure demon flesh to sizzle and bubble, daring another to step towards him or his comrades.*

*Even knowing the danger, he could not help but linger and stare. There was such power in his proclamation, his refusal to succumb to anything more than death. His end was on his terms, a bitter stubbornness that humanity would not be defeated. But that was an ominous promise. That light of hope beckoned forth its own darkness, that many more good men were to die.*

A touch on his chest brought him back. A prod to push him from the world long past in his mind, enough to make his eyes shoot open in the dark. Lin backed down, taking her seat in the camp. He pushed his back off from the tree, taking a few steps forward. Anuurae watched him closely as he joined them without a word, planting his elbows on his thighs.

"Thank you," Dul spoke softly to Lin.

She nodded again, returning to sewing up a tear in her undershirt. Scratching at the back of his hand, he could feel the eyes of another failing to part from him. Thankfully, the past few days had shown it was not distrust or resentment, surprisingly. The ostoran seemed to know it was not his choice to harm her. Instead, it had sparked her interest more, forming several new habits he wished had never come.

"You seemed to be having a terrible dream," Lin remarked. "But I didn't want to disturb you until it was late, like you asked."

He looked up, staring off into the shadows of the woods. Terrible was not the word he would use. Though he needed little sleep or rest, it was always the same things when he did. Little embers of the past drifting by, stirred up by the winds of the world. Somehow it always seemed to catch onto something, being more premonition than prophecy. And that alone was something he always struggled to decipher.

Whether the dream was a warning of him slipping further back, or perhaps a foretelling of a great battle to come ... such was hardly worth his energy. Whatever it would be in the end would be seen and lived, no matter what anxiety tried to tell him. Folding in his wings, he kept his grim stare ahead, feeling Kaerex in the distance, somewhere in the nearby town.

What mattered was that he had pinned their target here. Tonight would be the end of this spirit's journey, and the beginning of a new one for him.

"Are you alright, Dul? You've been ... distant again. Like when we first met," Lin asked.

He gave her a glance and nodded. Then again, alright meant different things for them. The last few days, he had felt the clouds shift. The pressure was different, the air itself ... strange. He had considered it to be the touch of Silvercry, akin to whatever Lin had described, but the two were different kinds of ominous. One perplexed and unnerved man, this ... it felt like a burden.

Not too unlike what he felt that day he dreamed of, which made sense. Now there was more consequence. Now he understood the weight of what he did. The only thing that hadn't truly changed was his control of Alshivex. Most of his power had been locked away by starving himself, hiding his full potential ... and danger.

Under Ophora's watch, nothing was made easier. A tingling shiver ran down his spine, earning a jolt and flex from him. His wings instinctively unfurled and flapped as he shook, nearly knocking both of his companions back. Blinking twice, he tucked them back in.

151

"My apologies. I felt a chill," Dul spoke, his lack of energy bringing his words close to a grumble.

While both were startled for a moment, both of his companions settled back quickly.

"You don't have to lie, you know," Lin told him as she once more took hold of the needle.

"You've already let it out. You don't know about the undead. You can be nervous, like anyone else."

He knew her words were meant to be sweet, welcoming and comforting, like a fine wreath of flowers, but he only felt the prickle of thorns. Anuurae tapped at her thighs at his side, the repeating sound echoing in his head and barring thought, allowing only anger. He gritted his teeth and scratched harder along his hand.

Upon doing so, the ostoran immediately ceased, drawing his eyes to her. There was a twinkle of guilt somewhere in his mind about the harshness of his gaze, yet the huntress did not wilt. Pursing her lips, she teetered back and forth with words concealed only by the silence of her tongue.

Taking his eyes back to the gloomy woods, the transition brought a concerned look from Lin. He curled his hands in, his fury confused to where it should be directed.

"Lin, just give him some space. I don't want to be rude, but you're smothering him," Anuurae spoke from the sideline.

Lin jerked her head back, squinting at the newest member of their party.

"Smothering? What do you want me to do, sit back and do nothing?" Lin slapped back.

Anuurae glanced down and nodded briefly. "He needs his quiet, alright?"

Dul perked up, cocking his head at the ostoran. Hearing his wish aloud was … strange. It was not often that one knew what he wanted even before he did. As he began to settle, he was able to process both sides. There were good intentions from both, but letting the effort go one way felt wrong. Placing his hands together, he worked at his breathing. Closing his eyes and pulling the curtains open once more, he found his center.

"Thank you, Anuurae. I … suppose I needed to hear it. Only a moment

… but a valuable one. I cannot lie, I am uneasy. There are many things to think about. Many that seep in from memory." Dul put forth some effort into his admission, an attempt at sounding steadier than he felt.

Lin sucked in on part of her lower lip, biting down. From her hesitation and the long look in her eyes, he already knew enough.

"It's not just your father, Lin. I know the stories from when I was young. The first unfelled, a member of Toren's congregation during the Devastation. Downed by demons, carted away, just to rise and return to battle. As strong as he was in life, if not stronger, he caused his men to kneel and weep before him. Few could even stand to look upon him, until his second in command informed him of his end…

"He went mad, killing his brothers and sisters until one of their own was able to put him down. The dead aren't understood, but throughout my time, all have been able to be returned to stillness." He spoke firmly, but carefully.

Until twin beams of rustic hues pierced into him, welling with tears, but filled with the sharp edge of wisdom.

"What else is there, then?" Lin's words coiled in his chest, forcing him to swallow the weight of his words.

*Not just your father.*

Anuurae shook her head. "You're climbing up the wrong side of the mountain. Think, as long as my kind have lived next to yours, have we ever been able to explain our instincts? Why ostorans always know the safer trails, or know what's a threat? We feel two different worlds, and it's fair to say it's the same for him. Don't try to force him to put it into words. If you want to help, you have to make an effort to understand him first."

Putting his eyes to the dirt as he listened, he hid away any surprise he may have shown. He had felt his eyes widen, and such was uncontrollable. Not since his brother had anyone considered his comforts so, or even crawled so far as to comprehend his inner workings.

*And this … in such a short time. Who…*

Looking back up brought him to a tense rivalry between the two, delivering him a pause. Lin began to back down, accepting her defeat at the hands of someone far more experienced. Going back to her throwing axes, Anuurae picked at the one empty ring. But no matter how she tried to occupy herself, she stealthily peered from the corners of her eyes at his wings.

Quick passes, taking in the tastes she could not hold back from temptation. Each time, she seemed to scold herself afterward. His thoughts level, he once more recognized it was the same spark that had led him to tell her of the past.

With a newfound calm, he opened his lips: "What about my wings has your attention, Anuurae?"

The ostoran froze as she was, stricken by sudden paralysis such that not even the rise of her chest was apparent.

"Is it why they have just now appeared?" he asked.

"Or how it feels," she whispered ever-so-quietly under her breath, words which would have passed unheard by any human ear.

Dul blinked twice, thinking about the question himself. Supposing they did feel different things, it would be strange to them that he didn't know the disparity when he cut them off.

"It's like any other limb, I suppose," he began. "I don't notice when they're gone, and when they're grown, they mostly move on their own. I guess I don't think about it. It's how the magic works ... instinct, like your own. Feed and mend. What you see now is my work being undone."

As he finished, Anuurae found her ability to move once more, but the rustle of leaves nearby took all of their attention away. Emerging from the shadows, Rorke dragged himself into the clearing.

"Last of the people are in their homes."

He broke into the conversation without a single pause, rubbing some dirt camouflage from his face.

"Cultists are held up all over the town, so it's like you predicted, down to the letter."

Rorke continued before going for his bag and pulling out a waterskin.

One slug, and he smacked his tongue: "Glad to be out of there, but you'd best get moving..." Rorke blinked a few times, trying to shake off some of his apparent nerve. "... they're awful antsy to get their plan underway."

In return, Dul stood, setting his hands on the hilts of his blades and marching to the edge of the camp.

"Dul?"

One last call came to him. Lin swallowed hard behind him as his feet stilled.

"I ... do what you have to. But be safe, alright?"

Her request was simple, but safety was never a possibility in such a conflict. He gave a nod, at least assuring both of them that this would be the end of her father's suffering. Ducking down, he picked up his pace, vaulting a low fence as he made his way into the town perimeter. The initial song was easy to follow now that he had heard it before. There would be a place where the crackle of torches and lamps fell silent, and his ears told him that was left.

He ducked into an alley between two homes, jumping out into the road. He peered out, drawing his blades as he stared at the distant lights. The first flame was orange, but the next was certainly wrong. Discolored, bland, abnormally bleak. Letting mist leak from his skin, he followed the signs down the road. Even if the place was not the most fortified or well-lit, the town dimmed with every light passed. Stopping at the fifth torch, he started to hear it.

Faint, somehow distant, it was just as Lin said. Like a tongue slithering into his ears, moist and wet, a vexingly familiar voice called to him. His gut sank, telling him it was his mother, but he failed to understand. No noise formed anything coherent, but none failed to have a purpose. It was as if he were being asked a question but knew not it or the answer.

Grasping onto his weapons tighter, he continued on. The slick whip of a lie struck him, a sound between a man yelling and a woman crying. It seemed to shift and change, noise like the shape of smoke. It was shrill, cutting into every nerve on his neck. Then came a snarl, darting from the front right into his skull. A sharp snap caused him to dart and turn, but when he looked to the source of the noise, there was nothing besides the stone wall of a house just a foot away.

His heart beat faster as the light around him was blown out like a candle. He held perfectly still, trying to ground himself as the voices boomed around his head. Shouts quieter than a falling feather, mutters more deafening than a rockslide. His feet shuffled back as it became overwhelming, his shroud sputtering out. Then it came, a silver flash that banished it all.

Birds took off into the night, fleeing in erratic paths, even colliding mid-air. Returned to a grounded world, Dul gathered himself and looked around. His eyes locked onto the one bit of movement he could see, a thin pillar advancing steadily in the dark. He crept forward to intercept, gaining a clear sight of the marching bones, distorted as if it were surrounded with baking dune sands from the West.

With no doubt it was heading straight towards one home, the very same he could feel the tug of Kaerex's mark from. He slunk along a fence, his mantle once more restored. Taking a stop by the road, he waited. The bare skeleton took its time, airy and weightless strides being completed when ready, and no sooner. Studying his foe, Dul found only one abnormality.

The ribcage was split near the heart, cracked by the impalement of a flat object. Not until he traveled up did he see something else, however. He froze upon seeing the cratered sockets of the skull not affixed ahead, but precisely to him. Silvercry's gaze followed him, unbroken, through every step. In an instant, the distance between them became meaningless, the skull just inches away from his own face.

The bones posed in a low crouch; the jaw jittered as it slowly opened before him.

"Murderer," a hollow voice crawled out from the undead.

In a flash, Dul lashed out with one sword in an upward swipe. The spirit vanished, leaving only a meager cloud of dust behind. The torchlight around him choked, the circles of light shrinking and pulsing unpredictably as faint whispers returned. Dul leaped into the open, away from any obstacle, keeping his neck loose as he swiveled around.

There was a blinding flash of silver light, and Dul dove to the side. He felt a hot line form across his collar as he blinked rapidly. Again, he felt an attack coming. Rolling on his shoulder, the second strike was close- near instant as it slipped by. There was no preparation, no anticipation, just an unnatural execution.

His vision returning, he dropped the veil and turned his power to his blades.

Though before him, there was nothing. Just an itching feeling around the light of the moon, his foe not only having stolen his strategy, but exceeding him in skill. It was disturbing how quickly the undead had turned the ambush around, though few understood exactly what the unfelled were capable of.

Coming fully to his feet, Dul waited for the attack. It could come from the gray trees, or the pale home. From below or above, Silvercry had shown that was not beyond him. Neither was waiting … wearing down those with frail wills. Yet such cowardice did not suit one with his experience. Taking a neutral stance, Dul closed his eyes, feeling the gentle breeze sweep around him.

He closed off his ears, silencing their lies. The sweeping wind caught his hairs, brushing those on his neck ever so gently. The touch of nature was constant, expanding around him, forming a delicately predictable flow. It could not move through him, but around him … and the foe. His chest expanded out, and there he held. The wind settled, and still he held.

His ears pounded, but no lie would move him. But like a tug on his web, the smallest change caught him. Even without the wind, he felt the parting and shift in pressure. His blades moved faster than the lids of his eyes, catching a hard impact right in front of his chest. Caught by the bone swords, the unusual point of a white crystal was but a finger's width from his skin.

He could not call it a struggle as the spirit pushed in, unshaking of hand, unlike his own before such strength. Even more haunting was the glittering true form of the unfelled. Shimmering pictures of a man blinked before him, coated in a metallic sheen. Long strands of hair flowed in ethereal wind as hateful eyes dug into his throat more violently than the claws of a starving beast. The jaw creaked open again, a low hiss emerging from the undead. Even then, it was not the end of such a violent haunting.

*Such aim could not have been an accident.*

Taking one hand from its weapon, Silvercry raised a spell. Dul went for a kick in hopes of disarming the unfelled, but his boot passed through nothing as silver static erupted around him. More alert, his heart pumped harder as he thumped his boot back to the earth.

*If it knows to go for my heart, it's only a matter of...*

Sweeping his torso to the side, he gritted his teeth as his back was split open.

In that same motion, he carried his sword in a slash but found only the empty cavity of a long-gone stomach. As he prepared a lance right for Silvercry's skull, the boney feet propelled the spirit to the side. Dul's eyes widened as he threw his head back, the crystal edge clipping one of his horns. It ground against it, scratching the textured surface.

He bit down as he was allowed to settle again, alone under the watch of such a being. Even in his battle trance, he could hear the stirrings of the spirit rise again, though they did not obscure the light patter of feet landing behind him. Flying on the balls of his feet, Dul turned and threw up his blades in defense, only to find Silvercry some distance away, watching him in the middle of the road. Unblinking, flickering, spectral flesh slid and faded like coastal foam in swash.

"You..."

The winds spoke to him for the one with no tongue. The word repeated in an echo a few times until Silvercry lifted his weapon once more, planting the edge in his free palm. Displaying the weapon somewhat ceremoniously, Dul took note of just how odd of a tool it was. The hilt, if that was what it could be called, appeared to have been broken off from a handle, sharp and jagged at the end. The lack of a handguard raised questions about the leaf-like blade above it, or the battered portions of the edge. No matter the damage, the pristine tip would remain a potent threat.

"... I see true."

With those three more spoken words, the spirit silenced the world in a silver flash, stealing away the breath of the very land. Before Dul could blink, the spirit was before him again, his blue eyes darting down to the glowing and humming crystal weapon. Dul lashed out in a parry, redirecting the lance to his side. As if the attack had never happened, Silvercry slipped back to a pounce in an instant.

Barely deflecting the second strike with his second blade, Dul already knew the same trick was coming again. He curved his core before the third reset, allowing the flat of Silvercry's blade to glide along the side of his chest.

Biting down, he forced his body out of its drowsy lull. His biceps and back rippled as he struck downwards, kicking up a gust with the might of such a blow.

Silvercry faded from harm in a glittery twinkle of light, yet he had left behind a sliver of essence. His living blades drank deep, and the ground between the two was leveled. Pivoting around in a slide and slash, Dul made heavy contact with the crystal. The crisp clink echoed the contact that shoved it away in a shower of dust, yet he did not relent.

He drove his other sword forward, impaling the skull of the spirit. Like meat on a spit, he lifted the bones, just to be met with baleful spite in Silvercry's phantom eyes. The cracks and fractured pieces near his blade began to pull together, emitting an unearthly glow. Dul aimed for the neck with a quick chop, cracking vertebrae. All the same, Silvercry once more faded away.

Reappearing down the road, the slack neck began to pull itself upright, jittering as it started to fuse. With a shrug and flick of both arms, Dul hurled both blades into the dirt as the two prepared their next attack. For this prey, he knew now he had to adapt. The soul within was resilient, no chance he could subdue it with a body that cared not about being broken and could not bleed.

Flexing his fingers, his muscles and veins created a rough topography as he narrowed his eyes upon the magical weapon his foe carried. Dul took one step forward, a soft pat of dirt against his boot. Like the snap of a tripwire, the beaten skull rapidly snapped back into place, a scowl upon it no living man could match.

With a crackle, the empty skeletal hand was raised, and Dul's eyes widened as a strange arcane vortex formed in Silvercry's palm. He broke into a full charge, enveloping himself in a misty shield. Yet the spell needed little time to gather itself, and a pulse of invisible force rippled outwards from Silvercry as soon as the bony fingers curled.

Dul threw his arms up in front of his eyes, but the cast seemed to be nothing but a distraction, a farce he could not let impede him. But as Dul moved, he felt light. And something else was off, but no sense could pin what it was. Until he blinked, looking down upon himself. The questions of when and why seemed important, but the real problem broke through the confusion and shock. While bloodlust did little to aid his comprehension, it was clear that it was no illusion.

He was indeed seeing from higher up somehow, displaced from his own body. He tugged on his legs to move, and that they did, dragging themselves backwards sluggishly, as if drowned in mud. He pulled and strained, but every sputtering order was done through a wet and heavy rope. All around him, the distant whispers returned and closed in, slithering through the cracks around him.

Another step back, and the lights around him began to vanish, until the only pale light was the one before him. Silvercry smiled as he took slow and methodical strides, brandishing his murderous implement. The distance between them gradually shrank as his mind scraped for answers, but he found none to such an eldritch curse. Desperately he flapped his wings, each beat slowing and earning him less and less time.

Leaves rustled along the barren soil at his feet, branches crackled above, and the unseen forest wreathed him with familiar scents. Staggered breaths billowed thick, moist puffs he could feel all over, indiscernible if they were fake or his own. Colder and colder, he shivered as he fought a sudden onset of pain. Part of him fought against the magic, yet some of him couldn't. With that, truth and lies blurred into one.

*Is this too much blood?*

He could hear amidst the raging torrent.

*I can't ... not here. Not ... like this.*

A ragged voice taunted him. He thrashed against the noises, but the now dominant voice pinned him in place with a terrible presence.

*You can't leave Lin ... not now.*

He choked and sputtered as something heavy wrapped around him, burying him, and dragging him down. With the chill, fighting it became impossible. Only when he tried to open his mouth to scream did he find his voice had been taken from him. It took him under, surrounding him in a frigid place as the pressure grew. Like someone pulling a noose tight, it was a strangling, murderous sensation.

There were no longer lungs to burn, no mouth to breathe from, and yet he feared to not try. Deeper, tighter, the longer he was here, the worse it got. Until it all spiraled, and he could no longer think straight, if at all. As consciousness became a blur, he could no longer sustain himself.

Constricting until he ruptured and burst, the pressure relieved itself as he dissolved into the dark with only one thing to keep him company. A silver glint shone above him, bearing four eyes. The twin faces seemed so far away, yet close enough he could reach them. He tried to move, but melted away. Dripping down into a pool, all was lost in the nothingness.

And so he saw it. A dark-skinned creature and a skeleton. They appeared to be locked in a conflict, though it seemed oddly one sided when one considered the dark-skinned one was all but hunched over. The flickering skeleton took its weapon and thrust it up into the bent-over chest of its opponent, picking the body up with the force of the strike.

Wounded, the man dropped to his knees, his limbs going slack as blue blood dripped from the gash. Exposed ribs appeared to have caught the blade, leaving a nasty, possibly mortal wound. But there was a tug, a feeling of attraction. As the crystal was raised again, he saw deeply in its pale glint. When it struck the chest of the man, twisting into the bone, a strange sensation rose from far away.

The undead's weapon was brought back again, thrust deep, and there was a snap of bone. Sawing, grinding, the motions rocked the dark-skinned creature back and forth. The world pounded as he watched every swaying motion. Forward, backward, forward, backward. Eventually, the blade would get through.

Yet somehow ... there was hatred. He knew not either one of these beings, but somehow, he grew bitter. Like he had seen something like this ... lived it. Lived it for so long it had become a part of him. But who was he? And why did he just have to watch?

*You never wanted this.*

Words not his own came to mind, though they felt familiar enough. So did the resentment ... deeper than the most distant black waters. This pain was not deserved. But it was what was known, and how could he break away so easily?

*But where ... am I? What am I feeling?*

No one came to answer, but a trickle of rage. It cried out against this fate, battered its fists against him. The thundering blow of the crystal against his ribs echoed throughout him, and he thrust his hand out. The man on the ground did the same, clasped onto the forearm of the undead. And then he gave a twist. The pale framework snapped, unleashing a brilliant radiance.

The crystal weapon fell from the gaping wound in his chest as he pulled himself up, vanishing in a puff of sparkles. Every move felt delayed, a vexing turbulence between the two. But he did not need to understand to know his purpose. The undead before the man did not retreat far, standing before him.

The arm, hovering in place despite being broken, enthralled him. Forcing his hands open, he welcomed violence as a means to an end.

"You..." the spirit spoke, "... are not worth pity."

Held up with a fractal arm, the blade was poised to dig deep with the next attack as a spell circled around it. From above, he saw the move coming, the undead's quick dart to the left. Particular footwork, a path that could only lead one way. Throwing his left arm out, he knocked the blade away and flapped his wings. The gust propelled him forward, his other hand swiping at ribs.

Returning empty-handed, the edge came down upon his left shoulder. Skin and muscle were shredded, spitting out a gush of blood. Rising on both sides like cresting waves, he quickly collapsed his hands and wings together to smother the light. As expected, the material form before him dissolved away, but they both had their tricks.

Behind his winged curtains, his feigned grab turned to cusped hands near his one opening. In a flash, the spirit appeared within his span from below, burning eyes seeking to kill. Time nearly came to a stop as he witnessed the path to execution. The crystal slipped past his right hand, though his left was already prepared. Within his palm, he grasped the glowing crystal, the conjured magic blasting outwards.

It flayed the skin from his hand and arm, pushing upon his wings, but even then his feet did not waver. Without hesitation he clasped down further, the sting and burning agony of every move only a motivator. There was a tug against his unyielding grasp, and a wisp of a spell conjured too late. A puff of grains came forth from a crack in the crystal, an imperfection which suddenly grew.

With spite, he met the glowing eyes of the resurrected form, which finally showed fear. The whispers around them fell and faded as streaks of flashing silver light crashed through the endless sky, a herald, just as the one fragment that fell from the weapon told of dusk of destiny. In a horrifyingly shrill scream the weapon gave way, snapping in two. Bluish-white tendrils exploded outward harmlessly to all but one.

Dul blinked as he dropped the half of the accursed artifact he still held, the rapid shift in perspective no less disorienting traveling the other way. Memory began to conjoin itself, patching itself up and giving him a mild headache. He put the nonsense and questions aside, instead giving thanks for what he was.

With such twisted magic, not even the strongest human or tiquo would have stood a chance. He was able to survive the strikes long enough for his will to overcome the spell, for that was something no one could take from a demon. Until the end, they were unconquerable, unbreakable ... dead before they forgot what it was that they desired most.

Putting a hand to his chest, he felt a smear of blood, and the beat of his heart. The latter reassuring him more than anything else. As he attempted to walk to the seemingly inactive remains of Silvercry, he found himself irresistibly attracted to the weapon. Next to his boot, the three pieces sat silent, but the closer he looked, they were not completely still. Scooping up the lower half, he rotated the piece in his hands.

Nothing in Tavora had ever come close to such alien craftsmanship, and not one race here made any functional weapon from anything but metal and marrolith. The closest perhaps was apostolith, but even he knew there was a reason it was called fool's fate. No one could work it. And while he had never tried to crush any bare-handed, or even held any, he doubted they

163

were the same.

*Especially with...*

Rudely interrupting him, a crystal face glistened. It traveled deeper into the weapon, then swirled before vanishing. Faintly, it almost felt as if there was something else there- different from his weapon, but perhaps not entirely.

*... that.*

Glancing to both the other two shards and the skeleton nearby, he nodded to himself.

*Too dangerous to be left here. If one fell to such a foul curse, whatever this may be, I cannot risk another discovering it. That magic, whatever it was, surely worked upon me as well.*

Flipping the buckle of his belt open, he loosened it enough to shove the shard snuggly in before doing the same to the other. With the smallest piece tucked into his waistband, he plucked his swords up and dropped them into their loops. The left blade caught for a moment, and he shook his head. It had been a long time since he had damaged one of his tools, but it could not be helped. A material of similar hardness would always end with the same result.

*Next would be you.*

Bending at the knee, Dul placed himself next to the end of a legend. Had he not seen what the very bones before him had done, it may have felt like any other body. Yet it was unnerving. Those brave enough to talk about the unfelled had always said they could be indiscernible from the living. They could still bear their flesh, speak, remember, and know those they lived with. Tainted with madness at times, they could be unpredictable.

Even then, no matter the will that held them together, they could fall. Drop like they had in life at any moment. He held out a hand to grab Silvercry, but his hand was repelled at the last moment. He knew why his body was alight, and why he hesitated. Even if a burial was deserved, what he had gone through was no less disturbing. A tinge on the back of his neck suddenly drew him up and away, pulling his focus off into the night. A presence, one he had forgotten, was nearing the edge of the town.

*Damn!*

While most people would not come from their homes to investigate what could be an obrok in the night, his other quarry was already on alert. Slipping into the distance, Kaerex fled further and further. It was rapid, more than a march, and it was a sure thing he had not gone alone. Whether he had time to gather everyone no longer mattered. Now was the time to act if anyone was to be saved.

Burning a trail back to camp, he flung himself into the clearing. The three looked at him with wide eyes. Dul fumbled with his tongue to find where to start, switching between the three with scattered glances and thoughts fluttering by. Biting his tongue, he shut his eyes tight.

*When you cannot speak, act!*

Tearing open his pack, he pulled out a cloth and wrapped the fragments of Silvercry's blade, holding them out to Anuurae. Quizzically, she held her hands out, and he delivered the package.

"Go home," he ordered, pointing a finger out into the woods in an aimless manner.

"Eh?" Rorke let his confusion leak out.

"Dul?" Lin sputtered, tears in her eyes.

"It is done. But the others are already on the move. Go home, and seek safety," he commanded.

While the two women stood before him, completely stunned, Rorke shook his head and moved forward.

"I don't think you get it. Anuurae lives in Kressel's Charge. And you can't just dump that kind of news on Lin. Who do you expect to get her home safely? Or us? We're in enemy territory, here. And you just ... expect to leave?" the hero asked, throwing a hand out to accompany the growing frustration in his words.

With a heavy heart and balled fist, Dul forced himself to slow down.

"Do not pretend this decision is easy. I was unable to remain silent, and that is my failure. And because of that, the worst may come to pass. War is inevitable now, though ... maybe..."

His eyes came to the young woman he had saved, seeing a myriad of emotions ready to overflow.

"Lin … I've done as I promised. Whatever was in that blade, whatever power it was, I'm trusting Anuurae to deliver it to Toren's followers. I cannot keep it safe, and I hope the reward allows her to rest when all settles. The blade is broken … your father, free," Dul spoke his words as softly as he could.

All the same, she seemed ready to burst. But her new experience held her steady, and she took a few slow steps towards him. She pulled on his right arm, and he let her take the one clean limb. She squeezed his hand and wrapped around his arm, turning his chest into a furnace. Memories and sensation battled his unquenched bloodlust from battle, smearing mire and murk along a situation he knew was meant to be touching.

"I don't know what use this'll be," Anuurae piped up, "You say they're heading over now … does that mean there'll even be a home for me to go back to?" she asked him.

While it sounded like a strange question, it was delivered completely genuine.

"You must trust in Toren's followers. Even if those there now did not live through the Devastation, they have not entirely forgotten who they are. They will not fall so quickly," he assured her, but it appeared his words had no effect.

He attempted to make a move to begin his own path, but Lin did not break from him. He did not know whether to try and push her off, or to just continue on, but both thoughts felt sour. Inking lines streaked through him, tearing back at the scab of a wound that could never heal. When he had set his mother down, wounded, and watched her walk away, knowing that was the last. That whatever words that had not been spoken never would be, that all that could have been would now not be.

The changing of lives, irreversible, gut-wrenching. His whole body locked as he met her eyes again. The lies he told himself stared him in the face, tearing down every board he had ever put up. For as vile as he was, as much as he was the Great Enemy, there were those irrational enough to call him friend.

The damnation that could come with it, their own and his, was such an alluring mistress. To refuse her touch left one with longing, dreaming, wondering- not empty, but worse. Filled with lust. Even she could bring ruin to his purpose, now filling his head with thoughts to take them. To run away to the North.

He knew how to survive anywhere in Tavora and needed little comfort. But that was to forsake all he stood for, to condemn all others for his own longings. There came a twisting trepidation in him, the original dreadful tyranny. A decision had to be made. Consequence. Something that, once done, could not be undone.

And everything after, an unforgivable result of the last. Like the links of chain, bound to the previous, sealing anew with every link bent, life snaked on, but could never escape from the post struck in the ground. Reminding himself to take a breath, he glanced down to her hand in his. Without a sound, he slipped from her, grains of sand between her fingers.

In joined silence, the three stood as the enigmatic half-blood vanished with only a few drops of blood on the ground to ever speak of his presence. Rorke was the first to break away from his stare at the path Dul had taken, but even he did not have the fortitude to hide that he felt the same sinking feeling they all did. Still, living up to his reputation, he pulled his shoulders up and puffed out his chest.

"Well … this is it, then. Not where any of us imagined we'd be standing, but here we are. And … home…"

His gaze falling, Rorke lost what steam he had as he rubbed the back of his neck.

"Illeah, all of this…" he muttered under his breath.

Tucking the bag of shards in her pack, Anuurae shrugged and shook her head.

"We might as well get on with it," she muttered before tightening down the straps over her shoulders, "It wasn't bad advice … I don't know what home I'll have to return to, but it's better than waiting here for someone to pull my feathers."

Making her way to the edge of the camp, she pulled her hood up.

"Since I'm comfortable traveling alone, I'd best leave you two be. If they catch you without me, they might just believe you're travelers and let you pass."

Hopping up onto a fallen log, Anuurae took one last pause.

"Rorke ... this isn't a matter of tiny victories or pride. Don't get her killed,"

Anuurae's tone told her it was as much of a warning as it was a way of asking him to make a promise. Left with that parting message, Rorke seemed receptive of it, his long look unusually grim. With just the two of them left, Lin looked to him for answers. Rorke caught on with a glance and began to rub his knuckles.

"She's right. Has been from the beginning. But I don't intend to die when I have a job to do." Hardening his resolve, Rorke looked to her with a firm renewal. "I'm getting us out of here. Right to Kressel's Charge."

Despite the throb in her chest and fiery face, she still cocked her brows at him.

"I know what he said. It's not your home. But there's one thing they got wrong- war won't just be coming to one city. Kressel's Charge is closer, and home to people that are ... more reliable than me. If there's anywhere I can keep that promise, it's there, by delivering you to the Children of the Star..."

Taking his own pack up, Rorke swung it on and looked up to the sky.

"I hope it doesn't ... but if the worst comes to be, leave me this time."

# Chapter Eleven: Watcher's Vigilance

*Careless.*

The carnage at his feet had not deterred him from taking the most direct path to Kaerex, which was no longer optimal. For the shortest distance did not mean the least difficulty, or that it was free of obstacles. His nose had not sifted through the forest's scents, nor was his mind focused to key him in on the subtle signs of a disastrous encounter.

An eyelid cleared dust from the yellow-gold sclera it protected, unable to smear away the convicting glare underneath. Even if his face was obscured by his helmet, no matter how terrible he was with understanding emotion, he needed no great sense to comprehend his foe. The heavy mace sparked and hissed as smeared flesh sizzled along the enchanted surface of the core, pulsing with the power of light magic.

Knuckles popped as Shajhu tightened down his grip, turning away from his pulverized prey. No matter their inhuman strength, the torn bits of cloth and meat had stood no chance before such a beast. The tiquo made no sound as he flicked his tail back and forth, studying him from beyond his armor.

Dul remained completely still, making no effort to shift and ease the draw of his blades. After all, the black plates of Fynor's Blood adorning the mysterious warrior would not yield to him. All there was between them now was an invisible feud, two old foes clashing once more. Each blink, every breath, any miniscule twitch- each one sought even the slightest withdrawal or weakness.

Shajhu placed his feet perpendicular with his stance, taking an aggressive and fearless initiative. His posture with his shoulders, however, was too low to be ready. It appeared he wished for a show before beginning. However, Dul broke away for a moment, seeing the smoke rise in the distance. Not too long, and he knew he would smell it. Biting down, he looked back at Shajhu.

*There will be no escape. He has your scent, and will never cease, not from here, not to the cliffs of the North. But you can't stop! The longer you are here, the more that die!*

Balling up his own hands, he brought forth a tool that seldom saw use as the first play of a fight: "You speak our tongue, do you not?!" Dul barked at the tiquo, whose eyes narrowed as he spoke.

It was enough of an answer.

"I know you," Dul rapidly followed up, keeping his foe at bay.

"I have since the beginning. I was there when you broke free and marched along back to the war camps. I was there to hear your name spoken, Shajhu. To see you fight until the hooks in your flesh rusted away. I know what you think of me. I have no interest in-"

The great mace thrust headfirst towards him, casting a shower of white, glowing embers on the muddy floor.

"Cease your words," the tiquo fiercely commanded, the depth of his voice coiled with an intriguing accent.

"My hands have not clawed; my feet have not rested for centuries for me to learn that the defilers may speak."

Taking his weapon back in both hands, the juggernaut before him loosened his shoulders, ready if the need came to swing.

"I care not," Shajhu once more solidified his position as an unwavering bulwark.

As the magical embers darkened between them, his skin began to itch. The ripples of such magic so close to him was enough to unsettle his cursed body. As if dragged back by an overbearing force, his toes scraped the soles inside his boots, curling as he fought to stay still. With one final breath in, the world seemed to pause for just the two.

The thread stretched, the watch of both blue and gold seeing it fail. Tension rose as the cruelty of the world once more sat in. All that he had warned the others of, that which he spent decades avoiding, all the rules he had broken, converging to make this unsavory mess. Shajhu's goliath feet dug in as Dul's eyes caught on to the path he would take.

The tiquo hurled himself forward as Dul bent at the knee. The dark mace passed beneath him with a quick hop, yet the hands guiding it were not set upon one track. Keeping his momentum, the great tiquo warrior continued to whirl his weapon for a second strike. Dul's grasp shot to a branch above, and a swift yank propelled him higher. More charged sparks burst forth in the mace's passing, dotting the land beneath him.

Shajhu grunted, catching and switching the trajectory of his weapon swiftly. With a kick to the trunk, Dul sent himself flying over his foe. Where he was just perched, the wood snapped and burst, shattered like pottery before such a force. Without relenting, Shajhu advanced, this time leading with favor to a pommel jab. Bending his body around it at the last second, the sparse hairs of Dul's chest nipped at his enemy's pauldron.

With such closeness in his passing, Dul focused his eyes for weakness. Going under a rather admirable one-handed swing from Shajhu, he shot back up after, a blade of grass unable to be cut. Again, he peered above the collar of the alien breastplate.

*Cloth.*

A downward strike led him to leap back as cool, moist dirt splattered on his stomach and arms.

*Chain.*

Armor most certainly had universal principles between the races- after all, it was designed for the very same purpose. Straightening his stance, Dul refused to let the pressure earn a reaction from him.

*There must be a weakness!*

His mind began to tear at memories from long ago, back from the war. An inventory of all the savage ways he had to kill. Demonbone, while above most human metals in hardness and ability, still had limitation of form. He wielded swords, weapons not designed for piercing armor. He could ineloquently cleave steel by means of might, yet he now faced that which

171

stood unflinching against him. That which turned away claw, tooth, and limb, a ward his kind had never broken, if anyone ever had.

Leaning back, he felt the scorching warmth of the guiding light from another relentless swing. His pectorals blistered just from the close passing, reminding him that a mind not focused on battle was not keen to survive it. Stepping on the sparking embers, Dul hopped back, shaking his head.

The blood of the Aspect of Death was something no man had ever shaped. Not simply harder, but far more so and not even brittle. It would not break, bend, scratch- as death was, beyond the harm of paltry mortal hands. And for that reason, the plates would stand eternal, bound to the wearer by chain links of the very same metal.

But not every part of the user could be coated in armor. That was a fact- just as it was that he had seen such muddy, earthen looking cloth long ago. Layers and layers of fiber from the land beyond the Gate, which stood against the most unruly of claws. Neither his hands nor blades would suffice as they were.

*That leaves one option to take him down.*

Taking a deep breath in as his foe paced, Dul placed a palm over the burns on his chest. Like a hot iron upon his very soul, the scorching, feverish sensation peeled back his lips as an uncommon anguish took over. His nails dug in, popping the bulb of skin as fluid leaked between his fingers. If it was only for a single beat, all of his body tightened, Alshivex offering him the very solution he required. And for once, it was truth that his curse spoke to him.

Without it, he would never topple this obstacle. But truth was not so pure that it could not hide lies. After all, what was victory? To stomp out this life, and lose his control so that countless others would fall? To be held here was defeat, no different from becoming what he despised. Slivers of perdition struck his veins as the shadowed hand of a woman reached to him from behind jagged bars, a phantom of one that could not be saved. They wailed and wept, tears the world had long since been blind to.

With one hand trembling at his side, the other further grinding against his scorched flesh, he faded back to his old room. And there it was, his old door, barred by his own hands. Yet on both sides, were they not here in the same home, the same people, fighting for the same cause?

The impact of heavy footfalls whisked away the trance and drew Dul to the one charging him. In a surge of rage, he blindly sought to meet the attack, his wings tucking in as his arms swelled. The great mace came from high as he ducked in, clamping onto the textured handle. He fought the mighty blow, digging into the soft earth to push back. The sting of arcane light falling upon his left arm only bolstered his own conviction until he wrested a standstill between them.

"What respite does one need from words?" Dul growled at the tiquo.

"What fear you, Shajhu?" he huffed fiercely.

Mustering a counter, Shajhu shoved outwards. Disallowing the opportunity to slip from him, Dul kept steady. Even as holes burned down to his bones, pocking him deeper than the southern sands in a rainstorm, he did not yield. Then his foe realized the difference in height and began to lift. As his feet left the ground, Dul used a gust from his wings to aid his retreat. Shajhu stood still, eying him curiously, trying to uncover some ploy only he could imagine. Holding up his scorched arm, Dul made a fist.

"You ... see far less than I," Dul spat through clenched teeth.

Pointing his wounded appendage to the bodies, then trailing it to the direction the city lay, blood dripped from his elbow.

"Is this your will?!" he yelled out, his voice echoing into the woods.

His words provoked action as the tiquo barreled towards him, unleashing an upward strike he easily side-stepped. The mace came for his head, but Dul dropped at the knee. Flung in a curtain, a shower of embers lit up his back as the weapon sailed above him. While his balance was offset by the weight of such a tool, Dul dove up and hammered his shoulder into the stomach of the warrior. Shajhu stumbled back, keeping a clear and bitter focus on the demon before him. The tiquo assumed a defensive stance as Dul stood and let his wings relax, the webbing between them now tattered with holes.

"You see them as I do. You have to know what is coming. So is it purposeful ignorance, or have you convinced yourself this is right?" Dul once more asked, thankful for the calm the light gave him.

The more punishment, the weaker the pull of his power was. And as he stood defiant, his mind grew clearer.

"The deceiver's word is the poison which taints the water of the foolish tribe."

Shajhu presented his words as a mantra, with such confidence in his voice that it was as if he carried the decree of Tavora itself. Snapping his weeping hand to the dead followers of Orobrex, Dul glared at Shajhu.

"The fire you start now will be fueled by far more bodies," Dul spat out his words.

"Far less than your kind left in one day," Shajhu countered.

Cradling his injured arm, Dul shook his head.

"We ask not how many we leave behind, but how many will be left standing to remember," he recited the words from long ago steadily, straight from the mouth of one who now cast his shadow back over the tiquo. Shajhu froze before him, the illusion of any lie now gone.

"They are who you fight for. Those not yet given a name, but will know yours. Sons. Daughters. They are our legacy, and without them, what would we be?"

Taking a slight pause, Dul nodded.

"Nothing. Even across the land, the tiquo know this to be true," Dul left his quote there, having borrowed enough. "Kressel was a man few could match. Or tiquo, as your leaders proved then, and you once more affirm now. Follow your decree to the letter, no matter the cost. You remember, don't you? If not for that day, your ancients would have led a foolish assault into the southern front to chase a retreating foe … ignoring the reports of another horde just out of sight. Many would have paid for such arrogance."

With those words Dul took note of some of the slack that went into his opponent's grip.

"How long?" Shajhu spoke, his tone indicating it was more of a demand than anything.

"Since the beginning, I've done the same as you," Dul spoke softly before attempting to take a step back.

A bite of surging pain went up his left leg as it failed to hold his weight, and he dropped down to his other knee. With a quick glance, he noted the holes burned in his pants. One right behind the knee, many in the calves of both legs.

"And now you have what you want, don't you?" Dul said in a hushed, solemn voice.

"What … who are you?" Shajhu asked.

"As if you would believe me," the half-blood retorted.

Placing his one good hand on the ground, Dul pushed himself up and planted his maimed leg firmly in the dirt. It protested greatly, but it had been too long since he had tasted such grounding, pure pain.

"What are you waiting for?" Dul taunted the great warrior.

"Hesitation isn't your way. Strike me down!" Dul barked.

"Then fight!" Shajhu threw his verbal punch.

"It is not mine!" Dul snarled, beating his hand against his chest. "Can you only rebuke? Does it perturb you that I relent?"

As silence fell upon both of them, the tiquo did not break his gaze. Dul kept himself as close to unwavering as he could, but the front wouldn't last much longer. Stumbling down to a knee again, Dul let his wings drape, all strength weeping from his muscles. His head drooped; he closed his eyes.

"Take heed that the Sons of Blackwood seek to cull Toren's men. Kressel's Charge will only be the first. They are desperate," Dul grumbled as he heard footsteps grow closer. "You've tied my hands, so what say you, tiquo?"

Dragging his head up, he stared at the titanic warrior from the dirt. A shadow from a creature twice the height of man, the executioner cast the surety of the end upon him. Slit yellow eyes hidden underneath the decorative plate helm said nothing more, the expression of man entirely absent from the coarse canvas. Intuition said there was a chance he was thinking the same as him. Yet there was no such guarantee. Law was law to the tiquo. They had killed more than a few people for disagreements or petty thievery.

"A demon that speaks … still a demon," Shajhu remarked, his heavy implement in hand.

175

"Then do what must be done," Dul grasped a handful of soil as he wore a slate expression.

The reach was perfect. One strike to his head, and it would be over. Yet … the mace remained where it was.

"Undo the damage you have done. Go to the city. Seek the one they call Kaerex, kill him … stop the Sons, and this senseless war," Dul spoke flatly.

"I have your scent, demon," Shajhu fiercely remarked before placing his mace on his shoulder. "I did not forget Kressel. I do not forgive my mistakes. You are not beyond my judgement, and I do not leave this lightly. You will answer when I call, by sun or moon."

The tiquo turned as he spoke, looking off to the West.

Abnormal was not a word for it. Thousands had fallen before him, under many skies, harrowed by the name Shajhu. There were many forms the Great Enemy took. But none had ever spoken the language of man. If it read minds, then it should have spoken in the language of his kin, if it wished to truly unsettle him. Yet it already had, crafting both tools and clothes out of the remnants of its own kind and refusing to even draw its blades.

Such a thing knew much, considered threats, had a world view. Not a simple being, not even as blunt as the leaders of the demonic packs he had fought. The closest he knew were perhaps the ones that had ordered him to be strung up, but that did not answer for the lack of savagery or violence. And to think such a thing was not self-interested, but working with them during the war … it was no traitor. No bad egg from the clutch. It even smelled different.

Which begged the question of how it had evaded him for so long. Not a single trail, clearly not a pattern of killing by any means. And … he had left it behind. It had not only spoken, but done so with fair artistry. It knew he had been tracking the humans from the dark woods, playing to his own knowledge. Their harassment of his kind had not gone unnoticed.

Out of the other fifteen sentinels, six had to retreat beyond the Gate of the Star back home to recover from their injuries. Blotting out the eyes of his people was certainly a sign of ill portents, and something he would not allow. He had suspected play with foul sorcery from the beginning, and now with such a thing opposing the prey he sought ... he could not be wrong.

It was bitter, all of it. Having to leave a demon behind, but if it spoke only truth, then time would be of the essence. With the many flicks of his tongue, he had recorded the identity of the dark-skinned one, and that problem could be solved later. Now it was time to go to the core of all this struggle and find the missing pieces.

Amid his thoughts, Shajhu's eyes snapped ahead to the copper tinge his nostrils sensed. More of Toren's own sat on the ground, another skirmish with the defenders once more losing. Having finished sacking the supplies, more men bearing the scent of the tainted land emerged to greet him. Letting his mace roll off his shoulder, Shajhu placed his other hand at the ready.

Through his limbs, he let his soul cascade into his righteous destroyer, the embers of Nacotz bursting to life from the sacred core. One of the robed ones shouted and called to his approach, but it was only the cries of dead men. Shields down, polearms were laid out as men took a knee and braced.

Like fruit under the foot of an ogre, their line was crushed as he barreled through shoulder first. Bringing his mace up, he made brutal contact with the robed man. The crackle and pop of bones brought with it a splash of blood until the corpse freed itself from his mace, flying back and crumpling in the dirt.

A barrage of arrows then assailed him, shafts snapping and others flying astray in an almost humorous test of his armor. With a backward swing, three more were dispatched in a shower of fluid and sparks. Others danced back as they tried to brush the burning fragments from their leathers, but the bravest among them was the one charging him from behind. Turning his tail to the side, the fool did not relent. With a solid slap, he heard the crack of ribs.

It never ceased to amaze him how something like a human could survive this world. They had not been shaped by the carnal world of Tiquatzek's humid jungles, and then Tavora left humans behind, so ... fragile. As the survivors began to realize the odds they had in this scuffle, they backed off, letting his racing mind put together different possibilities.

To do anything with demonic magic, one required sacrifice. War would bring it, a veiled disguise for some hidden power.

*But what can hide from Nacotz?*

Another robed man charged him, which he beat across the face with the back of his hand. The strike sent the man recoiling back, nearly spinning on his feet. His foe's body twitched and rumbled, pink energies pulsing around his twin axes. The human spat out a finely mixed glob of bloody shattered teeth, then returned him a maddened face. The crimson dashes from nostril, eye, and cheek did little to disguise the insanity in its midst. Without a care, the animal sought to match him with a leap. Raising his mace, Shajhu flattened the ignorant spawn in the mud.

*Beyond the stink of the lands the Great Enemy still taints, they are not the ones. So, who? What could orchestrate this? What would pit a demon against his own? It ... it cannot be a human. This stench, it itches my nose. All this wrongness, it flares my spines.*

To re-affirm that, all along his back his spines once more pressed against the fabric wrapping. Letting out a hiss, he tried to combat his anger. A true hatchling under Nacotz had no use for such a thing. Such respect for culture is what kept his people unified, unlike man. It did not take long after the Devastation for their fickle minds to bicker and squabble, fracturing them and threatening their race with war ... again.

Such is why he had this task. Of all his people, only he was trusted to prevent the Great Enemy from returning at any cost. All others, even the Majnuetlan, had placed him above for this very duty. And this trust ... it was something he would not betray. For it was not just for their homeland, not for the Sih, not for Tiquatzek, not for the tiquo. His was a vow to the world itself, that such a plague could never again threaten to consume all that was!

As the remaining soldiers routed, Shajhu slowly waltzed down the rough path that was called a road by the locals. The curved nails of his feet dug into exposed roots as his agitation surged. Was it because he had become lax in his duty that this had come to pass?

*After all ... a demon knows more than you.*

His right hand became deathly tight around the shaft of his weapon.

Deeper within his knowledge of the current human climate, he was near certain there was an answer. Something he misunderstood. Someone he didn't entirely examine. In the North there were the greatly secretive followers of fire, who served under the ideals they created around one woman.

Alyra, an icon of love, and the one who had apparently freed all of man from the Piraph by stealing their arcane ways. They played a small part during the Piraph Devastation, but even then, they were no less fanatical than now. They had refused his requests to enter their capital city, and recently taken on a new leader. He had met the man once- Irathael Bloodbrand.

Closing his eyes, Shajhu disregarded him. The gathering of people were strange, but their values were no front. Irathael alone was proof of that, even if he kept a fair deal of his intentions secret. Behind that mask, he had held his ground, one of the few humans he had ever attempted to coerce and felt a considerable pushback. Such conviction was a sign of purity, and their faction was all but currently absent with their deal with the ogres of the so-called Beastlands.

And that left three, or rather two. Toren's followers were the defenders here, and though they were not as skilled as any Natlik he could pull from his own ranks, they performed a similar role as he. Sadly, they were weakened now, and he had to admit, it was an optimal time to attack. The isolated homeland of the humans could have been suspect, but he hadn't sensed a trace of taint there ... despite that, the one puppeteering this had to be there, or in Mordiv's Hold.

His eyes flashing ahead, it finally hit him.

*You failed to find one. There could be two.*

Now he could see it. The Hold and its desperate people made the perfect distraction and tool. War brought the needed blood. And behind it all, tucked away in the heart of the human race, disguised in the Lesal Bastion itself, the orchestrator. It all presented itself as too perfect. After all, the "Sons of Blackwood" as the demon had called it, made sure the heartland was cut off from the very bringers of light that could uncover such a hidden fleck of rot.

*So, to stop this ... I must once more follow the words of that man.*

Kressel, timeless in his wisdom, was one he could never forget, or escape. However the demon had heard that speech, managed to get so close to their armies ... a story he must hear. The human commander was the only one the Majnuetlan had ever listened to, and for good reason. Without him, humanity would have hardly stood on their own two feet during the war.

Pulling his helmet down and tightening the strap, Shajhu barreled toward Kressel's Charge, unwilling to rest even as the light of day faded around him and rose once more. And as the trees thinned, clearing out, he smelled it in the new morning. Battle. It could even be heard, echoes of men shouting and metal against metal.

Breaking out into the open, he trampled through a farmland fence as he sat eyes upon the great walls. Long ago, he had been in this very place and stood among the ranks as lightning flashed above and horrors untold battered against the thousands of men and women that stood with them. And now, once more, smoke billowed from its buildings, and corpses dotted the ramp that led upward.

Yet never ... never had the barrier-city been struck from within. Panning around, he took note of how untouched the land around was. None of the crops stomped down, burned, the conflict was isolated. Taking his steps slowly, he gazed at the wood and straw buildings the workers lived in. A few frightened eyes watched him from cracked doors, some of which shut with hushed whispers as he marched by.

Rounding a corner, a gathering of men grumbled and pointed, many of which hoisted crude weapons or tools in their hands. Some had even mustered a piece or two of old armor, but this was no fighting group. Still, they could be useful. His approach was met with the men scrambling, going wide eyed, but he was certain they were familiar with him in his treks through here in the years past.

"When did the fighting start?" Shajhu asked calmly.

The farmers looked at one another, as if trying to decide who was to speak for them. Their lack of leadership was more apparent when one of the younger among them took a few steps forward, a wood splitting axe in hand.

"The guard left not long ago. Things were burning out in the woods yesterday ... I saw some leave to check on it."

The boy presented himself at the head, shrugging off the hand of what was likely his father grabbing at his shoulder as he came closer.

*Traps.*

"Have there been any strangers here?" Shajhu inquired again.

The boy shook his head.

"Quiet. But up there..." the boy rasped the last bit out, swallowing hard as he took a glance.

A few of the men chattered and shared his sentiment in the back.

"Stay here. Tell everyone, including the soldiers, to stay out of the woods," he ordered, setting his path for the city entrance.

With every step he stretched and rolled another muscle, keeping himself limber. He cast aside the thought of how much his armor weighed upon him, and how little rest he had gotten lately. His watch was reason enough to continue on. From below, he gazed upon the towering stone walls, seeing moving shadows scrambling about. Eyes were upon him, but such was to be expected.

The closer he got, the more he could see, yet so far it was unclear if it was friend or foe. It appeared to be pure chaos, as the glint of polished armor ahead told him that survivors of ambushes or attacks were still struggling to re-group or strike where they could. As he came up to the ramp, he took note of the many bows being drawn at him from above. He squinted to the guards, wondering for a moment if they had been compromised from within.

But without a release of arrows, it appeared it may have just been nerves. As he finished the long walk up, he noted that the shields of the guards pointed inward to the city, not out. Crude wood barricades had been fashioned from scrap, barrels, and crates, making the situation look even more desperate. A woman quickly approached him, a silver sword and shield stitched on the sleeve of her shirt.

"Hold, tiquo!" she firmly ordered, a shortsword thrusted in his direction.

Even with what she had mustered, he could see the bloodied cloth under her helmet and weary lines on her youthful face.

"Light-Captain, report," he ordered, disregarding her order entirely.

The formal address caught her off-guard, as did his refusal to stop until he was bearing down upon her.

"Eh..." she squeaked.

Just as he had heard at the training yards countless times, he repeated with more force: "Report!"

The combination of shock and hammering routine struck finely, as she blinked and shook her head.

"We've been isolated from contact with other patrol groups, and I'm down to seventy-three men. I don't have the strength to push in, or spare anyone to send out. I've taken a position here to prevent enemy runners from leaving, sir," she released her words.

"Where is your commanding officer?" Shajhu pressed.

"That'd be me now, sir." The woman barely managed to speak her words steadily.

Glancing into the city street, he had but one more question he needed to ask: "Where are the Silver Commanders?"

The Light-Captain shook her head.

"They were supposed to meet at the First Chapel. I don't know if they made it. No one's brought news."

Shajhu nodded, knowing every step forward would be reactive from this point on.

"Hold here, and gather any men you can. The enemy waits in the woods. There will be no retreat," he ordered before stomping forward upon the stone bricks.

Glass crackled on his entrance as he found the empty structures around him looming in. To his left he could see a pale hand poking out from wooden rubble, to his right an old structure seemed untouched. Flicking his tongue out under his helm, he sampled the battlefield. Dust, ash, and death came in three courses, but to tell the freshness of each kill was impossible. It was everywhere- an overload that caused him to shut his mouth.

Coming to the first intersection, he slowed his pace before entering the sacred site. An abandoned cart sat by its lonesome, not a single sign of a struggle nearby. Shajhu blinked, remembering just how many battles had taken place right where he was. Not once had the humans lost, or even come close to breaking when the Great Enemy had made it this far.

His veins felt cold, his limbs heavy as the words of the demon weighed heavier. His skin itched again, but he had already shed the week prior.

*What men could do this?*

Taking the path right, urgency pushed him on, just to see a barricade laid out. Men in black cloth took quick notice of him and notched their arrows as a commander barked orders to those around him. Shajhu kept up his march as arrows splintered upon his sky-fallen plate, and yet his foe was not deterred from stringing up a second volley. Before they could finish, a dark blur flew over the makeshift wall and came to stand before him.

The pale-skinned brute hefted a two-handed axe that still dripped from a fresh kill. He expressed his individuality from the rest of his kin by scratching a spare hand at the left side of what remained of his face, while the other remained a firm scowl.

"Orobrex be praised," the man remarked with a voice that could have been no more pleasant than thorny undergarments. "Come, brothers, sisters. Kaerex has brought us here to find our purpose again."

Shajhu stopped as the man held his hands out to his sides, summoning forth his kind to crawl from the wreckage. They collected around the man like a priest, and perhaps he was. The robed ones were clearly not demonic, even less tainted than those of the dark woods, but now it was clear that Orobrex was not just a man. It was difficult to tell with humans, and their strangeness about their aspects and magic.

But as an entire line of cultists gathered, it seemed much more plausible that he had greatly underestimated that which his mace crushed in one blow all the same. Swirling his head around, the scarred mass on the left side of the man's head beat with red splotches.

"Feel the river of change. How it carries you, Children of Madness," holding his axe high, the man summoned red mist around his axe. "Bring nourishment. Let me see the yellow of daisies sprout from the skull of this offering."

The crimson magic coalesced for a moment, then burst, the wave sending his host into motion. Without fear, Shajhu watched them dash and sprint, mere steel sent to stop him. Yet unlike before, the robed ones scattered, some slipping to the side to surround him. He watched left as one of the thinner of the bunch slipped a greenish dagger from a fold, which he immediately recognized as a human-made malarite alloy.

*The little one thinks he can puncture stone with his stinger.*

Winding up his mace for a swing as the swarm coiled tighter around him, the crunch of shattered glass drew Shajhu straight ahead. He shifted and thrust the shaft of his weapon out in a thunderous collision. Dust kicked up around them as the dull edge of the priest's axe ground and rattled, indented by the force of contact. The one-eyed mass gleamed at him, rough lips no longer concealing the jagged, pink teeth of a carnivore.

Yet such an attack was never meant to harm him. It was only the call of a pack hunter. Shoving the foe back, Shajhu turned and braced, his weapon held high, his feet perpendicular to one another. A warhammer smashed into his bracer, and paltry puffs of air came from his woven folds as sword and axe hopelessly dragged along. But his ears heard the patter- muffled, wrapped human feet carefully obscured among the cacophony.

Turning his grip, he brought his mace back in a swing from below. There was an insignificant bump from contact, though he knew not what he struck, until he hurled the body into the air as his strike finished. Without pause, he returned to a stable stance, the malarite dagger falling down before the assassin. Flopping upon the bricks, folded at the midsection, the corpse did not even twitch. Still, his company did not even flinch to look upon him.

Banging the pommel of his axe against the ground, the grizzly leader beckoned forth more of his magics: "Bathe yourselves in his word!"

As more energy pulsed from the congregation, Shajhu flicked his tongue. He fixated upon their pattern, tracked those that shifted behind the frontline in careless moves.

*They mean to hunt like this? Tiquatzek would devour them before dusk.*

As the third cultist on his right took a step forward, Shajhu widened his feet and lowered the angle of his mace. As the dance began, he swung left, away from the one drawing his attention. He caught the woman behind him mid charge, sweeping her aside in a juicy crunch before carrying his weapon overhead.

The high swipe obliterated a skull before it as he coursed life into the relic in his weapon, the curtain around him like a wall of glittering scales. In that same motion, Shajhu broke the offensive strike of the next man, catching his breast with a tail strike, throwing the pest away. Transferring the sky-fallen metal to one hand, he swept wide with titanic force, the extended reach culling down four, leaving but one standing as he slapped the handle of his mace back into both hands.

Planting the pommel, his weapon cracked the stone brick underneath, displaying the relativity of its weight. It seemed even the most faithful among them finally understood the difference between them as they backed up towards the barricade. As he stood watching, those with sense behind the priest fled their post. The flesh on the left side of the man's face twitched, old muscles trying to express something upon the mutilated cheek.

Shajhu began his advance with slow, heavy steps. His mace rested again in both hands, and with it he felt holy fervor. This was true and pure deliverance. Passing by an overturned cart and into the hasty fortification, the robed leader charged him. With a half-hearted swing, he battered the man away, sending him tumbling down the road. Shajhu watched as the man held his ruined body up for a moment with his right hand, which still grasped the broken handle of his axe.

His single eye was a wildfire of fury, pitiful for what he was. With one arm bent and limp, unable to stand, he would be nothing but a meal for scavengers. Tilting his ear, Shajhu ignored the man as he listened in on what sounded like the start of another conflict nearby. That presented him with a choice- seek out the leaders and find answers for his own quest, or to become the one these people needed.

# Chapter Twelve: One More Drop

Dul's boot shuffled through the leaves as he caught himself on a low branch. He pushed off, staggering to the next trunk. His palm smeared against the bark as he heaved, noting the distance to the next tree to be more substantial than any before. Even with his vision blurring, it wasn't hard to tell this was a challenge he had to be careful about. Leaning his weight further into his current support, he closed his eyes and shoved with both arms. His wobbling legs managed to carry him forward twice, almost three times, until he felt himself falling forward. He held out his good arm, swiping, but catching nothing.

The impact against the forest floor was barely cushioned, but he was thankful he had not hit his head. Digging his hand into the soil, he pulled himself forward, half-kicking with his better leg. Coming closer, he slapped his palm into the next trunk, grinding his nails into it as he fought to pull his weight up. His chest lifted from the moist forest floor until a surge through his back to his left foot dropped him flat. Grunting, panting, he thought of what a pathetic mess he had made for the sake of his own stubbornness and curiosity.

It was second nature for him to abuse his wretched ability to recover from wounds, but he had also never experienced such potent light magic. Though he should have seen enough to know that his kind shouldn't chance it. Especially from a tiquo, since from what he could tell, it was their race's specialty to wield that magic. Nearly all of them had to some degree in the war. Biting down, he grabbed at the tree again and clawed his way up. One pull, a tug, his chest was up again.

Slinging his mutilated arm around, he forced his fingers closed. The back of his hand dripped as his palm slid, slick with his own life. Despite the tearing sensation in his elbow, he committed, successfully getting his waist up. Sliding his knee in, the stress forced him to take a breath to relieve the building pressure. Such was enough that he began to topple, catching himself on his rear. Blinking once, his eyes opened to see what he had left himself to work with. Legs full of burned holes, arms pocked like a tree full of termites, wings tattered as if stripped by the claws of a pack of magsies.

All refusing to seal.

Closing his eyes, he knew what had to be done. Without a single delay, he slipped a sword from its loop and cut the straps of his pack free. Leaning in, he opened his eyes and sat the sword on the side of his leg, wrapping the leather around low and high. Tying clean knots, he braced for a second before jerking the first one tight. It brought forth a long exhale, but as he gripped the second, he would be ready.

The slick "fwip" clamped down on the improvised splint and stabilizer, holding the first step in place. The second step brought his pack around, where he flipped it open and pulled forth every cloth he had. Tugging his second blade out, he placed the handle between his thighs and worked out several strips. Dul wrapped them around his arms and legs until the supply went dry, making sure the fit was more than snug up close to the joint of limb and torso. While it was unlikely he could completely stop the bleeding, limiting it would still offer some benefit.

Cutting up the rest of his pack, all that remained was a mediocre patch kit that he had possibly used once to clean up a tear in his pants. But as he popped open the box and looked over the contents, what he had would possibly cover a hole or two out of the sixty, maybe seventy new ones. Setting the box aside, Dul closed his eyes and leaned back.

*You're still not close to the city. And how do you expect to fight like this? Unable to even stand?*

There were a thousand ways he could berate himself. Should he start at the fact he had embraced his curse and fought with hardly a care for so long?

This was punishment for that.

*Or was it saving that girl?*

His hands tightened into loose fists. Truly, it wasn't all her fault. He had been watching her, curious about why she made so much noise when traveling. That had by happenstance brought one of his kin to him, who was then attracted to her.

*Doesn't that mean it was my fault all along?*

What did it mean to save someone from a mortal threat that you yourself created? Dul let his head go slack against the bark, his horns scraping into it. No, all of this was from selfishness. Never could he escape his own damned desires.

*"She was too young to die."* Part of him had said.

Another part just wanted to do right. But those reasons were all too impotent compared to the truth he had to acknowledge. He'd seen so many lives pass over so many decades that it wouldn't bother him for long. But this one reminded him of his mother. Made his flesh quiver to rise and protect. And yet, he had then made them a part of his world. Brought them strife. Sullied her innocence by showing her carnage, and his vile self.

*But she was kind. She needed and deserved your help. If you did nothing, she would have died.*

**Isn't that the problem?**

*One life is all she has to live. Do you even have the right to choose for her?*

The words spat out from the darker depths of his mind.

*Silvercry was a distraction. You could have discovered this without her or him, and cut the heads of the beast before it awoke.*

His entire body hardened like stone.

*Without killing, you have no purpose. You're nothing but the tortured creature they see you for. If you fail, what separates you from the rest?*

**Why should they see you any differently?**

The voice grew louder as he dragged his knuckles in the dirt.

**What would you be?**

In a rage, Dul howled as he threw his weight forward. Thrashing his arms, spreading his wings, blue lines coursed through from his chest outward. His feet stumbled forward to catch his weight, the tip of his blade digging in aside his boot. Throwing his right leg in front, he picked up momentum. Slinging the mass of his left arm and leg ahead, he was faster.

*Mother, why do you love me?*

Gritting his teeth, he hardened his pace to a cadence.

*You're my son. That's the only reason a mother should need.*

The blotches of the bandages stopped growing as he covered ground.

*But...*

Flapping his wings, he broke into a sprint.

*But? I don't see a way around it, Darius. You're my son, and don't let anyone else tell you otherwise. And that means it's my job to ensure you're safe and happy.*

Hearing his old name warmed his whole body.

*It's all I could want for you. Tavora may try to say something else, but you're strong. Strong enough that you can move the mountains before you.*

Tearing through the foliage, Dul flew onto the open trail. Angling his weight and wings forward, he propelled himself at full speed.

*Long ago, it was his light that showed us the way back home after Alyra gave us inspiration. But why did we walk from our cages? Why did mothers and fathers place their lives down, risk their children to return to a world they barely knew? I ask you, this night, brave warriors. What venture do we undertake? Her story ended as she held her lover that was her world, and burned all to blackened dust before her rather than kneel in chains. Many see it as just an act of defiance. A fight for oneself.*

*Do you see such an act so simply? To the unknown she went, ready to cast all of the world aside! The first to do so, for her love! She overcame all! That is the strength in will, to turn passion to purpose! From the heart, man becomes more than what we are! We look to our sky above, stand upon our soil and stone, with Toren's guidance at heel! It is our bravery against that which will come that wrings a future from nought, taking from the oblivion that wishes to overtake all Tavora! Stand with me as the Great Enemy comes in force this day, knowing both why we stand and why we fall! For those that must be taken from us will not know the end of their reach, as we will not be overcome! Your blade strikes in their memory, brothers!*

Kressel's voice once more boomed in his skull. Standing on the balcony of his chapel, thousands before him, every speech he gave failed to lose its power to this day, even if he were one of the few to remember them. The blend of earthen greens and browns streaked as Dul threw himself towards destiny, but he couldn't stop the flood in his mind. The waves sloshed and pulled, unburying and disturbing older and older sites. And then came a more recent strand, further compounding his aching limbs.

*She can barely hold that sword.*

It was about all he could think of when she tried to impress him. As persistent as she was, Lin was but a young chick in the nest, not ready to leave. He could not bring himself to berate her, such was her birth that she belonged to Illeah's kinder side. But with that fervor of hers, she had persevered at his side until he succumbed to her wish.

*Traversing the woods is not a matter of speed. How far can you see? What aren't you seeing? There are many that see you. And that is the danger of this place. You must stop, listen, smell, track. The one who rules this place is the one you will never see.*

With a point up, he had shown her the orcots above them in the canopy. A jolt of fear, just from seeing a group of the small, furred predator, had shown him enough to know how much work he had ahead of him. But she had become a fair swordswoman, stronger, and bolder at his side.

*And that's why she'll survive.*

Like a shard of glass jammed into his knee, the sting of the wound was sleek and acute. Dul bit down as he stumbled. A bandage became heavier as a fresh flow of blood dampened it, and he closed his eyes. Letting out a staggered breath, he dragged his leg along in a slothful, long arc.

*But you trusted him. Left her with such a man in that place.*

His treads slapped into the bed of leaves underneath him as his pace slowed, and he felt his body tremble. Swaying like grass in the wind, his balance gave. Crashing his shoulder roughly into a tree trunk, an involuntary anguished gasp escaped his lips.

*I won't accept this.*

For all he had been through, every visceral battle, every lonely day in the sun, he had never once been unable. Planting his feet wide, he stared ahead at the blurry stalk in front of him.

*This ... is only the beginning. You ... won't stop now.*

Falling forward onto one knee, he slammed his good fist into the dirt. Blinking, he looked at the indentation. The imprint was shallow, as if made by just an ordinary young man. His entire body alight, he lowered himself down, prepared to drive himself back to his feet. Yet as he breathed in, it was as if he were impaled by a spear. Coughing, he collapsed onto his side. Laying there, he felt more than the usual physical and mental torment. It was as if Tavora itself was attempting to crumple him up, squash him, roll him out. It was unbearable, the crushing collapse of body, mind, and soul.

Tears came to his eyes as he shook, silently cursing himself for his zeal. Even more became clear as he closed his eyes. That when the voices of the demon blood within him were gone, he was nothing. All the confusion, the thirst, the might and conviction came from his curse. Those feelings were as much his identity as they were his burden. A company most foul ... and all he had. As the cold streaks ran down his cheeks, Dul curled up on the forest floor. Amidst the collapse of reality upon him, isolation joined the fray. Burrowing into his ribs, slithering through his throat. He had not a name to cry out for, not a hand to reach for.

*What could the world wish of me?*

Among all else, he had to wonder. It must've not been that crazy to believe he had been the subject of some ... trial. Some joke from a being of greater power. There was only one, no other like him. Not a single other demon had ever done such a thing, or perhaps even been capable. And he had been given such a long life, perfect for some twisted being to watch over him. And that ... it could be his father. Not his human one, whom he never knew, but the otherworldly one.

The one that had spoken to him twice, given him this name. Dul'Hahn. And that was all. Some semblance of connection in that Hahn signified something like a familial bond. It was enough to make him yearn, to feel in times like this, something besides the genuine hatred he bore for his kind. Enough to tie a rope around each wrist, so that others could watch him slowly be torn apart between two worlds.

*Mother ... I don't want to go.*

Like a whimper, he let a disheveled cry out from deep within. He closed his burned hand, as if to refuse the day he had let her go. But like everything else, it was to pass him by, as he could do nothing. He never could have had a life with her, nor one with any of them. It was a fate without choice. To go on. As he had kneeled in the room he grew up in so long ago, the walls around him ravaged, the roof torn open, so too would this one be ripped away.

As he had told the ostoran the truth. There was never any plan to stop. He had to defend his home- Tavora. He had to bleed so he had something to paint over the lies, to convince himself that duty was enough. Stagnation, slowing, remembering ... it brought back the self-loathing, betraying his mother's wish, his purpose. Downward, deeper, unraveling his heart and soul until he once more considered the ultimate betrayal, which only ever ended in him seeking more blood. As the pool under his side grew, any will to snivel or whimper faded, and all became a haze. Draining down into the soil, falling away, he descended into nothingness.

Eyelids crept open as he scrunched his face. Sensation sprouted like water flowing through dry canyons, bursting from the cracks. His arms trembled and his hands opened, his legs extending. A heavy, dry exhale came from deep within his chest as more than his body awakened. Stomach empty, soul deprived, the first sensation was that of hunger.

His left arm crawled into vision, sealed and coated in dried blood from wounds now forgotten. Thrusting his palms into the earth, the shower of forest leaves fell from him, returning a cool, tingling chill of early afternoon light. Some moss and dirt clung to him in a ragged cloak of filth as he stood still, gathering thoughts from his pounding skull.

*Time.*

The days could not be known, but it was more than a few from the leaves that covered him.

*Wounds.*

In a fury, he ripped his sword free of his leg, shaking his head. The mark of the star was gone. Before he could think of anything else, the wind caught up, throwing a myriad of scents into his nostrils. A sharp inhale. His lips peeled back, revealing his bared teeth.

*Food.*

Like an electric crash throughout his body, all was snapped back in place by desire.

*The fight still goes on!*

Faster than the thought could complete, his feet set themselves in motion. Vaulting over a tree, grasping onto a branch, he scattered some nearby muri and received hisses from the orcots that had been stalking them. His speed increased as he ducked down under a low branch and blazed through the brush, passing by looted corpses surrounding a cart and crates.

With one slick motion, he dove into a roll, deftly drawing his second sword before his back touched the ground. A foul shroud engulfed his weapons as he felt the tug of nearby souls, his eyes capturing the red of dyed robes as his boots propelled him up. The edge bit without loss of momentum, his dash continuing onward.

The men staggered and dropped behind him, their essences flowing into his empty vessel, a euphoria few other things could match. Yet he could not afford to linger and play with mere lookouts. Burning his trail onward, the bones in his back had already begun to shift. Kicking up and out into a clearing, he changed his route for the road, despite protest from his civil side. But caution had been forsaken months ago.

If he had to turn to the North for some time while humans and that tiquo exhausted themselves to hunt him, he would. The cold would be a fine shield against all but the most devoted, and the animals of the land undoubtably had him covered for the rest. Whatever needed done now was a worth the price. That he knew. Because the Sons of Blackwood being defeated meant that contact could be made with Lesal again. Four heads reduced to three, of which those that remained could reconcile.

This action would hopefully bring forth at least one with sense that could re-unite humanity again. Avoid disaster, like something as foolish as unnecessary conflict with a far more powerful force. Calling to his mystic cloak as his vision caught the clearing, Dul burst out into the outskirts of one of humanity's barrier-cities. Grinding to a near halt, he surveyed the destruction.

Closer to him, it seemed the most critical portion of the city was still untouched. The fields had been spared from fire, the houses pristine, the workers having assembled a militia of sorts. Creeping closer, there were rather admirable walls being erected from spare wood and metal. While they would do little to a follower of Orobrex, their effort deserved praise. And thankfully, that all meant not only could he pass by this and focus on the heart of the problem, but that the foe's plan was still predictable.

Their armies would be stretched thin. While many here did not expect to live long, the strategy their commanders came up with was still in play. Strike deep and shallow, close and far, take the land, and establish a supply line straight through. The city would provide food for those who held it and bring it back home. Sprinting up to the wall, he leaped up and thrust both blades back into their loops. With ease, his hands brought him to the top, where he put his boots on holy bricks for the first time in over a century.

Taking an alley deeper in, he peered into the streets to see an echo of the past. Bodies in the streets, doors torn open, debris and dust everywhere. Turning his gaze left, he caught a glint of a metallic reflection in an alley. The soldier tugged a mace free from his belt, nodded to someone out of sight, and shuffled closer. Down the street, a large cluster of dark clothed soldiers approached. Climbing up, Dul picked a perch on a balcony to obtain a better view. His ears picked up a few others moving about nearby.

*Ambush ... not the preferred tactic for these men and women. It must not be going well.*

As the first Son of Blackwood approached, the man pulled his arm back and readied a swing. He let the heavy head go, smashing the face of the unsuspecting soldier. Pushing in, the follower of Toren was joined from the other side by a rush from five men with spears. A group of archers emerged from hiding up high under refuse, pulling their strings tight. The enemy's frontline, now compressed in the open, received the first volley.

At the same time, a hearty war cry emerged from the rear: "By my wrath, I deliver his light!"

Brighter than any torch, white radiance flared to life in the rear as an imbuement spelled the end of this group. The Sons, split between a much more orderly execution, had not a single leader rally them. Instead, the robed followers of Orobrex burst towards the front. One quickly smashed her way through the spears in the front, another with a two-handed hammer challenging the man with his mace.

Though the shield of the righteous man lit up with some arcane assistance, it was battered aside by the heavy steel. The strike of his mace came faster than the foe could recover from, but the contact with a bicep did nothing to the man of madness. Forced back, the enemy's frontline opened up as the Sons sought cover, and to vanish into buildings to hunt the archers above. Their support scattered, Dul knew the attack now relied on whoever was behind the maneuver in the flank.

Within a few seconds, the drop of another body revealed at least one positive. Rather than polished steel, the man in emblazoned plate wore an unmistakable work of Toren's smiths. Behind the light, caught between the darkness of the ocean and the beauty of a clear sky by day, blueglory protected the man. Such an alloy was only given to their higher ranks, meaning that this fight here was not just from scraps of the more common recruits.

The two Sons of Blackwood facing them backed up as he pressed on, the beard of his axe dripping. Another broke the flank of the cult, carrying a body upward on a longspear as he strode forward. The man flung the impaled corpse away like a farmer offended by a rotten bale of hay. Behind the visor of his helmet, he fixated upon the servant of madness before him. As soon as the enemies at his side fell, the follower of Toren charged with his spear.

Though the slim and unarmored cultist was much faster at darting aside, so too did the footwork of the veteran follow in his shadow. He kept his opponent at a distance, disallowing a rapid flank with how he traced with the tip of his weapon. With a roar, the seasoned spearman maneuvered with grace, unleashing two rapid thrusts, pushing his foe even further back. A swipe denied the cultist's attempt to slip under, and with a change of grip, brought forth death. The tip of the spear buried itself in the stomach of the cultist of Orobrex, who was released, just to be finished off with a second thrust.

As the final cultist in the street went for the execution of a soldier who had now been forced to the ground, a bubble of light deflected the warhammer. Taking rapid strides up, Dul laid eyes upon a man who had seen his fair share of combat. Unwavering, he approached his fallen comrade and the foe. His greatsword in hand, he showed not a care as the cultist switched attention to him. Once the cultist entered the reach of the blade, Toren's faithful servant had already started his swing.

The greatsword, burning with light magic, cut through both arms of its target without pause. A second slash split the robes and flesh underneath open from shoulder to waist. Helping his fellow man up, the defenders gathered.

"A few managed to get away," one veteran remarked.

The leader nodded once, looking to his fallen brothers.

"Indeed, they have. But we must trust in our own to make it back to the barracks. We unfortunately have no time to care for the dead or our wounded. We must make our way to Inflector Oram and assist him in his endeavor to take out the main patrol force. Only then can we set our eyes back on the city entrance and stop any more enemy reinforcements from coming from this side."

As the light from the magical imbuement faded, the soldiers appeared to issue a silent farewell to those they would have to leave behind.

"Yes, Augur," the axe-wielder responded solemnly.

"Come, Vanguard," another veteran ordered to the infantryman at their side, who still rubbed his shield arm as blood ran from his pant leg.

Still, the brave man tried to muster what he could and stand with his superiors. As they faded away, they left him with the only information he needed for now. The Sons of Blackwood had secured the southern city entrance, and that was their lifeline to getting men in and out.

Dismounting to the street, Dul found himself submerged in a low-hanging fog of essence. It drifted towards him, pulled helplessly in by the yearning maw of his being. Lurking in this morbid shroud, he made his way through the stained streets.

Not even the bravest of scavengers dared pick at this field, wings or not. And that reason was clear as he approached the intersection ahead. Sentries in every niche, crude barricades now entrenched with soldiers lining them with polearms. Guards cut off the way through with newly gleaming tower shields. A few men of rank stood near the entrance, giving officers orders as their men stood ready. Among all of that, their savage allies lingered about, ready to commit to their martyrdom. With men carrying supplies in and out of the nearby buildings, there were likely thousands at the ready.

*They believe themselves to be secure. Let's see how they respond to an attack from within.*

A quick pounce landed him on a ledge, where a path to the roofs was revealed. Scaling a collapsed section, he slid along the destruction above the guards. Across the street, his eyes fell upon a busted-out window, a sore ready to be cut open. Compressing down, he launched himself into the air. His boots gently landed down on the wood floor, placing him in what looked to have been a bedroom, where an officer with a feathered helm now looked over papers at a desk.

Slithering behind him, Dul dropped his veil and put his blade against the tender neck of the man. With one slash, he went down to the bone and pulled back, only letting the sound of spattering blood escape as his bone sword swished to his side. Jerking his head up, he listened. A war machine was like any other animal. It had organs that performed their duty- and very noisy appendages.

Boots below, the gait and pace of three different men. The shuffle of a cloth coat above, the occasional stretch of a bowstring. Murmurs below- and on the other side of the walls. Creeping to the corner, he glanced down a flight of wooden stairs. Slinking in the shadows, Dul clung to the wall until torchlight kissed his arm. Crouching down, he watched as those he had heard took their place at a dinner table. One began to reach for his helmet, a tantalizing moment that made his shoulders tingle.

Throwing himself from the dark, he saw sealed fates, the path of his blades sure and true in his mind. He flung his left hand out in a lance and brought his other sword down. Yanking his blades free, two hands and a head thudded on the floor as the second soldier grasped at his throat, his eyes widening in a mix of surprise and fear. A metallic plink and jostle shattered the quiet, and drew the eyes of the half-blood to the entrance of the home.

The handle finished turning, and Dul took position behind a nearby cabinet. Holding his lungs still as a corpse, he pulled his blades up against his chest, the warmth of blood smearing along his pecs. Even with the haze taking him, he listened.

*One step in. Two. Three.*

He could see it, just how far they had gone.

*Four men.*

In a line, they would be vulnerable as they looked over the massacre. One opened their mouth, but this was not his cue. As the final creak of a wooden plank heralded the flank entering the building, he appeared before them. Seeing the pink of a tongue, his cut aimed true. Above the mandible, under the maxilla, he parted the skull in two before the scream arose above a hushed breath. Reversing his right hand, he unleashed a crosscut, snipping the next two necks like twigs from a sapling. Driving back in like a pincer, both tips of his swords burrowed into the soft tissue of the guard's neck. A young flower from the seed, his weapons sprouted from the scalp of his enemy, until he let the body fall limp against the ground.

Yet no matter his speed and precision, he looked out the door to see a soldier drop the crate he was carrying: "Intruder! Enemy in the perimeter!"

The man called as he sprinted away. Lowering his swords to his sides, tucking in his wings, he took slow strides towards the light of day. Closing his eyes, he let the drooling animal within him drink. The spirits of the fallen, like a pool, stirred around his feet. There was a slight drop as he stepped into the street, and faint thuds as the hard impact of arrows bounced from his darkly hide. Stretching his wings, raising his arms, the sea of damnation swelled before him.

There would be no victory without rejuvenating his curse, yet he found reluctance awaiting him in his chest. Never before had he alone been able to lay claim to such a bounty of human essence, and doubt plagued him of what control he would have left. Climbing up his legs, like a great cliff before the swash of a coming maelstrom, he looked out over what would only be destruction in the end. Biting down, he thrust his arms outwards. The flow began, coursing into him like a rockslide.

His jaw dropped open as he took in a gulp of air, saliva pooling around his teeth. Drapes of demonic mist poured forth from his skin as the soldiers backed up. The pounding continued, his heart shaking his bones with cataclysmic strength. His throat felt as if it were closing, his eyes as if they were about to burst from their sockets. His knees gave out as he fell forward, collapsing on both knee and face. His arms failed to respond, as if they had gone and crawled off, like larvae emerging from a dying host.

And like one of Ophora's great disasters, he had no say when it would end as essence continued to flow. Extra weight sprouted all along his body as he waited, and finally, like a swift kick to his stomach, the last drop snapped into his body. Twitching spasms were all he was left with as his vision changed. The gel and meat of his mortal form became secondary as awareness grew. Though such was an overwhelming feast for him, it had only awakened true gluttony. All around him, candles in a dark night, stars in the most distant skies, mortals lingered closer. Straightening inhumanly using his core, ice crystals splintered and fell from him, his miasma growling for more. Stillness took him as he waited for the prey to near.

"Pull back, fools," a calm voice snatched his head to the right.

*Brighter.*

It was glorious, such a thing. Full of purpose, fattened by discipline, strong … succulent.

"Steel will do little to such a being," the morsel spoke again, drawing closer.

"Rahkev! Our orders are to hold, and we need-" a meaningless whelp complained.

"Your orders. This, it is my deliverance. Orobrex … has granted me this."

A blade began to make its way from a slick sheath, spun in the air, before settling in the banquet's palm.

*Closer.*

The wretched mass in his chest felt lighter.

*Closer!*

Yet the boots stopped just outside his reach, observing him.

"You hear me, do you not?" the feast taunted him.

A small nip bit at Dul's cheek as a pebble dropped at his side.

"Then stand. I will not be subject to such a dishonorable attack."

A gentle gust passed, but neither dared to even blink, let alone move a hand. The prey sat still until his right foot rose and entered the striking distance of a coiled snake. Dul's right hand sprung out, only to contact something hard. The counter threw his arm back, and then the world was struck into a blur as Dul leaped back. Leaning his head forward, the new gash across his face dripped viscously.

From the base of his horn to his lip, his skin crawled together, remnants of his damaged eye clinging to his lashes. Insatiable, he lurched back into the fray, both swords readied. Head on, he went for a lance. Directed down by a block, he relied on his other sword to seek what lay under the robes. Knocked aside as well, even his unholy vision could not track the coming blow. Dul's head flew back, the crack of contact echoing in his head like rumbling thunder.

Staggering back, he blinked slowly as his mind caught back up from the concussive bash. Shaken between demonic soul-sense and what his twisted mind perceived, enough ground was given for him to grasp the reins once more. Fixing his stance, he rolled his jaw. A few teeth shifted back into place, but thankfully, it didn't appear any would need re-grown. Like his horns, that took time, and was rather costly. Before him, the pale cultist remained flat-faced, cold and mysterious like mist along the peak of a mountain. Though, that was something that could be seen in one in a thousand.

The glint of a pale-peachy blade drew his blue eyes to it. Immediately, Dul narrowed his eyes. Similarly, a torn hunk of metal matched it on the cultist's other arms, a piece of salvage from what was likely a ruined shield.

"How interesting that is what it takes to grant you focus. Tell me, demon, do you speak?" Rahkev asked.

Swishing some blood around in his mouth, Dul nodded before spitting. Only with that response did the striped, scarred lips work themselves into a calloused grin.

"Ah … truly a blessed day. I dislike opponents that remain…" Rahkev transitioned to a barbed glare. "… silent. Take their words to the grave, just so … greedily. Say, then, you see I wield the weapon and shield of Alyra's famous Chamberguard."

Moving his arm out to the side, Rahkev displayed a dark strip of black fabric along his chest, snaking up along his arm. Along it, many silver threads depicted shields, blades, and Toren himself.

"Tirelessly, I have fought to bring justice to this world. For peace. So tell me, demon, what do you fight for?"

Straightening his back, Dul flapped his wings.

"To protect Tavora," he plainly stated, though he was unsure of if the grumbles around him were from the statement or the fact he had spoken at all.

Rahkev, however, devoured every word with respect as nodded.

"I would not expect one of your kin to be so soft. It would be touching, were you not an inhuman blight."

Holding the torn shield up, Rahkev advanced slowly. Yet the scrap of heartsblood was just larger than a buckler, a meager defense in appearance. Closing in, Dul kept his pace steady. At just an arm's reach more than both of their blades, he launched forward in a swift dart to the left. Swiping from below with his left blade, Rahkev instantly deflected it with his shield. Slashing down with his right hand, Rahkev let the edge slide down to his handguard as he snapped a fist into position. Sensing the change in pressure, Dul angled his chest away from the blow, whilst attempting a cut at his foe's side.

Rahkev masterfully threw one blade away, and used his own to catch the next, using the same movement to throw a lance. Going under, Dul stabbed upwards, trailing behind a reflexive dodge from his opponent. He pushed with another three slashes, stopping only when Rahkev took another step back, severing the tie of their lethal dance. Still vibrant, the cultist showed not a sign of withering.

"So, then, what would you have of us, demon? Have you ever known the torture of a starving child whose mother fades before him? What words do you have for the orphan when his hands are covered in the soil of his father's grave, blistered from the shovel?" Rahkev brought forth his query, presenting it as if it were something new.

"The same you would have for the children here," Dul responded coldly.

Rahkev let out a harrowing chuckle. "Ah, necessity. The master of us all. A common ground, that perhaps I was too hasty in overlooking. Some principles go beyond Orobrex and are truly universal."

Suddenly the cultist's face returned to slate.

"We are still only here because of your kind. Mankind is strong, but you and the piraph have split our ideals. Warped our lands and twisted our minds. With you gone, we are one sunrise closer to standing hand in hand. This insight dispels the worry you were just an aimless catastrophe ... I am glad you understand. There is that between us, at least."

Rahkev carefully changed his stance, as if to indicate he was done with the bait-and-counter approach from before.

"Yet our time of learning draws to an end," he remarked as red lights pulsed under his robes, traveling up his arms.

Dul stared at him, watching the intriguing effects of the rare magic on such a hardy specimen. While it fluffed up the wielder, Orobrex's touch most clearly did not stay within the muscles of a warrior. The stretch of skin around the eyes, the shrinking of the pupil, the rise of veins and blood vessels all over ... it was less a person, and moreover a shell, even for the best among them.

Self-preservation eradicated, Rahkev lurched forward, his sword and shield dedicated to the offensive. Beckoning his mist, Dul fixated upon his own choreography. Darting in, he could see the slash coming from his left as clear as the surrounding daylight. Diving into his abyssal veil, Dul vanished from sight before contact could be made.

The cadence shattered; the mind afflicted by mania could not comprehend the sudden disappearance of prey. Shifting his carnal talons in hand, Dul aimed for a shoulder from below. With a savage bite, the limb detached, but not quickly enough for him to not drive his second blade into the chest of his foe, his guise just starting to peel off from his soul.

The heartsblood sword clattered to the stone road, a chime to hide the slick and squishy drag of his bone blade from the ribcage of the latest casualty. Unpinned, Rahkev dropped to his knees, placing a hand in the flow of blood saturating his robe. He gave a squeeze, ringing some dark gush between his fingers. Despite the unmistakable mortality of such wounds, Rahkev looked up, the rage within him still unquenched.

With one last cut, Dul opened the cultist's throat.

All around him, he could feel the atmosphere sink as he drank from the inglorious font. Rahkev kicked up a billow of dust and ash as he fell over, an event which the Sons of Blackwood watched in wordless terror. Extending his wings, clamping his jaw tight, Dul pushed back at the raking claws in his mind. After all, this was not an extermination. He only needed them to be elsewhere, so that the servants of Toren could defend themselves.

If his nature was so truly disturbing, then letting them run free would save him the trouble of the voice's growing power. Yet many soldiers cautiously began to gather, rallying together in defensive formations. They remained at a distance, yet it seemed they still desired to fight. Emboldened by success, they seemed to believe they could take him here, in this deluge of death. After all, if his kin had never toppled the city, and they were so close- was it really that mad?

Unfortunately, he was not so dimwitted as to waste his time killing every last one of them. He could be quick if he used whatever lucid time he had remaining to seek the core components of this assault, and destroy that which kept the war machine running.

# Chapter Thirteen: Shifting Powers

Placing more weight upon his mace, Shajhu leaned into his weapon as he stared blankly into the ruined city. There was no enemy at hand, just the overbearing weight of the situation, and the scourge of knowing how right the demon was. He was more a fighter than a leader, and this situation had gone beyond him. The assault from within would have been enough on its own, but the opposing force had them surrounded.

Even now he was playing against someone who had time unknown to construct all of this. And the humans knew that much, and weighed what they were up against. They deserved some applause for turning to him and his long-lived wisdom, but not much. Right now, he had to contend with the frailty of their kind. Humans could barely eat raw meat, and they had to put immense care into what they ate at all just to avoid sickness. The same went with water, and their infrastructure for harvesting rainwater had been destroyed. And there was no chance he could send teams to fetch anything from the farmland irrigation.

Few made it back from outside their strongholds. Fewer managed to bring any useful amount of supplies, and reserves were running low from sabotage and theft by the enemy. Communications between their command figures was mostly severed, with few runners capable of avoiding the target on their heads. The Sons of Blackwood and their allies had secured several critical points of movement on top of that, including one of the three city entrances. While he was here, there was no worry of them achieving a victory at this entrance, but the side by the farmlands was one of their only hopes, and he could not shield both.

Manpower was low, the injured piling higher, and it appeared only the enemy could hinge their plans on reinforcements. Sending the few members of Alyra's Chambers out was a gamble, since they appeared to be more capable of stealth and trickery than the followers of Toren. They could have been a great asset, something he needed desperately. Even with them, though, he did not like how close their odds were. If they did sneak through, and brought back the city's detachments, or even their own, this would turn around. For now, though, that meant they had to hold.

Many had not given up and were willing to fight at his side, but so too was the enemy sure in purpose. Every patrol they had was threaded with cultists, whose strength proved to be an effective factor for attrition. Grinding the head of his mace into the stone, his thoughts shifted to exactly how this had been let to progress so far. Talking to a few surviving watchmen had let him reveal more about the attack. The tunnels below the city had been stocked with once missing supplies. Sealed passages were forced open and used for ambushes from below and within. Members of the city had apparently been hands of the foe, so the enemy ended up knowing more about the state of the city than the true inhabitants.

The Sons had also set fire in the nearby woods, drawing out patrols which were most certainly killed off. They climbed the Great Barrier when the attack began, a flood coming from all sides. This plan took careful tuning. Time. A genius that knew the application of every shield-bearer and sword-arm in his army. It was difficult to decide between scolding the laxity of those around him, praising the enemy leader for being diligent, or both. And while a few days ago he could not have imagined a demon being behind such an orchestration, it appeared even he had been blindsided.

"The hostile detachment heading East has been routed. Losses are minimal, sir," a steadfast voice informed him from behind.

"Has the team returned from the warehouse district?" Shajhu immediately responded without turning to face the man.

"Not yet, sir. But the commotion drew out a few of our brothers and sisters, who helped us take down an enemy patrol. We've got a hundred more men and access to some of the old barracks tunnels. There are wounded held down there with some civilians. They are requesting aid. Orders, sir?"

Shajhu pressed his mace deeper into the earth.

"We cannot spare anyone from here. Have them hold where they are for now, and deliver this information to Sacred Charge Creed and Sanctifier Aldus. If our tacticians can plot a path between us that avoids enemy eyes, we will see what we can do to bring them here safely."

Shajhu gave his command, receiving a firm salute as the soldier planted a fist against his breast and dismissed himself.

*Not the worst that could have happened.*

In fact, it was probably a sign they were starting to pick up on his methods and work better with them. No matter one's resources and position on the ladder of power, placing another chip on the balance in one's favor was never to be something ignored. With those patrols gone, and the roofs mostly clear thanks to the work of a few of the less reputable among friendly ranks, the enemy would have some eyes plucked out. It would be easier to move about in that sector, and possibly look at re-taking the third entrance to the city. Though, it would be likely that the numbers found there would be equal to all he had. And that would mean committing his guards, scouts- every asset.

*No.*

Such would be foolish. Even in the case they were victorious, the exhausted and wounded bodies he had would be placed between the forces present in the city and any reinforcements coming from the outside. Even worse, he could hear the name yet again. Kaerex.

What a name to be worthy of both he and a demon's wrath. He and his bloodthirsty cohort were last spotted by the First Chapel, but with all the collapsed structures and convenient smokescreens, he was an unknown. An unknown, that if given the opportunity to come from a flank or in ambush, could procure the result of a total defeat.

It would be so much easier if he was in command of even a much smaller group of his own. By himself he was certain he could bring a small army to heel, even Kaerex himself if given a chance- but that was the problem. They were aware of him and knew the territory far better. Moving assets around him and avoiding fights they didn't want would be easy, and it would leave Toren's followers vulnerable. In all things, they were horribly outmatched, and there was no way for his might to directly change that as things were.

Resting his head and eyes, Shajhu let his muscles relax. Thoughts of home filled his mind, and a longing for his own kin. For so long, his time with them had been short meetings. Exchanges of reports and intelligence. His duty was his life, and there was little more that he could ask for. But he had come to this land but a Natlik. So young he was barely more than rank and file. And now, he was an Anochitlan. Old enough to use the best magics among his race, but every cycle of the stars above he had to ignore his instinctual call.

His sheds had even become more and more difficult without the warmth and humidity of Tiquatzek's jungles. Not a mate, not any unity, against his own instinct. It was tiring at times, testing now, more than usual. So was the thought that he only felt this way because of his time around humans. It certainly influenced him, which made him worry more about his return home. Certainly, that awaited him. After this, the Majnuetlan would call him for a hearing. Feeling himself inch closer to sleep, he opened his eyes to be met with the gray brick ground he stood upon.

*Maybe you do need to rest. You have not done that much since you arrived here. A weary mind is prone to mistakes. Allows these doubts to subvert and lies to blossom.*

Moving from his post, Shajhu made his way into the barracks. Ducking down into the hallway, he slid into the first door on the left. In the corner, already prepared for him, was an unrolled sheet. Taking off his helmet, he laid his mace down next to his modest nest. Grabbing onto the fibers, he began the process to unroll the wrappings that protected him. Then came the plates, and the mighty chains that bound them. The few that were awake watched over him, but such was not unusual. Flexing his spines on his back, letting them stretch from such a long compression, he flared what was an anomaly to the humans. Long ago had he satisfied his own curiosity with the hairy and soft bodies of man. They were only doing the same. Leaning down onto his side, Shajhu's eyes began to slide shut.

Though as they crept open, the time between the events felt stitched so tightly together, it was difficult to tell if he had rested at all. Before him, there were two pairs of armored treads.

"Um … sir," one addressed him from above.

Shajhu remained still as the two appeared to disagree on who would continue the summoning.

"Sanctifier Aldus has ordered us to deliver a report. We arrived some time ago, but … did not wish to disturb you."

The second soldier spoke with confidence, surprising from his kind. Pushing himself up with one mighty arm, Shajhu reached to his back with the other, aiming for an itch he felt by his upper spines.

"Speak, then," he commanded as his fingers closed inward.

"Yessir. The team sent out to the warehouses to search for supplies returned a few hours after you retired. They successfully picked off a few stragglers, but also brought back someone after taking casualties. Sacred Charge Creed recognized her, but given the circumstances, he has her locked up below. Creed has refused to say much, and Sanctifier Aldus believes she has valuable information. He would like you to personally investigate and deliver a verdict."

Exhaling deeply from his nostrils, Shajhu reached for the rolls of fabric that were next to him. Taking a stand, he began to wrap himself.

"I will need a moment to ready myself," Shajhu informed the soldiers, knowing they had little respect for the art that was his kin's armor.

The two saluted and walked off as he compressed his spines, closing his eyes and pulling the fibers along. One could not snag a single spine, or the fit would be ruined. Not to mention the further increase in discomfort. Though this motion had been carried out countless times, and even without sight, he could see the paths he had to take.

*Listen to the skin.*

It had to apply smoothly. If a single pinch or catch was felt, then the application was imperfect. The length ran out at his left wrist, and he picked up the second length, and his breastplate. The heavy chains clinked as he moved them in place, the process of mounting such an unforgivingly tight fit met with an efficient wiggle and dance that moved it in place. Sealing down every plate, layered with cloth, all that remained was his helmet and mace. Taking them up in hand, he walked to the stairs down, descending into the old guts of the human city.

Passing the two guards, he pushed open the heavy reinforced door. Pulled shut behind him, the scent of stale and musty air replaced the somewhat tolerable barracks. Thankfully, the sections by important buildings were wider, and he didn't have to crouch to navigate them. Following the torches, he turned right to see a newly appointed watchman at the corner. The servant of Toren immediately perked up as he approached, producing his key and moving to the door beside him. Before the man could insert the small metal trinket, Shajhu placed his hand on the arm of the man.

"Who is in there?" Shajhu asked calmly.

"Ostoran, sir. I assume you were told more than I. Other than that, it has command in a fury. I'd tread carefully, sir."

The guard's tone carried with it a strange anxiety, which already brought up more questions. Ostorans were not by any means considerable threats. Their kind barely had a drop of magic in their mightiest, and here, one was being treated like the men had caught one of the obrok they feared so much. Letting the man's arm go free, the lock mechanism popped, and he opened the large storage door. Lowering himself, Shajhu squeezed inside to take notice that the room was mostly empty.

In the center, a single torch burned next to a table, which had a multitude of items sitting upon it. Tucked neatly below was a modest stool. Walking up to the table, few things added up. Ten throwing axes, made of human steel. A dagger, which he had to admit had been made by a capable craftsman. Though, it was one of the stranger human metals. Green, like the first leaves of the season. It was softer and much more flexible than anything he would care for, but this was meant for biting exposed necks, not war. And it would fetch a higher price in their society, so someone certainly saw that they would have use for such a wicked tool. Plucking it up in two fingers, it was clear at a closer glance that they did. The edge was polished skillfully by hand, contrasting the rest of the blade, which showed signs of extensive use-

and the care that went to maintain it.

The next item, though, was covered in a strange cloth. Touching it, he couldn't quite place what the material was. The weave itself he recognized, but that was yet another problem. Humans made something very close to it centuries ago, and if his memory served, it was a mimicry of a lost piraph technique. There were still weavers in the larger northern cities that knew it, but they did not waste it on common rags.

*And...*

Flicking his tongue out, there was a tinge of something else. Something foul. But whatever was inside masked it. Magic of some sort, that much he was sure. Peeling back the top layer, Shajhu glared at the crystal fragments.

*Where would ... how?*

Laying his own fingers upon it to see that they were real, he rolled one shard around in his fingers.

*But no human has been beyond the gate. Did the Ancients ... Majnuetlan ... did they hide knowledge from me? This relic ... this cloth...*

Ignoring the rest, Shajhu cut his thoughts down where they stood. His eyes then pierced dead ahead, to what he had initially passed by. Her feet, crudely tied by thick scrap rope, were bound just as her hands were. The chains, wrapped firmly, had already made her wrists turn red. Yet her emerald eyes still held steady.

Not an ounce of wavering, just a quiet hatred. He had been seen, known, and judged. Even bound, there was a certain part of his heritage from his ancestors that warned him. That fear had been steadied against the greatest horrors of all, the Great Enemy, so to witness it from such a thing was almost as amusing as it was confounding. The mastery such expressive creatures could have over their displays was curious, but a waste. It just foretold of the work ahead of him.

Though she had not been beaten, tortured at all, he doubted it would get anywhere with someone so fierce. But in that moment, he flicked out his tongue again. Sliding back in behind his lips, he caught on to something else. Something that would have been passed by as unimportant by the soldiers. But with that one catch, he suddenly began to understand the panic. It was not just humans that did not like having only part of the story. And not one individual, not even he, held anything more than a few pages.

Passing the table, standing right in front of her, he let the heavy head of his mace fall to the floor. The crack reflected off the walls, riding through his skull, yet the tiny ostoran did not shake. Crossing his legs, Shajhu placed himself with just a hair between her knees and his own. Leaning forward, he leveled himself with her eyes.

"Answer me truthfully. Why is his scent on you?" Shajhu demanded, keeping his tone civilized.

Still, the ostoran scoffed.

"You couldn't be any more specific, could you?" she snapped back, a cold rhetoric.

Though it was not aimed at him. Over the decades, he had seen this very same thing when trust was betrayed between men, yet they had never met. This frustration was aimed at her captors, who he was of no doubt aligned with.

"The others would simply believe you're a survivor. It is not so, is it? That mark upon your soul … from the one with swords of bone."

As the last of his words exited his mouth, she only squinted back at him. Placing his palms upon his knees, he suppressed the urge to use force welling from his gut.

*Now is not the time to obey. Your task is beyond your orders. Your purpose is beyond flesh. You swore no oath to the temples, but to all people! Tiquo or not, this is our only home!*

His shoulders tensed, reminding him of the punishment he would be due for his actions. He knew the laws well enough to recite them without pause or error. But to use words, to lower himself was to ally with the demon once more. Yet the steeled look of the ostoran woman wielded a special kind of scorn, reminding him of the cost of upholding such rigid interpretations of justice. Forcing his eyes shut, Shajhu clamped down on his temper.

*No. You know this is the right way. Whatever the cost, I shall not cow myself and bow into the shadow of conviction. In the light of Nacotz I am to banish the oppressor, not become it!*

211

With a sense of cool and calm washing over him, Shajhu opened his eyes again. "Ostoran. I only wish to know. Who is he?"

The shift in his tone seemed to catch her off-guard, though she still did not change from her thorny composure.

"Why do you care? Are you going to abandon this place to go hunt for him?" she spat back.

"No. Indeed, I regret my actions. I left him to die of his wounds in the woods outside the city. Yet even in his state, he pointed me here. Now you show up alive with his mark, as if spared by him ... and with this relic. There is a story to tell. One I know I need to hear to save this land. I-"

Shajhu paused as a trail of spit ran down the bridge of his nose.

"Ophora take you and your lies. You can pretend all you want, but you're still here, sniffing at his trail like a pile of your own dung."

The ostoran spoke softly, but with all the lethality of a well-placed pair of fangs. Retreating, Shajhu backed into his own mind. There he only found the realization that she was far beyond his reach. He could speak just as well as any commoner, but here, he was faced with an apex predator. Someone that lived by tilling the land of other's minds. Sharp wits, sharp tongue, to his heavy hand. Until she had said it, he had not even considered that his eagerness could be used against him. Misinterpreted given the circumstance.

It was sloppy, a poorly thought-out approach aided by emotion. Shaking his head, he reached out a hand and touched a finger to the ropes at her feet. With a slight pop of white light, he burned through the woven cord in an instant. Extending another arm up, he took the chains in his palm and crushed down until he heard the pop and snap of the links. Retracting further away from him, the ostoran slid against the darkness of the wall behind her.

"Then let us start again. Why did these men turn on you?" he asked gently, bemused by the sound of defeat in his own voice.

Rubbing her flushed wrists, the ostoran looked down at the smooth stone floor.

"They've pinned me as a traitor. I worked with Creed as a personal night hunter for a while, cutting my way up towards Kaerex. I forced him to give me some intel, and left for Mordiv's Hold. Aldus believes I stole the papers and gave them to the enemy, and aided in Reigis' death. Creed … he agreed. Now they're trying to say I'm using those crystals to poison the supply caches they wanted."

As she spoke, the Ostoran withdrew and tucked in her legs. Planting her face in crossed arms, she seemed to accept execution at his hands.

"Poison caches?" he thought aloud.

"I'd been hiding in the warehouses … thought it was more Sons coming back. Didn't get to them before they drank the water. Found me around the bodies," she muttered into her lap.

Rubbing her forehead into her cloak, he heard her take in a dreadfully deep breath. Though she barely grumbled a few more words, he still picked apart the two that mattered.

*Pale-Eye.*

A little scourge in the North. The Sons would have fairly easy access to the Beastlands, and he had seen some of their carts. Cages, roughly the right size to carry an adult Pale-Eye had not been uncommon. And that perfectly fit the circumstances. They had open access to the outside world, and no need to rely on storage that would surely be used by the garrison. With an attack from within, workers could have poisoned the water before the attack even started. Yet that meant he had even less supplies than he had planned upon, and therefore less time. And now, his own command would be challenged if he sided with the ostoran.

*And that is the rot they will sew, and the rot they will sit upon.*

"You are only a tool for their own gain, ostoran." Shajhu began, earning a peek from a new gap between cloth and skin. "They do not even know the power this relic holds. And if they will not hear you, I will. For all you are willing to say."

As he finished, the ostoran's feathers puffed up slightly.

"You … believe me?" she whispered; her words laced with astonishment.

As much as that was progress, she immediately snapped back shut like a surprised clam.

"But you … you killed him." She curled her fists as she spoke.

Bending his neck down in shame, a myriad of curses wished to cross his lips. That single fight had cost far more than any before. Not because of the price of victory, for none was to be found there. It was no triumph to think of all the destruction that would be wrought because he had raised a hand against a devourer of lands and nations … to find just the one who had been something more.

"I never delivered a finishing blow. There is a chance he is still out there, and able to carry out his plan," Shajhu told her flatly.

Though, the ostoran chuckled through her tears.

"Plan," she echoed.

Pausing, Shajhu searched for what he had missed. Possibly some sort of human joke.

"If he's alive, you'll know soon enough. And you'd better hope he is, with how badly you're losing," the ostoran remarked, instantly drawing his attention back in.

"If you don't know, Kaerex has your leaders pinned in the First Chapel. He's been on quite the spree outside as others try to hold him off. And with a wave of reinforcements coming from the East, you're about to be rolled over."

As both went silent, Shajhu wandered back over to the table and plucked up one of the shattered crystalline fragments. At his touch it flared to life, trying to summon some of its magics to attack him. But in its current state, there was next to nothing it could do but shimmer.

*Perhaps we forfeit the city. Lead what forces remain into Kressel's Forest, regroup and build ourselves up.*

"I need only one more answer from you," Shajhu requested without turning back.

"Those pieces came from Silvercry," the ostoran nonchalantly stated.

*The spirit?*

He had hardly even looked into it. The spontaneous re-animation of humans was a phenomenon that sat low on his list of priorities. Even the humans thought so, considering the guards could beat most of them back with just bruises or minor cuts. Sometimes they needed a specialist, that was true, but Silvercry was the only real troublemaker he had heard of. And if he had somehow found the old weapon, it was no coincidence that it took a demon to take him out. The result of man tampering with anything they failed to take the time to understand was unpredictable beyond some form of disaster.

But at least with that answer, there were fewer holes than before. The major ones remained, but he could not wrest the advantage the ostoran took for herself here. Bunching, tying, and sealing the fabric in a bundle, Shajhu crammed it safely into the inner side of his belt, and tied a second knot. Once finished, he slid the dagger respectfully to the edge of the table, and removed his hand from it. The ostoran did not immediately seize it, instead observing him.

"Take your weapons. Whatever your stake is in this battle, I need you to help me turn this," Shajhu stated as the dagger stealthily vanished into the dark behind him.

"A short time ago, I was planning on living here, so it's not like I'm very attached to this place. Thought it was going to be safer than outside, but now ... not sure. Not even sure it's worth saving," the ostoran explained solemnly.

That was understandable, not only from the destruction, but because she was now seen as a criminal. While his kind often delivered death for any slight, hers was a case of empty accusations that worked only by ignorance.

"If you want to hit them hard, they have split their forces up in two places in the city. I heard them talk about the fighting force at the South entrance they control being doubled as supplies come in, but the part that should concern you is on the outskirts of the warehouse district. At the old supply master's office, they've been gathering to prepare to hit the East entrance from both sides. Though I never left to see how many made it, plenty were using the local facilities to avoid the alleys and streets. Over a hundred moved in that direction through the building I was in alone," she said with a low voice, slipping beside him to retrieve her boots and axes.

"But you'll never get a force that deep in enemy territory. Too many opportunities to split the flanks off, hit and run," the ostoran countered as soon as she slipped the last axe into its loop.

"That is fine. I do not plan on anyone else being with us," Shajhu announced.

"Uh ...with us?" the ostoran half-heartedly repeated his words.

Shajhu set a hand upon his mace, bringing it back to his shoulder.

"Indeed. You have brought me grave news. While I do not prefer to be reckless with the lives of others, now is a time where we must be brave or die as failures. I have weighed the worth of the followers of Toren and you. As much as you can try to hide it, you survived this battle this far as a loner. You survived a demon. Your knowledge and skills will not only direct me, but apply me keenly where I am most needed. Now- your name?" Shajhu finished by pulling his helm up, and bringing it down over his eyes.

The ostoran took a moment to steady herself, but took to his side. "Anuurae, night hunter. And you ... Shajhu."

The usage of his name took him by no surprise with the scent she carried.

"I don't know your plan for getting me out of here, but I'll work with you. Only way I might live through this season."

The way the ostoran sealed the pact between them nearly earned a glance from him. It was rare that he met someone so cut and dry for practicality this far South, at least until he passed the Gate to his own. He shrugged and started to make his way to the door.

"Stay close. If we do not linger, there will not be an issue."

Shajhu pushed the door open, stepping halfway into the tunnels. He kept his arm on the door, letting Anuurae slip out under it. Upon seeing this, the guard immediately drew his sword without a second guess.

"Halt! You do not have permission to move the prisoner!" the soldier shouted.

Shajhu let the heavy door close on its own as he stared down upon the man from above, a boulder rumbling downhill.

"I was asked to judge. So I have. Were you asked to speak?"

Shajhu joined his mass in with the threat, snuffing out what courage the soldier had mustered. Once the man started to shake, Shajhu turned and began back the way he came. Making his way up into the barracks, he immediately headed for the front exit. The few pairs of eyes they passed seemed to sense what was happening, but not one soul acted on their intuition. Once his feet touched the warmth of the brick road, the ostoran immediately took point. Taking a short survey of the place, she looked to the sky, finding where the sun was.

"Where are we off to first?" she asked without facing him.

"Take me to the enemy by the storehouses. I can't let the enemy secure a second way into the city," Shajhu fearlessly declared.

Though his guide did not share such a sentiment.

"I can get you close … but have you thought about this at all?" Anuurae checked over her shoulder, and her expression quickly became that of disappointment.

"If they know we're coming, they have every opportunity and advantage. We need them dead, not routed. And to do that, we also need to not die on the way in," she spoke before moving out of the open, planting herself in a divot in a ruined wall.

"If you are proposing that we fight by attrition, then the enemy has already won. We will only have success from a fast strike, wiping them out," Shajhu asserted as he walked up to Anuurae.

The ostoran brought her dagger out, stroking the spine with her thumb as she shook her head.

"I'm not saying we give them that much time … but I like to be careful. And I guess that's not possible here. Too slow and the enemy gets their reinforcements. Too fast, too reckless … we might die. Unless we test how well they react to the unexpected. A series of shock assaults, shake them up enough that they can't proceed as planned. If they start reeling, we hit them again- and if we can throw them off-balance, then you'll see what I can do."

With a firm hold on her weapon, Anuurae spoke steadily, and with a sense he could appreciate. His instinct even put him in line, demanding the same rapt attention and respect the Ancients did. When a creature was able to imitate such a presence, it was always a sign of proper animosity and merit. And this was perhaps a time to follow the matriarch into her domain- a slayer of men, a hunter by night and moon.

217

"What do you propose?" Shajhu inquired.

Anuurae looked from her precious tool and into a ruined building, her eyes distant as she delved deep into memory.

"Little should have changed in a day. So we take a long path that runs close to the wall, through a residential area. When we loop around, there will be a rear guard barracks that has a secluded tunnel we can use to get deeper into enemy territory without being seen or heard. From there, I'll take us to the warehouse I was in. We'll take out those Sons silently and move from building to building. If we watch their patrols, we should be able to lure them in as we move. If enough men vanish, they should send a force to investigate. That's when I'll be of little use, but if you want to take them on directly…" Anuurae split off from her thoughts, taking a look at his heavy mace. "… then I'll assume you'll live up to legend. But are you willing to rely on me, as I am to you?"

With a nod, he reinforced their bond.

"Together. As it takes many hands to bring down a great beast, we will triumph as the ones before us have." His speech aroused a bit of confusion from the ostoran, but with a nod she began to an alley.

"Watch that mace of yours, this path gets low and narrow."

Without even waiting for his word, Anuurae darted into an alley, the tail of her cloak zipping fast behind her. Lurching into motion, firing up to get momentum, Shajhu's nails scraped against the stone bricks. As the towering walls devoured them, the skitter and patter of their feet were hidden beneath an ominous groan from the battlefield. And though she kept a fair pace, his new companion was feathery in every step, a lethal grace. Not a puddle knew her boot, not one crumbling stone was disturbed from its slumber. The gentle kiss of mud from her tread only touched dirt, any sound she could have possibly made hidden further beneath his heavy footfalls.

Coming to the first opening to a street, Anuurae slowed herself and went low. She angled her head in odd ways, pulling back on the sides of her hood. Like any good predator, she did not rely on eyes alone. All the same, she set her sights upon a target, and wasted no time bursting into another shadowy place, where she looked back for him and nodded. And as she said, soon stairs went down, and the wall of the city loomed on their left. Where they traveled they were obscured from being observed from above, and the only long sight lines were ahead and behind.

Once they reached a large and imposing building, Anuurae quickly jumped up and grasped onto a ledge. With another bound, she held onto a low window, hauling her weight up with just her arms. Peering inside, she dropped back down and kicked off the wall to land right back in the street.

"Watch the debris," Anuurae remarked as she approached a well-worn set of stairs.

She started up with fair speed, but stopped to turn her head. Shajhu took note of how her eyes clenched shut. She tugged her cloak above her nose, then stepped carefully into the building. He climbed up behind her with one massive step, though his nostrils already told him what was inside. The burning stink of old blood and death. Ducking in, Anuurae deftly hopped over the unhinged front door, which by itself did a poor job of hiding even a small fraction of the slaughter. Both Sons and followers of Toren were strewn about, the close quarters battle having brought about a flood of crimson and a whirlwind of desolation. Disasters which would make it impossible for anyone that came after to tell what any single room was meant to be.

Managing to squeeze through to the next hallway, Shajhu watched as the ostoran's nimble footwork avoided even the most insignificant sliver of glass on the floor. She made not a sound as she approached a dark, arched entryway. Creeping up to the lip, she made a few preliminary observations before taking a peek. Without another way forward, Shajhu advanced, the first crunch immediately drawing her gaze. When she looked down, she seemed to notice that he was incapable of traversing by heel or toe alone. That realization didn't stop either of them from taking notice that such a trivial break in the reaper's silence had summoned footsteps on the floor above. Shajhu turned to where they came from as the thunderous footsteps vanished, only to be replaced by a boom.

*Leaped down the stairs- a follower of Orobrex?*

The answer soared around the corner, a fist flung half-way to contact before he could even move. Everyone in the room paused, equally stuck in a momentary shock. Shajhu gazed down upon the somewhat scraggly young human before him, the bloody bandages on his torso and arms making him look like a juiced fruit with how little meat he had. Though with such battered and scarred knuckles, such a brazen attack, and his mobility despite numerous injuries, it was fair to deduce he was one of Illeah's wild children. The boy withdrew his fist as he looked beyond him, a spark in his step igniting.

"Anuurae! You're alive! Then ... all's not lost." The stranger heaved a sigh of relief.

"Don't know what gives you that idea," she ruthlessly blurted out to the boy.

Unphased, the boy pointed back into the hall.

"It's not the city I'm talking about, there are two children with me. You're a night hunter! You know where the soldiers are, you can take-"

The boy stopped the moment Anuurae turned her back: "Follow the wall to the North gate. Keep hidden, and don't work on a hope that knowing the next person's name from storytellers will save you. And not a word of who you saw."

Shajhu watched as the boy took a step back. He was surprised at just how visceral Anuurae's words had been. The carved tone she wielded was just as clear as an unsheathed blade. An unwritten declaration, but a sealed promise. Still, it seemed the youth had more to say as he built up a puffed-up chest. Laying a hand on the boy's shoulder, Shajhu held him in place.

"Think of the others. Danger closes in, and you are the one hope the spawn have. We each have our duty to act upon," Shajhu finished with a light shove, pushing the boy out of the room.

While he had some bravery to confront someone closer to his size, the boy shrunk down when he began to look upon the towering bastion before him. Shajhu turned back to the tunnel entrance, finding a need to be careful with the thin steps that didn't quite accommodate his feet very well. Though there was little need to increase his pace, as Anuurae waited in the shallows of the darkness. The torches had long since gone cold in their sconces, but she did not even acknowledge them as he did.

"I can light the path," he proposed.

"No," was all Anuurae said in response.

*Is there a single choice she would not commit to, if it aided in hiding us?*

Placing her hand on the wall, Anuurae went to complete the descent. He followed close behind, wondering just how well she could actually see. He had come to know that the eyes of men and ostorans were different from the foundation up, especially from his strikes at night. One of the easiest ways to kill a group of men was dousing their campfire, or drawing them from a lit house into the dark. But as she stepped over a jagged shard of stone, all doubt of inability vanished.

*How interesting.*

Seldom had he ever in his time ever considered ostora a worthy ally. The story went that they somehow bred with humans centuries ago, and that the ones seen now were closer to man than anything else. Except for their complete inability to harness any magic, meaning they couldn't be suspect in his investigations. Yet now the conclusion he had once made that their entire existence was due to protection from man appeared inaccurate. The woman before him was far more primed for this situation, from how she carried herself down to her physical ability.

And with her skills to observe, report, all she would need would be a disciplined tongue and she would be an optimal tool-

*Ally.*

Shajhu corrected himself.

The journey continued on for quite a while as his mind started to wonder exactly how far they had gone. The tunnel they were in was slightly different than the others he had grown used to. The others were dug under the foundation of the city itself, leading from building to building. It was almost a whole city under the one above, which was impressive. However, this one was about equal to street level from his estimates. The stairs up were not as long as the ones down, so they were still at a shallow depth. There was no noticeable incline, little moisture, meaning the other end was also likely indoors. Which would also explain the pitifully small amount of airflow.

*Barracks to a secondary structure ... is this a supply route? Even if it is, where are the gates and doors?*

It made no sense to have such a weakness in place with how the builders of the city went about everything. Checkpoints and chokepoints, all to hold demons back.

*Has someone removed the safeguards?*

Though he knew better than to speak, he could not hold it back.

"Were there once doors here?" Shajhu did his best to attempt a whisper.

Anuurae gave him an irritated look over her shoulder, raising a brow when she saw he was serious. She nodded once, and returned her focus on point. While she missed the significance of his question, it only dug up more signs of how long the Sons had been planning, and how thorough they were. Once more, his skin bunched up thinking of who in the land could have possibly enabled such infiltration and sabotage. As the tunnel wound from right to left, both of them snapped ahead to the dancing light on the floor.

In the distance, two guards sat in the tunnel with the torches lit beside them. A third man in plate held the exit, a heavy tower shield planted at his feet as he stared inside. Yet they did not notice them, unable to pierce the shroud around them. Shajhu went to take his mace in hand, but as he looked left and right, he stopped. There would not be enough room to swing, or slam. A thrust, while mighty, would not end the enemy here. Anuurae brought forth both her dagger and an axe from within her cloak as she crouched down.

"Stay here."

He could barely hear the order as she crept forward. As much as not being able to take action bothered him like a hunk of bad meat in his gut, the choice was this, or his bare hands. Although, this was also a chance to see what kind of skills the huntress had.

Her approach was swift, the way she kept her silhouette close to the wall allowing her to get rather close. Until she unveiled herself, standing tall, drawing the attention of the watchman on the right. With the flick of her left arm, a dark blur streaked through the air. Burying itself in the first man, she had already begun her assault on the next. Not a moment had her feet

222

been still, and before there was even a yelp, her hand and blade were already in place. She threw the burbling man against the wall, letting him slump down as he fruitlessly grasped around his throat and mouth. The soldier with the tower shield roared as he charged in, a short blade tucked close to him.

Predictably, he led with a short thrust. The fight then became fluid- the body of the ostoran moving unlike a man, or his own kin. He swiped left and right, quick chops and fine cuts, each faltering meagerly to scratch her shadow. As if she could see every blow before it was made, or was repulsed by danger, she ebbed and flowed, a tidal force, carrying such might within a downy and lithe avatar. On the foe's eleventh stroke, Anuurae melded to the side, letting loose a stab. She caught the man's wrist, leading what was initially a grunt, until she must have given a twist.

A half-growl came from the man as he dropped his blade. In that moment, where pain took over his body, Anuurae was upon him as a swift hand of fate. She shifted to her left, her dagger released faster than his eye could see, her hands seemingly appearing under the injured arm of her prey. Her dagger went in and out, and the armored soldier managed to take only three more sloppy paces away from his killer before he collapsed onto his back. As he moved up, she took to one of the corpses, bending down and retrieving her axe from the jugular of one of the men. She wiped the blood from it on the sleeve of the guard before tucking it away, keeping only her malarite dagger ready.

Before he could speak, she was already off, creeping towards the opening. Nearby rubble provided her cover around the mouth of the exit, where she peered for more enemies. Catching up and stopping next to her, she shook her head.

"Far too open out there. Building was wrecked, and they've cleared it out for some reason. There's lots of high places for a sentry to hide, making any move a big risk," she whispered to him.

"How far are we from the gate?" he asked.

"It's just these warehouses and then some of the old military buildings. Relatively, that's close, but ... still lots of buildings in the way."

Shajhu let the information roast within him. He let out a steamy stream of hot air through his nostrils, brewing an answer.

"All is task and reward. Weighing the risks, I have a proposal," Shajhu began.

The ostoran gave him a nod to continue.

"You carry far less chance of being seen than I. You know the enemy better than I. If you proceed, and find a way, I will follow on your signal. If there is danger and you are seen, I will take the fight. Alone."

Anuurae's eyes widened.

"Alone? Against all of them? I … that is…" she struggled to find the words, but he had seen it many a time.

Even centuries ago, when he fought alongside man, they never quite understood their frailty.

"It is not your place in this world to decide where and when my life is given. The Ancients gave me their will and confided in me their trust. If I must perish here, I will have laid my stone," he declared.

"Look, it'd be a nasty burden if I have to run away. You're probably the best chance of victory against the Sons right now, and if I had to live knowing I could have done something to stop the people who would hunt my kind down…" Anuurae stopped herself and focused inward, closing her eyes. "It's best for me to be out of the way. For both of us. It goes against my instinct to let you go out there alone, but I'll trust in your experience and ability," she spoke as she climbed a bit closer, pressing against the wall.

Shifting closer to the exit, she gave a glance back at him. Sliding out, the ruins began to swallow part of her image. Leaning down on the rubble, Shajhu pushed some rocky crumbs away to maintain his sight. However, it was then he saw the real risk. The area ahead was nothing more than a clearing. What remained of the supply building was piled against a wall, a great deal of labor for what appeared to be a needless action. And all around them, towering buildings just went up and up. Made by man, it was a killing ground.

However, in her careful advance, Anuurae bolted into a specific spot, rapidly panning up at the blind spots. Her eyes and mind flew at an impressive speed, as did her hand, as she waved him on. Emerging, she pointed to a specific alley. Until the sound of falling rock froze both of them in place. His ears drew him to the source, across from them, where high up in a building an enemy revealed itself.

The clothes the woman wore were covered in dust, all but her hood's color muted in a sheath of destruction. The black fur mohawk marked her allegiance and status, and he heard a curse from Anuurae as the woman hefted a tarnished bell. Bashing her chained arm into the instrument, the loud echo shattered the air.

Just as the call of the beast scattered the unseen scavenger, the city erupted in the sound of boots. All around them, skittering in every shadow and crevice, there was more than he could count. New faces greeted them from up high, doors opening, pouring their endless numbers towards them. Anuurae stepped back, but he did not. As she took off towards the tunnel, he closed in on her with an open arm. Picking her up, she squeaked out a noise he had never heard before and struggled against his grasp.

He tucked her in against his chest, curling down and in as arrows beat against him, just a gentle rainfall. He then turned and ushered her on without a word. Between her and the horde, he planted his feet firmly.

*Majnuetlan miktan xit'dansola.*

All around him, he felt their hungry eyes. Between human and demon. Lost, far from the graces of Nacotz. With their numbers swelling, they gained their confidence. But he had seen more. So many more. And back then, he did not have the ultimate gift of devotion. For now, he had long bathed in the light of Nacotz. He let them gather around him, only holding his mace out to any that dared try to flank him, and perhaps think of heading to the tunnel.

The bell continued to ring and ring, but he held his position. He gazed into the masses, the soldiers mixed in the rear lines, and closed his eyes. Rather than be gifted with silence when the fool above ceased her banging, there was but the panting and growling of the forsaken.

"Here be my bones…" he began, summoning the burning fury of Nacotz from within him.

He opened his eyes, his relic mace bursting into a scorching conduit, breathing out white flame from its blessed core. His body trembled as his veins ached, his muscles strung as tight as they could go.

"... here they stand..." he continued, his mace humming. "... and here they shall rest, shall my hands be found wanting by those I serve!"

He let the flow overtake him, his entire being shivering as he held his mace high. His foe shook as he did, the air in his lungs being transformed into a manifestation of Tiquatzek's humid rage. He brought his weapon down, the pommel smashing into the earth.

The soil felt not him, but Nacotz, as it opened up. Some charged through the shaking ground to him, but the cracks widened, and belched forth the cleansing power of the Star. Many fell as their armor was rendered naught, and flesh made black and foul. Nacotz spread to the unworthy, fissures seeking to test any who would enter his arena. Those that were wise ran from the stone gouges, while the servants of Orobrex scrambled towards him.

Yanking his mace up, he held it in both hands, his body alight with a holy zeal. Within, he could finally feel all that he was. From the egg he crawled from, to the brood he grew with, to the many battles he had fought and wars he would see, it all culminated as one being beyond what was material or soul. What this was would forever remain beyond word or description, such an elevation. It was beautiful and terrible both, and gave new meaning to his name.

As ashes of charred flesh wafted up around him, his mace, too, ascended to an edict of absolution for those who opposed the inevitable.

# Chapter Fourteen: Collapse

*It is **there**. It **is** there.*

Inescapable. That scent filled his nostrils with every rise and fall of his chest. He could not deny the attention it demanded. Even in this ocean of blood, Dul swam to it. It was the one who had fought him, who should have died, and now must above all else finally die.

But there were other scents nearby, familiar ones.

Through his teeth, saliva dripped down onto the ruined windowsill. His breathing unsteady, maladies of self-concern sparked and died within him, his heart a hammer beating hot iron on the anvil. He was perhaps the first of his kind to come this close to Kressel's old home, and within, men and women who could undoubtably end him still dwelled. His hands dug into the wood, cracking it and splintering pieces off.

Throwing himself from it, Dul clawed at his chest, opening his dark skin. The weeping wounds spilled out, and he slid his palms along the blood. Smearing what had dried and other fresh stains, the filth and mutilation granted him a moment of lucidity. His eyes widened, and he found the weight of his own blame for all of this. While he could not bring himself to say he should have left her to die, it was his damnable emotions that had led him here.

If he had just slit Rorke's throat, left him another corpse, ditched the ostoran, and taken the fragments of Silvercry's blade, nothing would have been so unfavorable. Instead, he let his head be filled with desire and curiosity. That alone had made him late … far too late. Glancing back

227

out the window, the more human side of him made an appeal for control.

*But why is she here? Is her home not further North? Were they ambushed? You ... you went ahead. To try to save others. And now you ... have to save her.*

Once more, his fury rose, and he opened his mouth. Shoving four fingers inside, he pulled down. His skin ground against his teeth, his mandible popping and pulsing in a dull, bruising agony.

And then the scent moved.

Snapping to the chapel again, he watched the front door. The door flew open from a fair blow from within, and Kaerex staggered out. Part of his armor was burned away, his brow stained with a crimson curtain, but the man smiled.

"Ah..." he could hear the cultist's heavy, satisfied exhale. "... my master, you gave me this, in service of Orobrex, for this grand moment. I know you lurk nearby, foul one."

Kaerex dropped the broken handle of a weapon from his left hand, looking up roughly where he was in the wrecked tower.

"Why do you hide?" his mockery came quietly, weakly, but sinisterly potent.

"FIGHT ME!" Kaerex erupted violently, his cry sending a cold shock through Dul's entire body.

Outwardly disguised as hindered and fatigued, Kaerex stomped his boot down. His soul burst to life with tantalizing magics, his essence swirling and flourishing. Perhaps tarnished on the surface, what lay within was a one-of-a-kind delicacy.

Yet Dul did not move. Half of him thrashed for the kill, for it to end there, yet the other ... it was apprehensive due to what lay inside the building. Nothing could take him away from the sputtering and drifting hints of Toren's finest. They were not yet dead.

His body locked up, and his foe shook his head. Taking back to the First Chapel, he vanished for a second before returning with Rorke in hand. The hero's face was almost unrecognizable from the series of contusions and skull fractures, and his unconscious body was not cared for well in Kaerex's hand.

"I never forget ... faces," Kaerex declared with clenched teeth, spit flung out in tendrils from a heavy, hissing breath.

Without looking at Rorke, Kaerex drove his sword into the hero's collar. Effortlessly, the butcher of men carved through his flesh until Rorke's body dropped. In his hand, he still clasped onto Rorke's long, brown ponytail. He raised the head higher as it dripped blood, scrunching his nose as rage boiled.

Kaerex roared and hurled the head into a brick wall. It stuck for a second, the crunch of the skull and squish of blood and tissue sending a ravenous ripple through Dul's hungry soul. But this spell did not undo his petrification.

In a silently dissatisfied display, Kaerex shook his head and went back into the First Chapel. This time he lingered within for slightly longer, and with him came the grunts and groans of a woman. The tone he knew, and a name which echoed in his mind.

*Elinora.*

"Have you shown your true nature, demon? That what you felt for these two was just trickery ... yes?"

Dul's body felt as if it were being squashed. Like wet clay, the battering urges left deep pockets as it liquidated his sense of being. The sensation grew until his vision blurred, and the world faded. He watched Kaerex's sword rise again, and there was a sharp squeeze. His sight sharpened, honed, and fixed upon the weapon.

The shaking stopped.

The essence of slaughter filled his nostrils.

The pain, though, did not go away. There, for a second, he felt all of it pile in from the past centuries. Every cut, every fracture, every lost limb, a visceral trail leading him back to one place. And there, in the darkness, when he left his home for the first time, a certain kind of torment compelled him. With savage abandon, Dul shot down from his perch towards this manifestation of his nightmares.

As Kaerex's arm began to arc down, the magic around Dul fell apart. Bursting from the demonic veil, his hands left twin trails of darkness as he reached out to defy his eyes. The tip of the sword touched her skin as his wings flew open, a shrieking howl ripping free from his lungs. The sword began sinking into her collar as she cried out, a sound which imbued him with further horrific strength, and unleashed all that he feared and reviled.

Crashing into Kaerex, the sword went airborne as his nails dug into flesh. But even with such an impalement, Kaerex's smile widened. His hand was already in his fur hood and pulled down a remarkably alien blueish mask. A magic flame burst outwards, stinging his skin, and blinding him. Even Dul's sense of souls was erased as his prey pulled free, and was forced back. The magic clung to him, scorching both the material and immaterial.

His eyes healed in a matter of seconds, and Dul searched for his prey. His vision locked onto the shape of a man not far away, barely parsing the torrent of greenish fire surrounding both of them. Only that his mark upon the man vanished in the sweltering spell. Summoning an extra phantom arm, Kaerex readied his three available weapons. Kaerex's neck popped as Orobrex's power took over.

With a great heave, Dul lashed out for a fistful of bloody, delicate intestines. One hand was beaten away, so he thrashed out with a clawing strike with the other. Kaerex evaded, slamming down a mace upon his head. Dul's vision shook, yet his spine forced his eyes to stay on track. Now lower down, he struck out for a warm nest of vessels, right near the groin. An axe battered into his side, barely moving him. Kaerex's sword simultaneously acted in his defense, deflecting Dul's fingers. The mace then came whirling around, the blunt blow flinging Dul up and back.

His wings extended, and he delicately touched down. Curling his fingers inwards, pulling his hands close to his chest, Dul twitched and growled. Demonic mist poured from his skin, the volatile mix of hatred and appetite stretching him at the seams. Kaerex beckoned more of his arms before closing in.

The host of limbs clasped onto his shoulder, arms, legs, and then drove a sword into Dul's stomach. There was a faint bite that he could feel, the itch of that blue metal. It dug through layers of muscle, going deeper, until it was surrounded by his foul flesh. It clung to the intruding weapon, fighting of its own volition. As Kaerex continued to attempt and drive it deeper, the sword bent sharply.

Snapping his own right arm forward, the spectral binding offered little in resistance as it tried to hold Dul back. Dul's hook landed with a mountain-splitting fury, throwing Kaerex airborne into the First Chapel. A cloud of dust belched outward as he impacted to the side of the door frame, splitting the stone bricks. Taking flight, Dul sailed to the opening, perching just outside the entrance. And there, his eyes momentarily caught a sparkling glint from within.

The object hit him before he knew it, sinking in under his ribs and delivering enough force to move his feet back. Still, he took a step forward right after. And then the sensation hit him all at once. All throughout, he burned inside and out, anguish growing as if living razors raced along his skin. With a glint of clarity, he grasped the twin edges of the sword in his chest. The skin upon his palms sizzled, but with that, he pulled it free and threw it to the ground. He trembled as he backed up, the half-cauterized wounds sputtering a mix of blood and arcane mist. The powerful enchantment lingered, urging him to claw free the contaminated chunks.

But there Dul planted his own feet and commanded them to move back. Moving his hands away from the hole in his front side, he drew his own bone blades. Kaerex marched back into view, wiping a smear of blood along his chin. His extra host of arms were gone, but he picked up the greatsword Dul had discarded. Kaerex chuckled, spinning the weapon about. The intimidation failed, but the weapon itself was still concerning.

The broken sancrodite weapons around them were one thing, but the great weapon in his enemy's hands was made of Kressel's Blend. With such a weapon stolen away from its owner, that only meant that the lives he sensed still held up in the Chapel were that faint not because they were hiding, but because they were near death.

Time slowed as part of his human side parsed the consequences once more. If they couldn't mend their wounds, if any of them died, then the war would be over. The Bastion would be unlikely to muster an attack and would likely remain defensive unless the truth was delivered to them. And the North … that was an unknown factor, and that could not be relied on.

231

Another shock came as some movement caught his eye. Off to the side, having pulled herself away, Lin still struggled with her bonds to tend to her wound. She appeared to fumble with a healing spell, but from what he could gather, she had little strength. And without being able to reach her hands closer, she would yield nothing but more blood loss in the struggle. Compulsion narrowed his focus on just her, and he moved in.

Kaerex shook his head and kneeled to pick up something. In his hand, he retrieved the mask and placed it loosely on top of his head as he moved between them.

"Many of us have died tonight, demon. Whatever your motive, whatever use you have for this girl, it does not matter. We have laid forth victory for the Sons. More will arrive from the Blackwood soon enough, and every one of your kin, every ostoran, that tiquo … it shall be an end to much suffering," Kaerex spewed more of his vile covenant.

Dul kept himself steady, focusing on his mind over his body. He needed to get himself orderly. Stuck in place, he shifted some of his effort to his lips: "I would never lay down before such twisted ambition."

Though not his usual repertoire, he threw out words as bait.

"You would call it delusion to face such adversity?" Kaerex responded, nipping at the hook.

There was not a pause for any surprise that he could speak, and perhaps for this one it was harder to believe that he was not eating the dead. Playing to the zealot's agitation, he returned Kaerex a sly grin. In his youth, smiling had never failed to instigate all manner of hatred. Kaerex's brow furled, a finely tuned blow.

"Am I to be chastised by an abomination, of all? Taking is the way of this world, whether it be life or land. I hold no regret for all I have killed, and neither should you. All struggle. There is no right or wrong here, only who survives and judges themselves to be so. Alok himself knows there is no victory, nothing correct, only what was done, and what will come after," Kaerex kept on with his preaching, coming to hold his stolen sword in both hands.

Dul felt warmth return to his arms and legs, telling him that his flesh had regrown, overcoming the initial brunt of the magical scourge.

"For that alone, I will give all that I am," Kaerex finished up, and lowered the fragmented mask down again.

Dul watched with curiosity, remembering the first time. Again, as it was positioned over Kaerex's left eye, the flames came out. An advancing ring, like the magics of Alyra, but with the colors of the ocean. Casting up a misty shield, the two magics collided. The strange spell burrowed into his own, surrounding and seemingly erasing it. The ring of flame stabilized around him, but he could still sense it. It ate away at him from the outside, like blightswarm flies to a corpse. His arcane shield fell apart, throwing him many questions. Never in his time had he seen such a piece, nor any such magic. But if it hampered and harmed him, it was likely Kaerex himself fared no better.

Keenly, Dul returned himself to the duel. One magical factor remained an issue, and that was Toren's emblazoned power. Nothing demonic would withstand it for long, lending him to a non-contact approach. As much time as he had bought, his control was still imperfect, bringing him to a fight of precision while inebriated in this stinking bath of death.

*But it must be done! Here and now, for these people ... to save her.*

Emboldened, Dul brought himself closer. Cautiously, the two paced. Kaerex widened his eyes for a moment, and sped towards him. The first swift swing forced Dul back, and with ease, Kaerex spun the blade overhead. Relentlessly, he advanced with a deft assault. The whirls, however fast they were, did not hide the next move from him. Seeing the thrust coming, Dul slipped to the side. A quick lash with his sword nicked Kaerex's arm, falling short of doing true harm.

Kaerex maneuvered the greatsword closer to himself, his defense quickly flowing into a counter. Dul kept his feet going, sliding back. The silver blade arced under his chin, gracing him with a patch of stinging skin just from its proximity. Yet his foe placed the blade too high, and low he went, stabbing into his foe's thigh. Quickly he receded, not daring to risk Toren's touch again. Kaerex kicked up more steam, growling as he entered a deeper fury.

Advancing with his whirling greatsword, the attacks were faster, albeit sacrificing his footwork in the process. His foe could not cover as much ground, allowing him to easily keep his distance. With such reach, though, the act lethally combined offence and defense. Dul's predatory eyes peeled apart his prey as he waited for his moment. Even as it meant backing up further, putting more space between him and Lin, there would be an opening.

He watched the sword come around, traveling up and leftward, and his body tensed. Every muscle was already prepared; he lanced a bone sword forward. The cut was clean along the back of Kaerex's hand, severing tissue and vessel with the utmost impunity.

Kaerex tried to recover by transferring the weight of the sword mid-swing, and in doing so, opened himself further. Those few wasted fractions of a second allowed Dul to pull his other sword back and foresee the path to his enemy's neck. His sword tunneled beyond blade and arm, the aim slightly off, but at no degree in his mind that would fall lower than the grade of lethal.

Bright light then filled Dul's eyes, blinding him, as all senses exploded into overdrive. Not one thing could be singled out as something wrapped around his limbs, tugging him down to the earth in a surprise attack. Something stunk- not his nostrils, not the rot, nor the burning, something far more terrible. His teeth ripped into his lower lip, feeling the magic of his kin nearby. Slashing wildly at it and all around him, his swords bit into nothing, just for the bindings to dissolve away.

Throwing himself to his feet, Dul blinked rapidly as his vision slowly wiped away the murk that had been cast upon him. His chest rose and fell heavily as he scrambled for anything to know just what had happened. His ears rummaged for the sound of footsteps, yet grabbed nothing beyond the crackling and pops of some sort of deceptive spellcraft. And still, something bothered him more than the fact he had not been struck down by Kaerex while he was vulnerable. The attack seemed a mix of Tyxivol and Alok's Theatre.

What mages would wield both, could wield both- the threat would most certainly usurp even his fight here. Another blink and his vision came back, somewhat blurry, but he could see the unholy glow. Atop Kressel's home, he traced it to one figure.

*One mage? But ... who in this land could bring to bear such sorcery?*

Then a sniff brought it. Something that curdled his blood and banished all other thought. Even just that insignificant scrap, the smoke from an extinguished candle, he knew it. It most certainly had changed many things about itself, but not its identity. Dul's entire body rippled, his veins pushing against his skin as his mouth opened. While certainly not impossible, he would not entertain it further without knowing for certain. And the taste ... his tongue, nose ... and now, as his vision cleared, his grip loosened.

Looking down upon him, he could not mistake eyes that were not far from his own. That sapphire glisten, alight with an untold secret. And bound in demonic chains, he held a dangling Kaerex. Dropping one of his swords, Dul reached out to him. He could find no way to make his tongue work, the boulder in his throat made no more manageable by the choking noose around it.

*Brother...*

It was beyond him what he would even ask first. Where or how might have seemed important, but more so, why ... why he had hidden for so long. He may have not made himself easy to find, but if there was one capable ... but all that could wait. If Caelin wielded the power of Alok, he most certainly had Illeah's Breath at his disposal.

*He can heal her! And with both of us ... this war could turn. Together, even the tiquo would be rivaled!*

Straightening his own head, Dul prepared to speak. His petition was struck down as Caelin gazed into him. A look that recognized, and pitied. It was ... disappointment that shone above all else as Caelin cast open a portal. In a blink, he and Kaerex were gone. Abandoned in the wreckage, Dul froze. For a moment, he genuinely felt nothing. Not emptiness, neither in limb or mind. Until it all fell upon him. The moon, the sun, the sky, all upon his shoulders. It was unbearable, horrible in too many ways at once to endure. Falling to his knees, his heart felt the betrayal before he could acknowledge it. He clawed into the ground, throwing dirt, debris, and cobble about. He curled in on himself, digging his fingers into his cheeks. He ripped into the skin, down to his teeth, letting out a cry that flooded the city. It bounced off its many walls, duplicating, echoing, flaying him open.

*Brother ... too much...*

His tears fell to the stones as his wings wilted. His hands came lower, excavating his ribs to raw air. Rocking back and forth, his head pounded, not one side able to overcome the raw and pure chaos. Until a jolt of force shook him. Another, and another- impaling all into his back. The burning of Toren's light ravaged his insides, the arrowheads making scorching pockets within him. Falling to his side, he held himself up with his elbow. In the distance a few archers readied their shots. They let loose, and he was met yet again with infernal agony. Scrambling, he unpinned the wing he sat upon, and lurched for his blades. With them in hand, he ran, the rattle and clatter of more arrows following close behind. Retreating into the alleys, he could not bring himself to cast a spell to hide. Pulling the arrows from his flesh, he left a trail of blood behind as he ran.

His boots kept on through puddles and over corpses, outwards, onwards, in a confused rage at a world he no longer understood.

# About the Author

Caleb Laycock is a college graduate with a BS in marine biology, who started writing as a hobby. Continuing to work with animals, now including reptiles and insects, he is branching out into fiction. *A Demon's Heart* is his first novel.

**You can connect with me on:**

🐦 https://x.com/TextsOfTartarus

📘 https://www.facebook.com/profile.php?id=61567307716574

Made in the USA
Monee, IL
28 January 2025

812d8335-856a-4228-82bb-1f2b6f04e33cR01